RIGHT
BEHIND
HER

ALSO BY MELINDA LEIGH

Bree Taggert Novels

Cross Her Heart

See Her Die

Drown Her Sorrows

Morgan Dane Novels

Say You're Sorry

Her Last Goodbye

Bones Don't Lie

What I've Done

Secrets Never Die

Save Your Breath

Scarlet Falls Novels

Hour of Need

Minutes to Kill

Seconds to Live

She Can Series

She Can Run

She Can Tell

She Can Scream

She Can Hide

"He Can Fall" (A Short Story)

She Can Kill

MIDNIGHT NOVELS

Midnight Exposure

Midnight Sacrifice

Midnight Betrayal

Midnight Obsession

THE ROGUE SERIES NOVELLAS

Gone to Her Grave (Rogue River)

Walking on Her Grave (Rogue River)

Tracks of Her Tears (Rogue Winter)

Burned by Her Devotion (Rogue Vows)

Twisted Truth (Rogue Justice)

THE WIDOW'S ISLAND NOVELLA SERIES

A Bone to Pick

Whisper of Bones

A Broken Bone

RIGHT
BEHIND
HER

MELINDA
LEIGH

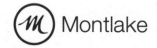 Montlake

Text copyright © 2021 by Melinda Leigh
All rights reserved.

Published by Montlake, Seattle

www.apub.com

Amazon, the Amazon logo, and Montlake are trademarks of Amazon.com, Inc., or its affiliates.

ISBN-13: 9781542007047 (paperback)
ISBN-10: 1542007046 (paperback)
ISBN-13: 9781542007061 (hardcover)
ISBN-10: 1542007062 (hardcover)

Cover design by Shasti O'Leary Soudant

Printed in the United States of America

First edition

For Charlie, Annie, and Tom
You are my world

CHAPTER ONE

June 1990

I squirm against the ropes binding my hands behind my back. Another rope binds my ankles. The trunk is tight and smells like gasoline and rubber. Nausea rises in the back of my throat. I suck in a lungful of stale air through the makeshift hood they've tied over my head. Curled on my side, I try for the tenth time to bring my bound feet through my tied hands. If I can get my hands in front of me, I have a small chance of fighting back. The way I'm trussed—like a Thanksgiving turkey—I'm helpless.

It's no use. There isn't enough space, and I'm not flexible. My shoulder presses against the wheel well. The arm I'm lying on is numb. Every time I shift my weight, a little blood rushes into my hand. Sensations of fiery pinpricks follow. I flex my fingers over and over to try to increase circulation, but my movements are limited.

I lie still for a few seconds, recovering my wind.

I shouldn't be surprised. My entire life has been leading up to this moment. Every bad decision, every thoughtless act, has brought me here. I have no illusions about what is going to happen to me. I'll be dead before the night is over. I think of my family. Will they miss me?

Sorry. For everything.

I'm no angel. I've done plenty of bad things in my life. I find it ironic that the one time I stand up for what's right, that's the decision that gets me killed. What was I thinking? What did I hope to accomplish? The thought of me becoming a decent man is laughable. The weight of my combined sins is too great to be balanced.

I'm a hopeless case.

The car lurches and bumps, and I assume we've left the paved road. It won't be long now. My remaining time can be counted in minutes. Nervous sweat breaks out under my arms, and I can smell my own fear. Not sure why. It's not like I'll be leaving a rich, full life. I'm barely getting through the days. My life is pathetic. What will I be missing?

The car comes to a stop, and the engine cuts off. Despite my attempt to meet my end with calm, bile surges into my throat, and I begin to shake—not little tremors, but humiliating, body-racking quakes.

My life might be for shit, but I don't want to die.

Stop it.

Honor isn't possible, not for me, but I can at least die with some sort of dignity. I don't want to meet death crying and whimpering. It's the very last thing I'll do. I should try to show a little class and act like a man.

I hear the trunk pop open. Humid night air rushes over my sweat-coated skin, lifting goose bumps on my arms.

"Get out," he says.

"Please." As if I weren't humiliated enough, I hear myself beg. *Have some pride.* But a primal survival instinct overrides my need to be dignified. I can't stop it.

I hear a switchblade snap open. Terror supercharges my heart. I have no control over it as it beats like a frantic hummingbird's wings. But he doesn't stab me. He slices through the ropes around my ankles. I shift my legs and feel the hot surge of blood flow as my feet come to life. I'd like to kick him in the fucking face, but I can't see, and after at least an hour in the trunk, my legs are too weak.

The hood is ripped off my head. I gulp fresh air like I've been underwater.

"Fucking get out of the trunk."

I hear dogs barking, big dogs. One begins to howl, and the others join in, as if they're a pack ready to join a hunt. The thin sound lifts the hairs on the back of my neck, and dread balls in my gut. They are not friendly pets. These are hungry beasts conditioned to rip me or each other to shreds the second they get an opportunity.

"Move it," he snaps.

"Why?" I find my voice and hope I don't sound as scared as I am. "You're going to kill me anyway."

"Because if you don't, I'm going to hurt you first."

I've seen him in action. That is not an idle threat. For emphasis, he pokes me with the tip of the knife. The point bites into my shoulder. I feel blood well out of the wound and run in a warm trickle down my arm.

I work my legs over the edge and lever myself into a sitting position. With my hands still bound behind my back, the task takes work, and I'm breathing hard. I settle there for a few seconds, taking in the night and what will surely be my last moments on this earth.

The shadow of a barn looms over me. I look up at the sky and spot the Big Dipper. My senses heighten. The stars seem brighter, and the scent of pine in the air is sharper. Clouds pass in front of the moon, darkening the summer night.

"Walk." He barks the command, sounding as vicious as the dogs.

When I hesitate, he pulls the gun from his pocket and jerks it in the direction of the barn. I shift my weight to my feet and stand. My knees wobble, but I keep them under me. My first few steps are shaky, but they steady as I move. I glance at the woods behind the barn and think about running.

Do I have anything to lose?

I dig in a toe and get exactly three strides. A hand fists in my hair and my head is yanked backward. I fall on my ass. Pain rings through my tailbone and up my spine.

He grabs my arm and hauls me to my feet. "That was pointless."

Yep.

There seems to be no end to my stupidity tonight.

With my arm chicken-winged, I'm half dragged toward the barn. He steps in front of me and pulls at the door handle. Despite the door's age, weight, and lack of maintenance, it rolls open with little effort. Can't find quality construction like that these days. The world is going to hell.

Am I?

He herds me inside, closes the door behind us, and turns on the light. The barn is mostly used for storage. I see a tractor in one corner, a pile of junk in another. A few animals occupy a pen on the far side of the space. They don't like the intrusion into their quiet night. Straw rustles with their nervous movements. A goat bleats. An old pony pokes its nose through the slats and eyeballs me. Ridiculously, I hope the gunshot doesn't scare them.

He shoves me. I trip over something and stumble. I can't catch myself with my hands behind my back, and I go down. My knees hit the ground, and my teeth snap together. Kneeling, I smell manure and realize I tripped over a pile of animal shit.

The woman is already there. Is she dead?

He walks in front of me, lifts the gun, and checks for a round in the chamber. Ready. "All I wanted was loyalty. Was that too much to ask?"

"Apparently, yes." I don't even understand why I decided to draw my moral line tonight, after having very few ethics my entire life. I wasn't even going to die on a stupid virtuous hill, but down in the filth where I've spent most of my days.

Maybe this is what I deserve. I want to go out bravely, but I just don't have it in me. I used up my single drop of courage making the decision that led me here.

"You tried to betray me," he says.

"I tried to do the right thing." What the fuck? I'm dying anyway. I might as well go for it.

Our eyes meet. His are as cold and dark as always. I don't bother asking for forgiveness. He doesn't have an ounce of mercy in his soul.

"Go ahead. Kill me. We both know you're going to." I try to summon some courage, but it feels more like defeat.

He pulls a pair of bolt cutters from his pocket. "Oh, I'm going to kill you, but first, you have to pay for your betrayal."

He cranks my arm behind my back and lifts my hand. I struggle, panic scrambling in my throat like an animal trying to claw its way out of a trap. I hear the snip of bone. Pain explodes in my finger and travels up my arm at light speed. My own scream sounds far away. Tiny lights swirl in front of my face.

Snip.

I scream again. The agony reaches a level my brain can't comprehend. My heart beats so fast, it feels like it could explode. The sheer terror of suffering more pain fills my chest to bursting. My body shakes uncontrollably, as if it's no longer connected to my will. Fear becomes a separate entity.

Snip.

I'm beyond words now, whimpering and grunting like a prey animal as he moves in front of me again. He lifts the gun and points it directly at my head. I snivel. I have only one thought. *Do it. Please, just do it.* Tears and snot run down my face. I have no control over the reactions of my own body. There's no dignity now. He's won.

And he knows it.

He looks down the barrel. Just above the sight, I see the corner of his mouth curve up in a cruel almost-smile. He's in no rush. He's enjoying this, dragging it out, savoring every second.

I have nothing left. I just want it to be over. I want to stare him down. I want to be brave. I want to be the person I've always imagined I could become. But that's just not me. One attempt at virtue can't undo all the bad things I've done. I'm a coward and a failure. In the end, I close my eyes.

No good deed goes unpunished.

CHAPTER TWO

Sheriff Bree Taggert stood in the road at the end of the driveway. Her stomach turned, a faint queasiness rising in the back of her throat as she stared at the house. Upstate New York was in the middle of a heat wave. At noon, the air was oppressive and humid. A sense of claustrophobia closed over her, which made no sense. She was outside. But the trapped feeling wasn't due to physical constraints. It was the memories that came with this house. The only place she feared being trapped in was her past.

The roof sagged, and years of wind, rain, and neglect had peeled the paint from the wooden clapboards, turning the exterior to a weathered gray. Untrimmed trees and overgrown foliage blocked the sun and left the house cast in deep shadows, even on a sunny afternoon in mid-July.

Bree inhaled. The scent of decay and dampness lingered in her nostrils. Twenty-seven years before, this had been her childhood home, but she had no warm or fuzzy memories attached to it. Inside those rotting walls, her father had shot her mother and then killed himself while Bree and her siblings had hidden in terror. She shuddered, the memories she'd banished to the dark corners stepping into the light to show themselves.

She glanced at her younger brother, standing on the other side of her. At twenty-eight, Adam was tall and lanky, with unruly brown hair that curled over his ears.

"Sorry I'm late." She did not tell him why. He didn't need to hear about the college kid who'd OD'd early that morning. Bree wished she could forget his face, already blue by the time her department had responded. But his image, and that of his sobbing parents, would haunt Bree for some time.

"It's OK," Adam said.

Sweat dripped down Bree's back. "I'm almost surprised the house is still standing."

It should have been razed to the ground.

"Old houses are solid." Adam didn't take his eyes off the house. "They don't build them like this anymore."

The three-bedroom, one-story bungalow squatted on a large chunk of mostly wooded land. A thick canopy of fat branches crisscrossed over the house, casting shadows between the tree trunks, the eerie landscape worthy of the nightmare that had occurred here.

Adam nudged her with an elbow. "Are you sure you're OK with going inside?"

"Yes." Her answer was automatic, not honest, and the lie burned like acid in her chest.

She would never be OK with what had happened in that house, but she had managed to mostly put it behind her.

Now, every instinct in her body told her not to cross the threshold. The memories on the other side were the monsters under her bed.

Adam closed his eyes for a few seconds. His face scrunched in concentration. "This place feels familiar, but I can't remember anything specific. I can't even picture her face."

"I'm sorry." The atmosphere felt familiar to Bree as well. Dread pooled in her belly. "You were just a baby when she died. I wouldn't expect you to remember her."

He turned to her. The yearning in his hazel eyes brought unshed tears to hers. As hard as Adam was trying to recall their childhood, Bree was working just as hard to forget it.

"Are you ready?" he asked.

No. Bree eyed the front porch. "Is it safe?"

"The structure is surprisingly solid."

"You've been inside?" she asked.

He looked away and shrugged. "A couple of times. I fixed some stuff."

Guilt weighted Bree's shoulders. She should have come here when he'd first asked months ago. He shouldn't have had to face this place alone. Though he stood a full head taller than her, he was still her little brother.

It was her job to protect him. Bree had failed their sister, Erin, and she had died. Bree could not repeat the mistake with Adam.

Her mouth went dry. She didn't want to replay anything about the first eight years of her life, the years she'd lived in this place with her family—or the violent night that had ended that period. Once she entered, she would no longer be able to repress her memories. No more excuses. Since their sister had been murdered back in January, Bree had left her job as a homicide detective in Philadelphia, moved to Grey's Hollow, and taken charge of her eight-year-old niece and sixteen-year-old nephew. Back in her hometown, she'd done her best to distance herself from her childhood tragedy. She'd never even considered visiting this house until Adam had asked. But her brother had stepped up to help with the kids. He'd done everything *she'd* asked of *him*, and he'd made only this one request in return.

"Let's do this." She stepped over the property line. Skirting a puddle, she strode toward the house.

Long-legged, Adam moved ahead. Thunderstorms had pummeled the area the previous week, and low-lying areas had flooded. Her brother's strides were eager, while Bree's feet dragged in the sole-sucking mud. Once, the driveway had been gravel, but the small stones had long since been ground into the earth.

Adam jogged up the stairs to the porch. Bree didn't allow herself to pause until she stood beside him.

The porch boards didn't sag under their weight. Some of the planks had been recently replaced. He moved toward the front door. Bree noticed the door, hinges, and lock were new. The doorframe had been repaired. How many times had Adam been here? Discomfort curled into a ball in her chest. She'd let him face the horror of their past alone. She'd let him down. She wouldn't do that again, no matter what it cost her.

Something creaked. The hairs on the back of Bree's neck bristled. "Did you hear that?"

Adam shrugged. "Probably the wind. It's an old house."

His reasoning was plausible, but Bree's instincts weren't happy.

He fished a key from his pocket and unlocked the door.

Bree touched his shoulder. "I'll go first." She moved in front of her brother. Her hand went to the service weapon on her hip.

She took a deep breath and went inside.

The living room was empty. Behind her, Adam shuffled a sneaker. The throw rug had rotted away to a few shreds of fabric. Dirt and leaves gathered along the walls. But Bree no longer saw the abandoned house as it stood today. She was transported back to the very last night she'd been under this roof.

Adam said something, but his voice was muted by the imagined sound of her parents fighting and the smack of her father striking her mother.

"Bree?" Adam jostled her arm.

She shook herself. "Sorry."

His gaze turned hesitant as he engaged in some internal debate. Bree said a quick prayer that he'd change his mind and haul her out of there, but she suspected it didn't matter. The damage was done. She was remembering.

Everything.

His jaw went rigid. "Which room was mine?"

Bree turned to walk down the hallway that led to the bedrooms. She passed the room she'd shared with Erin and stopped in the doorway of the smallest, the nursery, now empty. "This one."

Adam followed her into the room. She ran a finger over the grimy wall and uncovered a patch of faded baby-blue paint. "She was excited to be having a boy. I remember watching her paint over the pink." She pointed to a scuff on the wall. "Your crib was there."

Adam pivoted, scanning the room, his face creased with concentration. "I don't remember anything."

For the best.

Bree turned on her heel and went back into the hall. She halted in another doorway. "This was their room."

"Is this where he killed her?" Adam asked from behind her.

"I don't know."

"But you were here," he protested.

Bree whirled to face him. Anger heated her face. "I didn't wait around to watch him do it."

"I'm sorry." Adam looked away.

Bree breathed. "No. It's all right. You have a right to know, but I was only eight. My memories have definite blank spots."

She glanced back into the room. Despite what she'd told Adam, a clear picture formed in her mind.

"They were fighting in there," Bree admitted.

And that's the spot where Daddy pinned Mommy to the wall. One big hand curled around her throat. The other held a gun, the muzzle pressed against her forehead. In the warm, humid air, clammy sweat broke out between Bree's shoulder blades. Her heart thudded against her ribs in a thin, panicky rhythm.

Don't make me hurt you. You always make me hurt you.

Memories assaulted her. Bree grabbing her siblings and taking them under the porch. The winter wind blowing through thin pajamas. Terror shaking their very bones.

The echo of a gunshot.

She flinched.

She moved back down the hallway to the kitchen. She could sense Adam behind her, but she didn't narrate her recollection for him. How much did he need to know? Did he really want these images in his head? Once they lodged there, they'd remain forever, like a tattoo—or a deep scar.

"Daddy had a gun," Bree said. "I took you and Erin out the back door."

Even at eight, she'd known they needed to hide. She'd recognized the murderous look in her father's eyes was different from his usual anger, which had been bad enough. A shudder passed through her bones, shaking her from her athletic shoes to her uniform shirt. The house was empty, but Bree's hand hovered over her service weapon, as if she could go back in time and save her mother.

She flexed her fingers and lowered her hand.

There was no one to save today.

Adam moved toward the back door. Bree followed him out onto the porch. He'd replaced boards here too. They descended into the weedy yard and turned to face the house.

Bree pointed to the porch steps. "There was a loose board. I'd hidden under there before." She didn't have to elaborate on what—no, who—she'd hidden from. Adam knew, even if he didn't remember.

"Then what?" He looked like he was holding his breath.

Bree shivered hard. It had been cold that night. She felt the icy dirt beneath her bare feet, and the bitter chill seeping through the thin fabric of her pajamas. "A gun went off."

The dogs had been barking. One had howled. The sound memory rippled over Bree. Despite the summer warmth, goose bumps rose on the skin of her arms.

"How long were we under there?" Adam asked.

"I don't know. A while." Long enough to get very cold.

"What happened next?"

"I'm not sure." Bree sensed a blank spot in her recollection. Had her eight-year-old self shut down with shock at that point? She vaguely recalled slamming doors, loud footsteps, and shouting.

Another gunshot.

Daddy?

Did it really matter? She knew enough. Her father had killed her mother and himself. The three siblings had been split up shortly after. Adam and Erin had been raised by their grandmother, while Bree had been sent to live with a cousin in Philadelphia.

"The sheriff came." Bree had never set foot on the property again— until today. "He took us to the station and called the family."

Adam stared at the house. He looked disappointed.

"I'm sorry I can't tell you more," she said.

"No. It's enough." He reached for her hand. "Thanks for sharing that with me."

"You're welcome." Bree squeezed his fingers. "What will you do with the place?"

If it were hers, she would burn the house to the ground. But she doubted Adam would. He seemed to want to maintain the structure as some sort of shrine.

"I don't know." His brow knitted, and his eyes looked lost. But then Adam had seemed disconnected for most of his life. Violence always left marks. Some scars were just less visible than others.

She turned to her brother. "I'm sorry, Adam. I need to go back to work." She scrambled for an excuse. "We had a tough call this morning." That was the truth.

Adam's shoulder jerked. "It's cool. Thanks for coming out here."

"We'll talk about it again, OK?"

"OK." Adam nodded, but his eyes were still disappointed. He shoved his hands into the back pockets of his jeans. "You'll tell me if anything else comes back to you?"

"I will." Bree gave him a one-armed hug.

Adam glanced back at the house. A damp wind stirred the branches overhead. Bree shivered. She glanced over her shoulder. The barn overshadowed the yard. Next to it were the remains of two partially collapsed sheds, their exposed wooden beams bleached like old bones in a desert. Beyond the clearing, an overgrown path led to the area where the dogs had been kept. Bree rubbed the thirty-year-old scar on her shoulder. Her earliest clear memory was of one of those dogs nearly killing her.

Something banged in the barn.

"Someone's in there." Adam started forward. "I've run off trespassers before."

"You should have called me." Bree reached for her gun. "Stay here."

But Adam was a Taggert, and they were a stubborn lot, always making choices that were the opposite of their own best interests. He jogged across the weeds at her flank. She reached the side of the barn, put out a hand to stop him, and hissed, "Stay behind me."

The door was ajar. Bree peered inside, but all she saw was darkness and dust.

Leading with her weapon, she eased around the corner just as something crashed into the doorframe a few inches from her face.

CHAPTER THREE

Bree startled as a rock bounced off the barn doorframe and landed in the dirt.

"Sheriff!" she yelled, then ducked as another rock came sailing toward her. It hit the wood with the force of a line drive. She pulled back behind the barn's doorframe. She was grateful the projectiles weren't bullets, but a rock to the head could do plenty of damage.

Pushing Adam toward the house, she whispered, "Go back inside. Call 911. Tell them I'm here and request backup."

"I don't want to leave you."

Bree's job would be easier if he was safe and out of the way. If he knew that was her reason, Adam would be insulted. So, she lied. "I know, but I need backup."

He pulled out his phone and reluctantly retreated across the yard in a running crouch.

Bree focused on the barn. *How many people are inside? Are they armed with anything besides rocks?*

"This is the sheriff," she called out. "Drop any weapons and come out with your hands on your head."

"Fuck you!" a man shouted. Another rock hit the door, rattling the old hinges.

She heard the barn's back door slide open. She peered around the doorframe again. A dark-haired man in jeans and a brown T-shirt was running into the woods, a small black backpack clutched in one hand. He weaved between the trees.

"Stop! Sheriff!" She quickly cleared the empty barn. She sprinted through the back door after him.

Ahead, he looked over his shoulder. His strides were unsteady, faltering as if he were drunk. Bree turned on the speed. She ran five mornings a week. He might have a head start, but she would catch him in no time.

The runner glanced back at her over his shoulder. Panic widened his eyes as he tripped over a tree root. He nearly went down, and it took him three steps to recover his speed. Bree almost had him.

So close.

She dug into the ground. Her quads burned as she drew closer.

Just a few more feet.

She reached out and tried to grab the back of his T-shirt, but her hand clawed empty air.

Finally, she dived at him, tackling him around the knees. They went down in the overgrown weeds. Bree's chin bounced off his leg. She tasted dirt and blood, but she hung on.

"You bitch! Let me go," he panted between gasps for air.

Bree's lungs burned. She shouted only two words: "Sheriff! Stop!"

He rolled to his back and tried to scramble out of her grasp, kicking hard at her face. Bree turned away. His sneaker glanced off her chin, and pain zinged through her jaw as her teeth slammed together.

Grabbing ahold of his pant leg, she hauled herself up his body. He wasn't fighting with any skill. His fists and feet flailed as he lashed out in wild desperation. Bree caught his wrists and pinned them to the ground on each side of his head.

"Ow! That hurts." He whimpered, but he stopped fighting.

"Hold still." She gasped for air and nearly gagged at the smell of his unwashed body. "Are you going to cooperate?"

He nodded.

Bree tentatively shifted her position, moving onto one knee beside him. When he didn't resist, she rolled him onto his belly and hand-cuffed his wrists behind his back. Then she shifted him onto his side and sat back on her haunches while they both caught their breath.

Wind rustled through the branches overhead, and the trickle of water over rocks reminded her there was a stream at the edge of the property. A quick memory surfaced—Bree as a young child walking barefoot in the cool water, smooth rocks underfoot, catching tadpoles and salamanders.

The man wheezed.

Bree took one last deep breath and refocused on him. "Are you carrying any weapons? Is there anything sharp that's going to stick me when I search your pockets?"

He shook his head. His body had deflated, as if the desire to fight had gone out of him. "Just a pocketknife, but it's closed."

She patted down the pockets of his jeans and tossed the contents onto the ground: cheap cell phone, folding knife, cigarettes, lighter, and wallet. She secured the knife in the leg pocket of her cargo pants.

"Do you want to sit up?" she asked.

He nodded and she rolled him over and helped him sit upright.

"What's your name?" she asked.

Instead of answering, he glared at her, anger rolling off him in palpable waves. Blood trickled from a split lip. He spit in the weeds beside him.

Bree opened the wallet and matched the driver's license photo to his face. His name was Shawn Castillo. She didn't recognize the street address, but it was in Grey's Hollow. "What are you doing here, Shawn? This is private property."

He clamped his mouth shut.

Bree sized him up. He was ragged in an unwashed and unshaven way, but his jeans and sneakers were expensive brands. The leather wallet felt pricey too. She checked his birth date on his license. Forty-eight. He looked ten years older.

"Do you have a vehicle?" she asked.

No answer.

"How did you get here?"

Nothing.

She tried, "Do you live with someone?"

His sullen stare didn't waver.

Bree gave up. "Well, Shawn. Congratulations. You are under arrest. So far, the charges are trespassing and assaulting an officer, but there might be more by the time the day is finished."

His eyes flickered at the word *arrest*. "I want to call my lawyer."

That was fast.

She raised an eyebrow. "So, this isn't your first time."

He didn't answer, but the hardened look in his eyes told her he had a record. "You didn't read me my rights!"

"I don't have to read you your rights until I question you. Stop getting your legal advice from TV." She glanced around. "Where's your backpack?"

Shawn lifted his chin. "What backpack?"

His denial sharpened Bree's interest. "The black one you were carrying."

She scanned the tall weeds and underbrush. He must have dropped it. *Must be around here somewhere.*

"I don't know what you're talking about." Shawn looked away.

Adam and two deputies jogged into the clearing. In his late forties, Deputy Oscar was one of Bree's senior deputies. Juarez was a rookie fresh out of the academy. Oscar was serving as Juarez's FTO, or field training officer. They would ride together for the first six weeks before Juarez would be turned loose on solo patrol.

"Watch him," Bree said to Deputy Oscar. "I'm going to look for his backpack."

Adam hurried over to stand next to Bree. His eyes narrowed with concern as he looked her over. "Are you OK?"

She looked down. Dirt and grass stains streaked her uniform. She plucked a dead leaf from the Randolph County Sheriff's Department badge on her shoulder. She rubbed a sore spot on her elbow and swept her tongue over a cut in her mouth. "I'm fine. Mostly dirty."

"Can I help?" Adam asked.

"Sure. The more eyes the better." Bree called out to the rookie, "Juarez, with me."

The rookie hustled over.

"We are looking for a black backpack about this big." Bree held her hands about a foot apart. "Either he tossed or dropped it while he was running, or it flew out of his hands when I tackled him. If you find it, just call me. Don't touch it."

Juarez nodded. "Yes, sir. I'm sorry. I mean, yes, ma'am."

Bree sighed. "Either will do, deputy."

"Where do you want to start?" Adam asked.

Bree turned in a slow circle, studying the clearing she'd chased Shawn into. They stood about a hundred yards behind the barn. Small piles of rotted wood dotted the weedy ground. Her gaze fell on a rusty metal bowl in the tall grass. Near it, an equally rusted chain was half buried in the dirt. Tension coiled in her belly as she realized where she was. "This is where he kept the dogs." She didn't need to specify who *he* was. Adam knew she meant their father.

Adam glanced around. "How many did he have?"

"Six or so most of the time. Some he kept for a long time. Others would come and go."

"What kind of dogs were they?" Adam asked.

A thirty-year-old image appeared in her mind: a half dozen barking dogs chained just far enough apart that they couldn't reach each other. If they had, they would have torn each other to shreds. She pictured a big brown animal with cropped ears and massive teeth. "I don't know.

He called them hunting dogs, but I don't remember any retrievers or spaniels." She shook her head, trying to clear the mental picture. She had work to do.

She waded into the high grass just beyond the spot where she'd taken Shawn down.

"Watch out," Adam said. "This grass is probably loaded with ticks."

Bree hesitated, one foot lifted. She hated the little bloodsuckers. She pointed a few feet away and motioned to the rookie and Adam. "Both of you, walk a line parallel to mine. Stay close. Some of this grass is high. We'll have to be right on top of the backpack to see it. So, go slowly."

They spread out and began making their way through the grass. Ten minutes into the hunt, they'd found no sign of the pack, but Bree did find two ticks crawling up her pant leg. She picked them off and flicked them into the woods.

Something black caught her eye. She walked closer. A small backpack was embedded in a patch of prickly vines. The nylon looked too new to be anything that had been in the woods for long. Pulling on gloves, she lifted a vine and disentangled the strap from its green thorns. "I found it."

"I found something too," Adam said from a few yards away. "But it's not a backpack."

Bree opened the main zipper compartment and found a plastic baggie containing a dozen round white pills. She was no pharmacist, but she'd seen hydrocodone before. The pills would explain why Shawn hadn't wanted to claim ownership of the pack. She closed the zipper and stood, lifting the bag.

"Bree? Could you come over here?" Adam was squatting near a shallow runoff ditch. Something in his voice caught her attention. Recent heavy rains had saturated low-lying areas. She walked to his side, the mud sucking at the tread of her running shoes.

Adam pointed to something long and dirty-white half buried in the mud.

"It's a bone." Bree squinted. "Probably from a deer—or a dog." Her stomach turned. They were standing near the place her father had put down the dog that had attacked her. Daddy had made her watch, after telling her she was responsible both for the attack and for the dog's death because she'd wandered too close. She'd been five.

This is why we have rules, Bree. Her father's voice echoed in her mind. An involuntary shiver passed through her. In her head he sounded like a character in a Stephen King novel—downright psychopathic. Was her recollection accurate, or was her imagination adding detail?

Did it matter?

Psycho or not, Daddy had been a lazy man. The dog had been large, and he'd probably buried it close to where it had fallen.

Bree scanned the shallow ravine and saw a few more bones seemingly exposed by the runoff. "It looks like this area flooded recently. There's a stream on the other side of those trees." She nodded toward the woods. "And we did have some big storms in the past few weeks."

Adam shook his head. "I don't think it's a dog or a deer, Bree." He waved to a spot about five feet away.

There were a few more bones. *Wait.* Bree moved closer to a large, rounded object wedged under a rock. She didn't want to believe what she was seeing.

Bree straightened, suddenly light-headed. The implications of their discovery swirled in her brain. "It's a skull."

"Is it human?" Adam asked, but from the tone of his voice, he already knew the answer.

A stick poked through one of the empty eye sockets. The remains weren't canine.

"Yes. It's definitely human."

Chapter Four

Matt Flynn threw the toy out into the pond on the rear of his property. The young, pure black German shepherd plunged into the lake and swam hard for the floating toy. She ignored the squawking ducks that half flew out of her way. Greta was 100 percent focused on her quarry. She caught it in her teeth, turned, and swam back to Matt. She ran out of the water, spit the toy at his feet, and shook. Water sprayed in every direction. Laughing, Matt wiped a drop of pond water off his face. She stood in front of him, tongue lolling.

"Good girl," he praised her, then poured water from a stainless-steel bottle into a collapsible bowl. She lapped up half the water.

Matt was fostering the young shepherd for his sister's dog rescue. With keen intelligence and a strong drive to work, Greta had been difficult to place as a house pet. Matt had been tempted to keep her as a foster fail, but he recognized all her pain-in-the-butt traits made her a perfect K-9 candidate. By the end of the month, she would be old enough to be paired with a deputy and sent to K-9 training, provided Bree could raise the money for her training and equipment. With July ushering in sweltering temperatures, he was using the month to get Greta accustomed to water and burning off her seemingly endless energy. He shouldn't have worried, though. Greta was fearless.

Matt picked up a towel and rubbed the excess water off her coat. Then he stuffed his gear into his backpack and slung it over his shoulder.

After clipping a leash onto Greta's collar, he commanded her to heel in German. *"Fuss."*

Matt's former K-9 partner, Brody, had been imported from Germany and already obedience-trained in that language, so Matt was accustomed to using German commands. He also felt using foreign words helped avoid any confusion on the dog's part, especially in the early phases of training. The dog was unlikely to hear the words from anyone other than the trainer.

She fell into step at his side as they walked through the large meadow and into the grassy rear yard that led up to Matt's back porch. His restored farmhouse sat on twenty-five acres, and the summer sun was afternoon-high. Greta was nearly dry by the time they reached the backyard. They walked past the kennels where Matt had planned to train K-9s before his sister had filled the entire building with canine rescues. He waved to his childhood friend Justin, who was walking a timid pit bull around the yard. Justin worked for the rescue. Justin had suffered terrible tragedy and was battling a drug addiction. He and the dogs were healing each other.

Matt went into the house. A second German shepherd, this one a traditional black and tan, rose from his bed and greeted Matt with a wag of his feathery tail.

Matt stroked his head. "I'm sorry, Brody. Next time you can come swimming with us, or even better, I'll take you after Greta leaves for the academy."

A few years before, Matt and Brody had been a sheriff's department K-9 team. A shooting had ended both of their careers. A bullet in Matt's hand had limited his dexterity—and his marksmanship. He could shoot a rifle, but his accuracy with a pistol had been compromised. Now, he consulted as a civilian criminal investigator, a position that did not require him to carry a handgun. Brody was simply getting older, although the shooting certainly hadn't helped the aging process.

Greta tried to nose her way between them, but Brody held his ground. Matt lifted Brody's big head and looked into his deep brown eyes. "Don't worry. She'll be out of your hair in September." After she was accepted into the training program, Greta would live with her new handler.

Brody let out a long-suffering sigh and gave his temporary house-guest a side-eye. The older dog liked Greta, but she also annoyed the hell out of him.

Greta moseyed over to the corner and stretched out on the cool tile. Swimming had tired her out. Matt went into his kitchen for a glass of water. He made a turkey sandwich and ate it while leaning over the sink. He felt the weight of both dogs' stares as he chewed. He was brushing crumbs off his hands when his phone buzzed on the counter, and he reached for it.

Bree's name popped onto the screen. They'd been dating for a couple of months. The smile that tugged at his mouth felt stupid, but he was always happy when she called him.

"Hey," he answered.

"Hi." The single syllable sounded stressed.

Matt remembered she'd agreed to see her childhood home with her brother today. "What's wrong?"

She blew out an audible breath. "Adam and I found human remains in the woods behind my parents' house."

"What? You're sure it's not an animal?" At one time in Matt's former career, he'd also been an investigator for the sheriff's department. He'd gone out on more than one call to collect bones later determined to be an animal's. Deer bones were similar in size to human, and bear and raccoon paw bones resembled those of a human hand.

"I'm ninety-nine percent sure," she said. "We found a skull. I'd like your help with the investigation. Do you have time to work a case?"

Matt checked the time on his phone. One thirty. "I can be out there in fifteen minutes."

"OK, thanks. The ME is on her way too."

Skeletal remains weren't as time sensitive as a fresh corpse. Bones weren't going to degrade significantly in a few hours, but the location of the bones made Matt uneasy. Were the remains related to her family? Or had someone taken advantage of the vacant land? He hoped it was the latter. Bree and her family didn't need any more tragedy heaped on their devastating past.

Ending the call, Matt quickly changed into a pair of dark-brown tactical cargoes and a polo shirt embroidered with the sheriff's department logo. He took Brody out to do his business, then filled the water bowl. After donning boots, he left the dogs snoozing in the kitchen and drove out to the Taggert property.

Bree stood on the side of the road behind her official SUV and two patrol vehicles. She held her cell phone to her ear. She didn't fidget or pace. She was 100 percent focused on her call. Bree didn't waste energy.

Matt stepped out of his SUV. Her gaze met his for a brief second. At the eye contact, Matt felt the now-familiar light punch to his heart. Then she returned her attention to the caller.

Bree was an attractive woman. No doubt about it. Average height, she was naturally athletic and leanly built. Her hair was brown, wavy, and thick. Today, it had been half pulled from its usual neat knot and fell to her shoulders, tousled and tangled and sexy. But it was her intelligence and another quality he couldn't quite quantify that riveted him. Pure physical attraction was great, but Matt needed more. He wanted what his parents had—a lifetime of connection and friendship—but he understood most people never found anything even close.

Bree lowered her phone. Those intelligent hazel eyes landed on him again, and he felt the connection with her in his bones.

"Thanks for coming, Matt." Her words were formal. She was never inappropriate on the job.

In fact, he could only hope that she wasn't so worried about a potential conflict of professional interest that she couldn't commit to him in any way. Bree's identity was tied to her job, but her dedication had nothing to do with money. Adam would support her. Though her brother looked like he lived in a tent under an overpass, he was wealthy. His paintings sold for obscene amounts of money. Bree's need to protect and serve came from her experience as a young victim of violence. The same childhood tragedy also made it hard for her to trust, and he understood why she needed to move slowly.

Matt came from a solid and secure family. Bree had been raised by a monster. It was not surprising he would be ready to make a commitment before she was. But he still feared she'd never be able to return his feelings. Not that it mattered. He couldn't change how he felt. His heart was in her hands.

She tucked a stray hair behind one ear. Tension bracketed her mouth, and her uniform looked like she'd slid into home plate.

"What happened to you?" he asked.

"Long story." As they walked around the side of the deteriorating house, through the rear yard, and past the barn, she filled him in on finding and chasing the trespasser. "He says he only went into the barn. The house was locked, and we found no sign that he'd broken in. He also says he doesn't know anything about the skeleton."

"How old is he?" Matt asked.

"Forty-eight," Bree said.

"Of course we have no idea how old the bones are." Matt stroked his beard.

"No."

It was notoriously hard to determine the postmortem interval, or the length of time since death, for fully skeletonized remains.

Bree and Matt passed through a small strip of woods and emerged in a clearing dotted with the rotted ruins of small wooden structures.

Bree pointed. "The grave is over there, in a shallow runoff ditch."

On the other side of the clearing, Bree's second-in-command, Chief Deputy Todd Harvey, was stringing crime scene tape between trees, marking off the entire area. At the edge of the clearing, Adam was sketching on a notepad.

Todd raised a hand in greeting, then went back to his task.

"Hey, Adam." Matt greeted Bree's brother.

Adam lifted his pencil. "Bree put me to work."

"Handy to have a real artist on-site." Matt skirted a rusty stake in the ground. They stopped a few feet short of the runoff. He could see a few partially unearthed bones, including the dirty-white of a skull.

"What was this area used for?" he asked.

"This is where my father kept his dogs chained." Bree waved a hand over the clearing. "It's been decades since I've been back here, but I think the grave would have been out of their reach."

"You don't know that the body was here when your family lived here," Matt pointed out. "The property has been vacant for how many years?"

"Twenty-seven," she said without blinking.

"Right. These remains could have been buried here at any time before or after."

Bree's jaw tightened. "I know that, but it would not surprise me to learn my father had killed someone." She exhaled. "He murdered my mother."

His heart cracked for her. She'd endured and overcome unimaginable horrors.

"I understand," he said, "but let's not make any assumptions. Anyone could have accessed this land over the years. I'm sure the current trespasser isn't the first."

Matt scanned the weedy ground and surrounding woods. "Have you searched the whole property?"

"Just about to do that now," Bree said. "So far, we just cleared for threats. From our initial sweep, it seems he's been camping in the barn. It looked cozy, so I suspect he's been there on and off for a while."

Matt sized up the grave. "Excavation will take some time. The grave wasn't very deep, and the skeleton isn't intact. The ME will need to sift a ton of dirt to find as many pieces as possible."

The small bones of the hands and feet often went missing after the connective tissue decomposed. Rodents and other scavengers dug up and carried away body parts.

A deputy walked onto the scene, carrying a clipboard. Matt didn't recognize him, but he looked young and still sported an academy buzz cut. There was a bounce in his step, and eagerness shone from him. Like a Labrador retriever puppy, he wanted to please.

Bree waved him over and introduced Matt to Juarez.

"Start a crime scene log," she instructed the rookie. "No one enters without signing in."

"Yes, ma'am." Juarez took Matt's information.

The medical examiner walked into the clearing. Dr. Serena Jones was a tall African American woman, and she covered the ground with long strides. Her assistant, a full head shorter, race-walked to keep up.

Dr. Jones paused at the edge of the ditch and scanned the general area. "What do we have here?"

Bree summarized. The ME crouched to examine the visible bones more closely without touching them.

Straightening, she propped her hands on her hips. "There's a chance of showers tonight. We need to protect this area." Squinting at the sky, the ME grimaced. "Let's hope it doesn't flood this ditch."

The sky was still clear, but the wind had picked up. Tree limbs waved above them.

Matt checked the weather forecast on his phone app. "Only light rain is expected, and we have a few hours before it starts."

"Good," Dr. Jones said. "We can do the site prep work today and be ready to excavate first thing tomorrow."

Bree called to Todd. He walked over and she explained what they needed.

Todd nodded. "I'll have a deputy transport the suspect to the station and bring a tent back here from the storeroom. Juarez is the FNG. He can babysit the bones overnight."

FNG was cop-speak for *fucking new guy*. The newest recruit always got the shittiest assignments, like directing traffic in the middle of August or cleaning vomit from the back of a patrol car. It was an everyone-pays-their-dues tradition. Handling the worst assignments with grace and humor would help the new recruit assimilate into the unit and build camaraderie.

"I want Oscar and Juarez working the scene," Bree said. "It'll be good experience for the rookie."

"Yes, ma'am." Todd nodded.

Bree turned back to Dr. Jones. "How much time do you need to remove the remains?"

The ME changed her position, moving a few feet to the left and leaning over the ditch. "I don't know." She didn't take her eyes off the bone she was studying. "I'm going to call the forensic anthropologist at the university." She pulled her phone from her pocket. "I'd like his help."

Matt sensed something had changed. "What do you see?"

"Look at this femur." Dr. Jones gestured to a long, thin bone that widened at each end. "This is the head that connects to the hip. We can tell by the angle of the bone shaft that this is a right femur." She pointed to another long bone a few feet away. "That is also a right femur."

Matt and Bree exchanged glances.

He digested the information. "There's more than one victim in this grave."

"Yes." The ME straightened and brushed her hands on her thighs. She surveyed the clearing. "We have at least two victims in this ditch. With comingled skeletal remains, I'd like the anthropologist's input before we excavate. I also want to bring in ground-penetrating radar."

Matt watched Bree turn to face the side of the clearing that led back to the barn and house.

Without turning around, she said, "You want to make sure there aren't more remains."

"Yes." Dr. Jones turned in a circle. "There's plenty of space out here for additional graves."

Matt and Bree left the medical examiner and her assistant laying out their equipment. They trekked back to the barn.

"Where do you want to start?" Matt asked.

"The barn," Bree said. "Adam keeps the house locked, and we found no sign that anyone had broken in."

"When was he here last?"

"I don't know." Guilt swept over Bree's face. "Apparently, he visits the place now and then, fixes things." She shook her head as if she couldn't understand. "He hasn't bothered with the barn, though. It's just an empty shell."

They circled the building, then entered through the rear door. Six large stalls lined one side of the space, with a loft above them. Two-thirds of the space was wide open clear to the roof at least twenty feet up.

"Did your family keep livestock?" Matt asked.

"Not really," Bree said. "My mother collected a few discarded animals. It was the one indulgence my father permitted her. We had an old pony, a used-up dairy cow, and some barn cats, of course." She gestured to the empty area. "My father used this area to store farm equipment." She sighed. "Knowing my grandparents, they sold the machinery. The animals probably went to slaughter. I never asked because I didn't want to know."

Since Bree's grandparents had separated the Taggert siblings after their parents' deaths, Matt doubted they had been the kindest of people.

The sadness on her face was heartbreaking. Matt wanted to take her hand. He wanted to hold her, but she'd never allow it, not when she was on duty and in public. The best he could do was make sure she didn't have to be here alone.

He surveyed the mostly empty space. "You said it seemed he was camping here."

"In the loft." She headed for a ladder and started climbing.

The wood was old and creaky. Matt waited for Bree to exit the ladder before he followed her. While a thick layer of dirt and dust covered the first floor, the loft had been recently swept. The space smelled faintly of mold, and a few watermarks indicated areas where the roof leaked. But overall, the space was dry. Matt had seen worse digs for a homeless person.

The makeshift camp had been set up in the far corner. An old lawn chair sat next to a wooden box. A battery-powered lantern and a flashlight occupied the box. A sleeping bag had been rolled out. Next to it stood a beat-up wheelie suitcase and an old-fashioned footlocker.

Matt pointed to the trunk. "How did he even get that up here?"

Bree took out her camera. "I don't know, but he took some time and care to clean and set up this space." She began taking pictures.

Matt pulled gloves out of his pocket and tugged them on. He squatted next to the suitcase and opened it. Both sides were full of neatly folded clothes. Matt riffled through brand-name jeans and shirts. "These are not Goodwill finds."

Leaning over his shoulder, Bree snapped a photo. "No."

"Sheriff?" Oscar called from the ladder. "Where do you want us to start?"

"In the loft. Bring plenty of evidence bags and boxes. Everything up here needs to be bagged and tagged," Bree answered.

Matt found underwear and socks in the zippered compartment. He closed the suitcase and moved on to the footlocker. The lock was broken. Matt lifted the lid. The trunk was full of random, odd personal items: a shoebox of baseball cards, a coin collection, a model airplane, a few cartoon character jelly jar glasses, and rocks. He moved aside a stack of graphic novels to reveal two cartons of cigarettes, a handful of match-books, a bottle of Johnnie Walker Black Label—and at least twenty white pills in a plastic bag. He called out to Bree, "Found more drugs."

Matt lifted the lid of another shoebox. Rocks. "Except for the alcohol and cigarettes, he collects things like a ten-year-old." He replaced the lid and closed the footlocker.

Bree moved to the sleeping bag, which had been neatly zipped over a pillow. She unzipped it and folded back the top layer. "Shit." She fell back onto her haunches.

"What is it?" Matt leaned over her shoulder.

Nestled on the pillow was another skull.

"Another victim?" Matt asked.

"Seems like it." Bree pointed to a small, neat hole in the skull. "And that looks like a bullet hole."

CHAPTER FIVE

It was late afternoon when Bree walked from the fenced-in parking lot through the back door of the sheriff's station. Several hours at a crime scene in a mid-July heat wave had left her feeling wilted. The anthropologist had brought several grad students with him, so the site assessment, mapping, and other pre-excavation preparatory work were progressing at a rapid clip.

In the squad room, Deputy Oscar worked at a computer. He'd left the scene before she had, but his cheeks were still ruddy from the heat.

She stopped next to his desk. "Where's Shawn Castillo?"

"In interview room one."

"Not in holding?"

Oscar looked up, but he didn't directly meet Bree's gaze. "Collins is booking a big, bad-tempered suspect. I didn't want them to mingle."

Though the interview rooms were normally occupied by witnesses, not arrestees, his reasoning was sound. The sheriff's station was simply too small—one more reason the department needed better funding.

Oscar added, "FYI, Castillo's lawyer is on the way anyway." He handed her the arrest report. "Your copy."

Bree read through it. Seemed complete.

She folded the report in half. "What about his background?"

"No priors."

Surprised, Bree asked, "Employed?"

"No."

Bree plugged his address into her phone's map application. "He lives in an awfully nice neighborhood for an unemployed man. And why was he camping in a barn? This makes no sense."

Oscar didn't comment.

"Let me know if you find anything interesting." She checked her watch. Matt should be here any minute. He'd been helping to set up the tent over the bones when Bree had left, his height proving useful.

She headed to her office. Once inside, Bree sat behind her desk, a battle-worn and scarred hunk of furniture the size of a Cadillac that she'd inherited from the previous sheriff. It was too large for the room, but Bree liked being able to spread out her files. Leaning back in her chair, she called Todd, who was still at the scene. After he answered, she asked, "Where do we stand on fingerprints on the drug evidence?"

"It all went to the fingerprint tech at county."

"Thanks." Bree ended the call, phoned the latent-fingerprint tech, and asked her to rush a comparison with Shawn's prints. "I'd like to know before I interview him."

"I can do it right now," the tech agreed.

"Thank you." Bree set down her phone.

Her administrative assistant, Marge, entered, a pen and notepad in her hand.

Bree tucked the arrest report into a manila file where she'd put her own notes. "Any messages or news?"

She was readily available through email and voice mail, but a few citizens of Randolph County still insisted on calling the sheriff's station and leaving a message with a live person.

"Two things. Neither of which are going to make you happy. One, the date and time for your budget meeting was changed again." Marge lifted the reading glasses that hung from a chain around her neck and placed them on her nose. She squinted at her notepad. "To tomorrow afternoon."

"It was supposed to be next Tuesday." Bree swallowed a curse. "I'm scheduled to attend the autopsy on that overdose victim tomorrow."

"I know." With her pen poised above the paper, Marge looked over her half glasses. "Do you want me to reschedule the budget meeting?"

"No. They've postponed this meeting three times." Bree huffed. She had already submitted a proposal. Now, two members of the public safety committee, Elias Donovan and Richard Keeler, wanted to discuss her proposal.

Marge went to Bree's door and closed it. Then she perched on one of the two guest chairs facing Bree's desk. "They know you want more money. They don't want to give it to you, but you are very popular right now. So, they are going to drag the process out as long as possible, try to wear you down, hope you'll cave on some of your requests just to get the process moving."

Bree knew all this. She'd padded her initial budget to allow room for negotiation. When she'd been appointed sheriff back in February, she'd taken over a department in shambles. After the former sheriff's death, the department had hemorrhaged deputies. Bree had hired a handful, but every patrol was still short-staffed. Equipment needed replacing. Staff needed training. The station needed to be updated. Female officers—including Bree—didn't have a locker room. She wanted to replace the K-9 unit the department had lost three years before when Matt and his dog were shot. All those things required money. Bree had to prioritize.

In the year the county hadn't had a sheriff, some funds allocated to the department had gone unused, and the county had reduced the budget. Bree would have to fight for every nickel.

Marge wrote a note, then looked up and fixed Bree with an unhappy stare.

"Let me guess," Bree said. "Your second point is worse."

"Much." Marge nodded. "The man Oscar just brought in, Shawn Castillo, is the brother of Elias Donovan."

"Shit."

Elias also sat on the county board of supervisors. He was a BFD in local politics.

"Yes," Marge agreed.

"They don't share a last name."

"Technically, I think they're half brothers or stepbrothers." Marge's face creased. "I don't remember which."

"What were the chances?" Bree sighed.

"With Shawn, they were pretty good," Marge said, as if she knew him. But then, she knew everyone. Of all Bree's employees, Marge had worked for the department the longest. "This isn't the first time he's broken the law, though he hasn't been in here for several years."

"He doesn't have a record."

Marge lifted both eyebrows, stared at Bree, and waited.

"Oh." Bree rubbed her forehead. She should have guessed. She needed more coffee. "He's always been given a pass because his brother is on the board of supervisors." The prior sheriff had been old-school—and corrupt.

"Elias has a lot of money."

Bree turned to her computer and accessed the motor vehicle records. She compared Elias's address to Shawn's. "Shawn lives on the same road as Elias. Their house numbers are one digit apart."

"Elias built him a guesthouse just down the road from his own, on his property. If Elias didn't house him, Shawn would be homeless." Marge humphed. "Personally, I think the arrest will be good for Shawn. He needs help, and if he's never held accountable, he won't get it. It's not healthy for a person to be given everything."

"Is Elias Donovan going to hold this against me?" Bree asked. She'd met Elias a few times, but only in a large group. She didn't have a good feel for him. However, she suspected today's events would not help her win him over.

Marge tapped her pen on her pad. "Honestly, I don't know. He won't do it outwardly. If anything, look for something passive-aggressive."

"Wonderful." The sarcasm tasted bitter on Bree's tongue. She hadn't even had the chance to argue for her budget, and she already had one giant strike against her. "What else do you know about Elias?" She'd tried to catch him after the monthly public safety committee meetings, but he always seemed to disappear.

Marge made a wry face. "He's been in county government for decades. He has the kind of money that allows him to manage his money rather than have a real job. He is the primary reason county taxes have not been raised in years. Basically, he gets elected every year on a no-new-taxes pledge."

"Unfortunately, operating costs don't remain the same."

"Which is why the county is broke," Marge finished. "No one wants to pay taxes, even if they like the services their taxes provide. Elias is smart, and he has charisma. Not everyone likes him, but when he talks, people listen."

"How did he make his money?"

"Elias was still a young man when his father left him a small inheritance. He was smart about investments. He bought land and commercial properties during the recession in the early '80s, and again in 1990. He sold off or developed that land after the market recovered. He went about it ruthlessly and definitely made some enemies. He'll seem refined, but be careful. He's a shark in business transactions."

"Is there a best strategy with him?" Bree asked.

"Other than going back in time and not arresting his brother?"

"Yeah." Not that Bree would have considered that an option.

Marge turned up a palm.

Bree conceded with a nod. She would never let budget negotiations affect her decision to arrest Shawn. She had to play along with local politics, but she couldn't allow them to change how she did her job. She wouldn't use a man's arrest as leverage against his brother. But would Elias use the incident against her?

"Moving on to the second committee member, Richard Keeler," she said.

Marge continued. "Keeler doesn't come from money, but he married into it. His wife is from the FitzGeorge family."

"Should I know that name?" Bree asked.

"They build custom sailing yachts. They also dabble in horse breeding."

"She's from old money."

"The company was founded in the 1800s," Marge said. "Richard went to the university on a baseball scholarship. He married Susanna FitzGeorge right after graduation. Everyone thought he'd go pro, and he was picked up by a minor league team for a year or two, but that was as far as his career went. He came back to Grey's Hollow and started working for his wife's family business. The factory is located in Hyde, on the Hudson River. Many people around here still worship him as a college baseball star. He has quasi-celebrity status. With his wife's money and influence behind him . . . Let's just say making him an adversary will make your life—and meeting your budget—difficult." Marge stood. "So, in short, you're going to have to squeeze them for every nickel, but you have to do it without making enemies. Be diplomatic."

"Not my strong suit." Bree mentally cursed Shawn Castillo and his crappy timing. "Tomorrow should be fun."

"Yeah. Good luck with that." Marge brushed the wrinkles out of her practical black slacks. "The good news is that I just made fresh coffee."

"Thanks." Bree rose.

Marge patted her own dyed brown hair, sprayed into a curly do. "You're going to want to fix your hair."

Bree opened the middle drawer of her desk, pulled out a small compact, and checked her reflection. Tackling Shawn Castillo had knocked out her bun. Sweat and humidity had turned her loose hair into a frizzy, fright-wig mess. She fished through the drawer for bobby pins. At thirty-five, she'd been a cop long enough to redo her bun without looking. Hair was always neatly secured when in uniform.

"Better." Marge nodded in approval.

"One more thing."

Marge raised a brow.

"I need you to pull some old records for me," Bree said.

Matt had said she shouldn't assume her father was the killer, but the remains had been buried in her family's old backyard.

"How old?" Marge asked.

"Before 1993. Any arrest records or case files for Jake Taggert and Mary Taggert."

"Are you sure you want to go there?"

"Positive."

Marge gave her an *all right then* nod and wrote herself a note.

"I want their homicide case file as well." If Bree could not outrun her past, she would have to face it.

"I'll have this today or tomorrow." Marge snapped her notepad closed. "Physical files this old are in the basement."

Bree cracked her knuckles. Time to deal with Shawn Castillo. With Shawn's file tucked under her arm, she left her office. She headed for the break room and filled a mug with coffee. She added a little cream to cool it enough to drink half the mug in three big swallows.

Matt walked in looking as worn out as Bree felt. Above his tightly trimmed beard, his face was flushed from the heat. His short, reddish-brown hair was damp with sweat. At six three, he was built like a Hollywood Viking. In a movie, he'd be played by Chris Hemsworth. His eyes were a piercing blue, and sweat that would be gross on anyone else looked damned fine on him.

Back to work, Bree.

"Coffee or water?" she asked.

"Are we killing time while he stews?"

Bree sipped from her mug. "I'm stalling while I wait for the finger-print examiner to call."

"In that case, I'll have both." He stopped at the watercooler, filled a stainless-steel bottle, and drank deeply. "And maybe a snack."

He bought a pack of Peanut M&M's and a bag of almonds from the vending machine.

"Everything settled at the scene?" She poured coffee into a second mug.

"Yes." He set his water bottle on the counter and traded the bag of M&M's for a coffee.

Bree opened her package and ate a candy. "I don't like leaving the remains overnight. It feels disrespectful. The victims have been waiting for years to be found. They deserve better."

Matt chugged his coffee, then started on the almonds. "Deputy Juarez will guard the remains overnight. Nothing will happen. What those victims deserve is justice, and proper excavation will ensure the best chance of finding out who they were and who killed them."

"I know." But Bree didn't have to like it.

Matt ate a handful of almonds. Turning, he lowered his voice. "How are you dealing with finding the remains at your family's house?"

Bree felt the scrutiny of his intense blue eyes. He saw right through her.

"At first it was a shock," she admitted. "But as I said earlier, I already know my father murdered my mother. If he killed a few more people, it shouldn't be a surprise to anyone." Bree took a deep breath. She'd been trying to outrun her horrific past her whole life, but it seemed violence was determined to snap at her heels. Would tragedy always be right behind her?

Shaking it off, she explained about the relationship between Shawn Castillo and Elias Donovan.

"That's unbelievably bad luck," Matt said.

"Right? I'll miss an autopsy tomorrow afternoon."

Matt caught her gaze. "Do you have another homicide case?"

"I don't think so. It was an OD, most likely accidental."

"Then why did you want to attend the autopsy?"

Bree shrugged. "Just in case the ME finds something suspicious." She pictured the victim's grieving parents. "His death deserves as much of my attention as any other unnatural death. I like to dot my i's and all that."

"You like to make life hard for yourself."

"Maybe I do," she admitted. "Randolph County has had a dozen overdose deaths this year, and it's only July. Something has to be done about the opioid crisis."

"Bree, you can't be everything to everyone. You're only one person."

Bree nodded. "You're right. I need to improve my work–personal life balance."

Marge knocked on the doorframe and poked her head into the room. "Shawn Castillo's attorney is here. I put him in with his client."

"Thank you, Marge." Bree mentally cursed. She had wanted to know if they had a fingerprint match before she spoke with Shawn and his lawyer, but she'd have to wing it.

Her phone buzzed. She glanced at the screen. "This is her." Bree answered, then asked, "Were you able to pull any prints from the backpack?"

"The texture of the backpack exterior fabric was too rough," the tech began.

Not a surprise.

"What about the objects inside?" Bree remembered plenty of smooth surfaces, including the bag of prescription pills.

"No," the tech said. "All smudged."

Damn.

"However," the tech added, "I found a partial thumbprint on the bag of hydrocodone found in the footlocker. That partial matches

Shawn Castillo's. I haven't finished with the rest of the evidence. I'm only calling because you wanted a match quickly."

Bree exhaled. "Thank you for rushing that."

"No problem, Sheriff. I'll keep you updated."

Bree ended the call, hoping more evidence would be forthcoming. Until then, she'd have to bluff.

CHAPTER SIX

Bree repeated the information for Matt.

"Good," he said. "A solid drug possession charge should allow you to keep him at least overnight."

"Yes." Bree checked her watch. She'd purposefully stalled until the judge would be gone for the day. "I don't want to turn him loose just yet. He looks like a flight risk, and we have no idea if he killed those people or simply found the skull."

"And decided to play with it?" Matt raised a brow.

"I've seen weirder."

Matt agreed with a nod. "So have I, unfortunately."

Bree chugged the rest of her coffee, set the mug in the sink, then turned to Matt. "Ready to interview Shawn Castillo?"

"Let's do it." Matt carried his mug with him down the hall.

Bree opened the door. Shawn sat at the table conferring with a middle-aged man in a slick charcoal-colored suit. Slick was the attorney, no doubt. His hair was jet black with the perfect amount of silver at the temples. He was writing on a yellow legal pad. When Bree and Matt entered the room, he flipped a page to cover his notes.

The room smelled like hamburger and body odor. Bree glanced in the trash can and spied a crumpled-up fast-food bag.

Shawn sat back, slumped his shoulders, and crossed his arms. He glared at Bree. He might be a middle-aged man, but he wore insolence like a teenager. A take-out drink cup sat on the table in front of him. Who had bought him food? Not the attorney. He'd just arrived.

The attorney half stood for a split second. "Lyle Croft. I'll be representing Mr. Castillo."

Bree introduced herself and Matt.

Lyle resettled in his chair and smoothed his tie. He offered no opening comment. He folded his hands on the legal pad in front of him.

"I have some questions for your client." Bree slid a Miranda acknowledgment and a pen in front of Shawn. She recited his rights, then said, "I need you to sign that you understand these rights."

Shawn glanced at his lawyer, who nodded. Shawn signed.

Bree put the signed sheet in the file and returned the pen to her pocket. "This interview is being recorded."

"Now I have a question for you." The attorney flipped a page on his notepad, then read off a list of the charges Shawn had been booked on. "Do you really think you're going to make any of these charges stick?"

He was taking the offensive? Interesting.

"I do," she said. "Shawn is being held on trespassing, assaulting an officer, drug possession, concealment of a human corpse, and tampering with evidence." Though Bree had no doubt Shawn would ultimately plead to lesser offenses. Technically, this was his first offense.

Lyle lifted the paper to check his notes. "He assaulted an officer?"

"Yes," Bree said. "He threw rocks at me. It's there in the report." She'd considered adding a second simple assault charge, but the rocks hadn't come close to hitting her brother. Some cops would have padded the arrest to allow for negotiating room, but Bree wasn't a game-player. She'd rather make her case on the evidence.

The attorney didn't seem impressed. His mouth curled in a smirk much like his client's. "Did you identify yourself as the sheriff?"

Bree nodded. "Yes. Multiple times."

Lyle wrote a note.

"Your client had prescription opioids in his possession." Bree faced Shawn. "Do you have a prescription for the hydrocodone?"

"Don't answer that, Shawn," the attorney said without taking his gaze off Bree. "How can you prove the backpack belonged to Shawn?"

"I saw him carrying it," Bree said.

"How do you know he was carrying that particular backpack and not one that looked like it?" the attorney asked.

Bree didn't break eye contact. "I saw the backpack very clearly."

"While you were running at full speed through the woods?" The lawyer's brows rose in doubt.

"Yes," Bree said without hesitation.

The attorney lifted his pen. "Did you find my client's fingerprints on the backpack?"

"No." Bree let him think he had the upper hand.

Shawn gave Matt and Bree a smug stare. Bree wasn't a violent person, but his privileged smirk was definitely slappable.

The attorney nodded but said nothing. "You're going to file the drug charges anyway?"

"Yes." Bree sat back. Did Shawn really think he could beat the charges by throwing his backpack a few yards? "We also found drugs in the footlocker in the loft."

The attorney lifted a smug eyebrow. "Can you prove any of the items in the loft belong to my client?"

Bree dropped the bomb. "We matched a thumbprint from the baggie of drugs to Shawn."

In the middle of writing a sentence, the attorney paused. Beads of sweat broke out on Shawn's forehead, and his personal funk began to smell like fear. Had he not expected them to find prints? Seemed strange. Everyone knew all about prints in the age of *CSI*.

Bree addressed Shawn. "Why were you at the Taggert property?"

He shrugged, his eyes wary. "I like it there."

Matt leaned forward, planting his elbows on the table. "We found a sleeping bag in the barn. Is it yours?"

Shawn's gaze darted to his attorney.

"Lying to us will only make things worse for you," Bree said. "We have your thumbprint on the bag of drugs from the footlocker. I have no doubt we will find additional prints that match yours. The things in the loft belong to you. There are hairs in the sleeping bag. I'm sure DNA analysis will prove they're yours."

"Do you know what was in the sleeping bag?" Matt asked.

Shawn gave his head a slow shake, but his hands were shaking. He knew exactly what they'd found.

"It was a skull." Bree let the tension build for a few seconds. "We found skeletal remains on the property. Did you bury those remains?"

Shawn stiffened. His gaze slid to the table. "No."

"Did you kill them?" Bree asked.

Shawn jerked. His head snapped up. "No! Why would you think I did it?"

"Because you were there, sleeping with the skull?" Bree batted his question back.

The lawyer touched Shawn's arm. "My client declines to answer that."

Bree cut to the chase. "Where did you get the skull, Shawn?"

Again, Shawn glanced at his lawyer, who shook his head.

"Do you know how they died?" she asked.

He looked away and shook his head, his mouth tight. Was he lying?

"Do you own a gun?" Bree already knew no gun was registered to Shawn, but he could have an illegal one.

"Don't answer that," the attorney cut in.

She swallowed her frustration. "Is this the first time you've been to the old Taggert property?"

"Don't answer that," the attorney said, but Shawn was already shaking his head.

"Why did you camp at the farm?" she pressed.

"I like it there," he repeated, mumbling.

"Why?" Bree asked.

Shawn lifted his gaze. His eyes lit with interest. "Bad things happened there. People died. It's a killing place."

The attorney looked disgusted. He leaned over and whispered in his client's ear, "Will you shut the fuck up?" Then he muttered something Bree didn't catch in a *don't know why I'm even here* voice.

"What bad things?" Bree asked.

"*You* know." Shawn's eyes brightened, as if he were enjoying the discussion. "That's where your daddy killed your mama, and they weren't the only people to die there."

The attorney looked like he was going to choke. "Stop talking."

But Shawn was engaged. He didn't want to stop. He leaned forward, his excitement palpable in the small room.

Bree shifted forward, mirroring him. She held his gaze and put some macabre interest in her voice. "How many people?"

"Lots and lots. At night, you can feel them." Shawn's eyes brightened further. His leg began to jiggle, the foot tapping on the floor in a crazed rhythm. He looked like he was going to explode.

"Did you kill them, Shawn?" Matt pressed.

The attorney grabbed Shawn's forearm. "Do not answer that question."

Shawn leaned back and crossed his arms. Was he paving the way for an insanity defense?

"Why were you staying in the barn?" Matt asked. "To be close to the people you killed?"

Shawn's foot tapped in double time, and he shifted on the chair as if he could barely keep his body on it. His gaze darted between Bree and Matt. Then he side-eyed his attorney and pressed his lips flat.

The attorney grabbed Shawn's arm again and held it in a tight grip. "Do *not* say anything else. You don't have to answer any of their questions. It's their job to prove everything. Don't help them."

"They don't know shit." Shawn's chin lifted and his jaw tightened in defiance.

The attorney told him to be quiet and addressed Bree. "Do you even know how old the remains are or how long they've been there?"

Bree shook her head. "Not yet, but we will soon." She stared at Shawn and threw out her bluff. "If you handled that skull recently, you left what we call touch DNA on the surface." It was possible, but hardly a given that they'd find anything.

Thankfully, Shawn couldn't restrain himself. "I found it. There's no law against finding things."

"Actually, there are laws against tampering with a crime scene and improper disposition or concealment of human remains."

"We're done here." The attorney checked his watch, then shot Bree an accusatory glare. "It's too late to get him arraigned today."

Bree had planned on exactly that.

"What does that mean?" Shawn's gaze darted between Bree and the lawyer.

"It means you can't get bailed out today," the lawyer said without breaking eye contact with Bree.

Shawn jolted, his shock palpable. "I have to spend the night in jail?"

"You're being charged with multiple felonies, Shawn," Bree said. Was he really this dense?

"Just one night." The attorney slapped Shawn on the shoulder. "We'll get you into court tomorrow, and I'll have you out ASAP."

Disbelief clouded Shawn's face, and he muttered, "Jail? I can't go to jail."

The attorney ignored the comment.

Bree opened the door and called for Oscar to transport Shawn to the jail. Lyle hurried down the hall toward the lobby. Bree and Matt were on their way back to her office when she spotted Elias Donovan in the lobby conferring with the attorney. Donovan was a tall man with short gray hair, a goatee, and wire-rimmed glasses. His expensive suit was obviously tailored to fit his lean body. Their gazes met across the station. A bright spark of anger lit his eyes before he turned his attention back to the lawyer.

Bree walked into her office. Matt followed and closed the door behind them.

She sank into her chair. "What do you think?"

Matt paced the small space between the guest chairs and her desk. "I don't know. The skull in the sleeping bag was freaky. I don't like freaky."

"Me neither." Bree tossed the file into her inbox.

"That was a weird interview." Matt stopped and scratched his chin.

"Yeah." Bree tapped her fingers on the desk. "I don't know what to make of Shawn. He's a tough one to read."

"His emotions were inconsistent."

"They were," Bree agreed. "He was cool and arrogant until I asked about the bones. Then he got excited. Did he like talking about dead people, or did it feel like he was playing with us?"

Matt stroked his beard. "He seemed confident his brother's attorney can handle the lesser charges. But murder is a whole different ball game."

A crash sounded on the other side of the door. Bree jumped to her feet and flung open the office door as the station erupted in chaos.

CHAPTER SEVEN

Matt rushed toward the door, but Bree was already through it. He was right on her heels. He burst through the opening and drew up short, assessing the situation in a quick glance. The squad room was complete bedlam. Chairs had been knocked over. Shawn and a much larger man were rolling on the floor trying to punch each other. The big man was heavily tattooed with a full Duck Dynasty beard.

The men stopped rolling with Shawn on the bottom. He gasped under his opponent's greater weight but somehow managed to slide out from under him like a slimy eel. He was halfway to his feet when the big man rose onto one knee and let loose with a backhand that knocked Shawn ass over end.

Shawn slid into a desk. The desk careened across the space—right into Matt's path. It hit him in the legs with an impact that was sure to leave a mark. A phone, a lamp, and assorted office supplies flew off the top and went sliding across the cracked linoleum. Shawn wobbled on his feet for a nanosecond before the big man charged him, taking him to the ground again.

Oscar and Deputy Laurie Collins rushed in and attempted to get past the men's kicking legs. Collins took a boot in the chest and fell back, gasping. Oscar went after Shawn—the lesser threat.

Typical, thought Matt as he vaulted over the desk.

To his right, Bree weaved around another desk, two fallen chairs, and more desktop debris.

The men rolled again. Their colliding bodies knocked Oscar back. Panting, Shawn weaseled out from underneath the bigger man. His opponent was twice his weight, but much slower. Matt had to give Shawn credit. He was a scrapper.

The fighting men scrambled to their feet and faced off. Oscar jumped into the fray and grabbed Shawn's arm, but all his action accomplished was to allow the larger man to land a solid punch to Shawn's face. Blood spurted from his nose. The big man pulled his arm back to fire another punch. On the backswing, his elbow struck Oscar in the chin, knocking him off his feet.

Collins got to her feet, but she looked unsteady. Her face was pale, and she was sucking air like a landed guppy. Oscar was down on his hands and knees. He shook his head as if to clear it.

Bree shoved aside a wheeled chair and headed directly into the fray. Matt tried to pass her. The second man was bouncer-big. His biceps were so bulgy he probably couldn't wash his own face. Not that his size would deter Bree. She waded right past her struggling deputies, the look on her face fierce.

"Freeze," Bree shouted.

No one responded. The fighting men were completely focused on each other. The larger man caught Shawn around the waist, twisted, and threw him to the ground. Then he rolled Shawn onto his back, straddled him, and raised a giant fist over his shoulder, preparing to pummel him.

Whipping out her baton, Bree flicked it to full length. Then she caught the larger man from behind in a seat belt hold. Her arms weren't long enough to encircle his torso, so she used the baton against his chest as leverage. But he was enraged. He tried to shake her off. Bree hung on as the man bucked. He rose onto his knees, reached over his shoulder, and tried to grab her. Ducking away from his clawing hand, she lost her grip and fell off his back. She was moving in again when Matt stepped between them.

He dived at the larger man, tackling him and taking him to the ground next to Shawn. At six three and two hundred pounds, Matt was no lightweight. But the other man had three inches on him, along with a fifty-pound weight advantage. In his peripheral vision, Matt saw Shawn roll to his hands and knees and crawl away.

In normal grappling with a much larger opponent, Matt would have gone for a rear naked choke, but chokes were not permitted as restraints. He'd have to find another way.

The man reached for Matt's head. Matt took advantage, catching the man's elbow under his own and stepping over him to straddle him, sitting on his opponent's hip.

Matt trapped the big man's upper arm between his own knees and wrapped it up tight. Then he rocked sideways, using the weight of his entire body against the big man's elbow and shoulder. The man's other arm was pinned under his body. With his shoulder locked up and his elbow hyperextended, the man couldn't move without damaging one of his own joints. Trapped in an armbar, the man struggled for a few seconds.

"Don't make me break your arm," Matt said. "I can sit here all day."

The man went still. Matt could feel his chest heaving.

Matt waited for Bree to appear at his side with a pair of extra-large handcuffs. The big man didn't resist as she restrained him. Then Matt hauled him to his feet and shuffled him to the steel bench at the rear of the room. Once the man was secured to the bench, Matt stepped back. "Do you want to add shackles?" he asked Bree.

Bree glowered at the man. "Yes."

Matt retrieved a set of leg shackles and put them on the prisoner. Stepping back, he assessed Collins. She was bent over, her hands resting on her thighs.

"You OK?" he asked.

"Just had the wind knocked out of me," Collins said between gulps for air.

Bree squinted at her deputy. "Do you need the ER?"

Collins shook her head. "I'll be fine in a couple of minutes."

Oscar leaned on the wall, breathing hard.

"Are you injured?" Bree asked him.

He shook his head.

Elias Donovan and Shawn's attorney rushed in.

"What happened to my brother?" Elias asked.

Shawn was holding both hands to his face. Blood seeped between his fingers. "My nose is broken. I can't see straight."

"Get him an ice pack," Bree ordered. Oscar hustled out of the room.

He returned with the ice and a stack of paper towels, which he handed to Shawn. Shawn mopped his face and held the ice to his nose. His eyes were rapidly swelling. Matt expected him to be defeated, but a strange glee lit his eyes. The expression on his blood-streaked face was chilling.

Baton in hand, Bree glowered at the two suspects, then her deputies. No one moved.

Donovan gave Oscar an equally withering look, then switched his grim stare to Bree. "My brother needs to go to the hospital. You'll be lucky if we don't sue you."

Bree met his challenge. "And Shawn will be lucky if I don't add additional charges to his growing list."

But legally, the odds were in Shawn's favor, even if he'd started the altercation. He'd been injured while in police custody, and his brother had the financial resources to pursue an agenda.

A deputy walked in the back door. Bree collapsed her baton and used it to point at the newcomer, then at Shawn. "Take this man to the ER. Make sure he is appropriately restrained at all times. Do not give him an inch. Make sure to tell the ER docs that he has a history with narcotics."

"Yes, ma'am." The deputy handcuffed Shawn and marched him out the back door. Donovan hurried out of the station, presumably to meet his brother at the ER.

Bree called out to the shackled man. "Do you need to go to the hospital?"

"No. *I'm* not a pussy!" he shouted back.

Bree turned to Matt. "You're not even out of breath."

Matt stretched his neck. "I'm durable. I get a solid beating every week in Nolan's MMA class. My brother has been using me as a practice dummy since I was born."

His brother was a retired professional mixed martial arts fighter and owned an MMA gym nearby.

They both nodded. Collins looked sheepish. Oscar remained stone-faced.

Bree pointed at Collins and Oscar. "Both of you, in my office. Matt, I'd like you to come as well."

Collins walked gingerly. Oscar didn't even have the brains to look embarrassed. He followed Bree, his posture still rigid, his chin lifted as if he were in the right, even though he'd failed to properly restrain or maintain control of his detainee.

This is not going to go well.

They trooped into the small office. Matt leaned against the wall. Bree sat in her chair. Oscar stood facing the desk, back ramrod straight, arms crossed over his chest. Collins sank into a guest chair. She rubbed her ribs, which Matt thought probably hurt more than she was admitting.

Bree pointed at Collins. "What happened?"

"I was fingerprinting my perp when Oscar brought that little asshole by." She jerked a thumb at Oscar. "The asshole called my perp a pussy. My perp then exploded."

Bree exhaled and turned her gaze to Oscar. "Why was Shawn not handcuffed?"

Oscar tried to shrug, but he was too tense, and the gesture looked like a muscle spasm. "I just hadn't gotten to it."

Bree frowned as she considered her deputy. Then she straightened her uniform shirt. "Don't let it happen again." She spoke to Matt. "Do you think Nolan would run some classes and practice sessions for my deputies?"

"I do." Matt nodded.

"OK, then." Bree fixed Collins and Oscar with consecutive death stares. "Let's make that happen. I understand that we've been short-handed and scrambling for shift coverage. Now that we have five new deputies, we need to make time for training. Defense skills are perishable. We all need regular practice." She breathed, clearly trying to be calm and proactive when down deep, she was probably pissed off in twenty different ways.

Both deputies nodded in relief.

Bree pointed at Collins. "Transfer your perp to the jail. Let them book him and hold him overnight. He's liable to pull an Incredible Hulk on our ancient holding cell."

"Yes, ma'am." Collins fixed her bun and hurried out of the office.

"Oscar, back to work," Bree commanded.

Matt waited until both deputies were gone and the door was closed. "You could have given them both written reprimands."

"They fucked up." Bree nodded. "But the truth is, we need more than one holding cell, we need more damned space, and I was being honest when I said we all needed more training and practice. It's my responsibility to make sure my deputies have and maintain the skills they need to do their jobs." She let out a tight breath. "But we did learn a few more things about Shawn."

"We did," Matt agreed.

"First of all, he's more aggressive and capable of greater violence than I would have predicted." Bree rubbed her elbow. "But I can't decide if he's a great actor or truly impulsive. Did he insult that man thinking he could get away with it here?"

"No." Matt considered Shawn's expression after the fight. "He wanted that fight. The big guy reacted exactly the way Shawn intended."

Bree frowned. "Why? Why would he want to get the hell beaten out of him?"

"By going to the ER, he avoided spending a night in jail."

Bree sat back.

Matt continued. "He looked pleased with himself."

"If you're right, then that's disturbingly manipulative. He was willing to take a hell of a beating to get what he wanted," Bree said. "Let's hope we get some answers about our victims tomorrow."

"Bones take time to analyze, and skeletal remains are not usually so easy to identify."

"Maybe we'll get lucky, but let's get a search warrant for his residence. Get another to search his phone. I want his financials too." She looked at her phone. "I'm going home. Put a rush on those warrants. I want to search Shawn's place tomorrow, before he gets home and disposes of any evidence. At this time, the charges against him aren't severe enough for the judge to deny him bail, not with his brother's expensive lawyer in his corner. Shawn will be out on bail by the afternoon. I really don't want a potential murderer running loose."

Chapter Eight

Early Friday morning, Bree leaned over Cowboy's withers. The warm wind whipped her face. Under her, the horse galloped across the meadow. Exhilaration flooded her as the paint's hooves flew over the ground. Cowboy pulled at the reins, and she let him have his head. At the far end of the meadow, she eased him down to a lope, then a jog. He pranced a little, still excited from the run. Sweat gleamed on his coat. Bree lifted her T-shirt away from her chest.

"Easy, boy." She patted the horse's sleek neck. "I promise we'll go for a longer run when this heat wave breaks."

She slowed him to a walk as they approached the hill. In the distance, sunrise glowed on the horizon. They crested the hill next to the huge old oak tree. Bree stopped beneath its branches and turned her horse around to view the meadow she'd just galloped through. Yellow wildflowers dotted a sea of tall grass. It was in this place that she and the kids had scattered her sister's ashes. Whenever she went riding with the kids, they stopped here. But there were times when Bree liked a quiet moment alone with her sister's memory. Doing that while sitting atop the horse she'd inherited from Erin seemed appropriate.

Was Erin watching over them now? Bree liked to think so.

Peace settled over her. Sometimes, the sheer wholesomeness of her new normal astounded Bree. Her entire former life had revolved around her job. She'd lived in an apartment with a cranky tomcat as her only company. She'd rarely dated and had seen no reason to include other people in her personal life. She'd seen her siblings once a year and talked to them on the phone occasionally. Thoughts of reconnecting with her family had always been considered under the heading of *someday*.

Then Erin had died, leaving Bree no time to renew her relationship with her sister. That opportunity was gone, like Erin's ashes in the wind. Bree could not let the same happen with the kids or Adam. She had rearranged her priorities—and her entire life—to put her family first.

She allowed herself a few minutes to watch the sunrise. Then she gathered her reins and touched Cowboy's side with her heels. Calm now, he walked on a loose rein and was cool by the time they reached the barn. She untacked him and brushed the sweat from his back before returning him to his stall. She would have fed the horses, but Luke insisted that was his job. On her way out of the barn, she scratched Kayla's short and sturdy horse, Pumpkin, under his blond forelock. Luke's bay gelding, Riot, snorted and bobbed his head until she patted his nose as well.

She crossed the back lawn, jogged up the back-porch steps, and entered the house. The kitchen was cool and smelled of coffee. Bree's best friend and former homicide detective partner, Dana Romano, was pouring coffee into a mug. After her retirement from the Philly PD back in January, Dana had moved to Grey's Hollow to help raise Bree's niece and nephew.

Bree bent down and removed one of her still-snug new riding boots. Ladybug came sliding across the floor. Her big, wet nose hit Bree in the face, and the dog's shoulder took her out at the knees. Bree crashed sideways, her hip hitting the floor with a burst of pain.

The dog stood over her, then lowered her shoulders to the floor and wagged her tailless butt, as if she wanted to play. Someone had docked the rescue dog's tail long before Bree had adopted her.

Laughing, Bree sat up and tugged off her remaining boot. "Ladybug, you are a silly girl."

Bree rubbed her hip, then scratched under the dog's collar. Ladybug cocked her head and leaned in.

It still amazed Bree that she wasn't terrified of the pudgy rescue. She'd been annoyed when Matt had tricked her into adopting the dog, but he'd been right. Ladybug was the least intimidating canine she'd ever encountered. Bree had formed a relationship with the mutt she never would have thought possible.

With a final pat for the dog, Bree stood. At six thirty, sunlight flooded the kitchen. Bree's black cat, Vader, sat on the sideboard staring at the scene as if he wanted to roll his eyes.

"Ladybug, breakfast!" Dana called.

The dog bolted. Her loyalty went only so far. Dana filled a stainless-steel bowl and set it on the floor. The dog ate her food in less than a minute. The cat looked away, clearly disgusted.

Dana sipped her coffee. It was barely dawn, and she was fully put together, right down to bright raspberry lipstick that matched her toenail polish. Her short, gray-and-blonde hair was artfully tousled. Bree had scraped her own hair into a ponytail.

"Good ride?" Dana asked.

"Yes. Feels good to get outside before work. Besides, riding is the best for clearing my head. If I'm not one hundred percent focused, I could fall on my face." Bree wiped the sweat from her forehead. She'd been riding a few mornings a week, alternating with running and yoga.

"Grab a shower. I'll make you a cappuccino." Dana turned toward her fancy coffee maker.

Bree showered and dressed in her uniform. She blasted her hair with the dryer for a few minutes and pinned it up still damp. As she went downstairs, an incredible aroma hit her nostrils. She entered the kitchen just as Dana pulled a baking pan from the oven.

Bree sniffed the air. "Are those scones?"

"Blueberry." Dana gestured toward a cooling rack on the counter that already held a dozen pastries. "Your cappuccino is ready."

Bree reached for a scone. It was still warm in her hand. She set it on a napkin and broke off a chunk. It melted in her mouth. She sipped the cappuccino.

"You should sit while you eat."

"Yes, Mom," Bree teased as she slid onto a stool at the counter. As much as she'd like to be at the scene first thing, she would take the time to have breakfast with the kids. She had no idea what the rest of the day would entail. Being home for a family dinner was always her goal, but never guaranteed.

Dana rolled her eyes. "Someone has to teach you self-care. Prepare for my evening lecture about not swimming for an hour after you eat."

They often joked about their relationship, but the fact was, Bree had never experienced any mothering. Her mother had died when Bree was eight. The cousin who had raised her had been lacking in maternal instincts. Ironically, it turned out that twice-divorced-no-kids Dana had mad mom skills, which she'd turned loose on Bree and the kids over the past six months.

Footsteps thundered on the stairs.

Dana smiled. "Luke's up."

Bree's sixteen-year-old nephew hurtled through the kitchen, dressed in jeans and a black polo shirt with a supermarket logo on the chest. "Morning."

"Morning," Bree and Dana said in unison.

"I have an early shift. I'll muck stalls after work, OK?" He grabbed a scone on his way to the back door.

"Sure," Bree said.

He ate his pastry as he shoved his feet into rubber boots at the back door. He wiped his mouth with his bare forearm and went out the back door to feed the horses.

Bree looked at the calendar on the kitchen wall, where the kids' activities were posted. Luke started work this morning at eight. An unexpected burst of pride surged in Bree. Luke woke early to feed the horses, even on his summer break. And he was balancing a part-time job at the local grocery store with playing on a travel baseball team. He'd taken his mother's death hard. Spring had been rough on all of them, but he seemed to be happier since school let out for the summer.

Like it or not, they were settling into their new normal.

Eight-year-old Kayla skipped into the kitchen. Not a morning person, she usually liked to have breakfast in her pajamas, but she was dressed in jeans and a pink T-shirt with a pony bedazzled on the front.

"You're up early," Bree said.

Kayla climbed onto a stool, her face serious. "I have a lot of work to do."

Bree put a scone on a napkin and set it on her niece's placemat. "Excited for Sunday?" Kayla had entered Pumpkin in the local 4-H horse show at the county fair.

Kayla nodded. Dana went to the fridge and poured a glass of milk. She set it in front of the child.

"I'm lucky." Kayla broke off a huge chunk of scone. "Maya Steiner's pony is so bad. Last year, he bucked her off in the middle of the ring. No one could catch him. Pumpkin would never do that."

Pumpkin the Haflinger was an angel. He was also too lazy. Bree sent a prayer of thanks to her sister for passing on a fancy mount and picking a safe and sensible horse for Kayla.

Kayla shoved the pastry into her mouth and mumbled around it. "But he's really dirty. Will you help me give him a bath tomorrow?"

"I will." Bree ignored her talking with her mouth full. Like Luke, Kayla finally seemed to be taking an interest in activities. Bree would not do anything to dull the shine of the upcoming 4-H show. The little girl washed down her scone with milk. "He does like to roll in the mud like a pig."

The pasture hadn't dried out since the last big rain.

Kayla burst into giggles. Milk shot from her nose. Her eyes opened in surprise.

Laughing, Bree handed her a napkin. "Next time, swallow before you talk," she said in a light tone.

Kayla grinned. "We have to give Cowboy a bath too. He can't lead the parade all dirty."

"Sure."

"Can we braid his mane too?" Kayla asked. "Mommy used to do it every year for the parade, but he never got to be in the front before."

Bree pictured Cowboy's long mane. "I've never done it, but we can try."

"Yay! He needs ribbons." Kayla finished her breakfast, then ran to the back door and stuffed her feet into her purple boots. "I'm gonna clean my saddle and bridle today. I'll do yours too."

"Stay outside, so I can see you, OK?" Dana called to her.

"OK," Kayla yelled over her shoulder as she raced out the back door.

"All ready to lead that parade?" Dana asked with a grin.

"I guess." Bree had been roped into leading the opening parade and giving out the Best of Show awards at the end of the day.

Dana snickered. "You'll live. It's made Kayla really happy, and it's good for the voters to see you as an active member of the community."

"I know," Bree grumbled. She didn't love politicking, but she would do anything to make Kayla happy. "She's really coming out of her shell." Grief had sapped her niece's energy for most of the winter and spring. But her smile had returned with summer.

"Her whole personality has changed," Dana agreed with a smile.

The kitchen went quiet. Bree finished her own scone and drank the rest of her cappuccino. Through the window, she watched Luke carry his sister's saddle out of the barn and set it over the fence. Kayla dragged out a small bucket of water and the saddle soap.

"Digging out the remains today?" Dana asked.

Her tone was casual, but Bree felt her keen focus. "Yes."

"Is Matt working the case?" Dana asked.

"Yes."

"Don't you usually go out on Saturday nights?"

"We do, and we might this week, as long as the case doesn't get in the way."

"Don't let it. You need to spend some *romantic* time with Thor." With two kids in the house, she and Dana had begun talking in code, but the waggle of Dana's eyebrows made her meaning clear. She pointed at Bree with her spatula. "Time when you're not talking about a homicide."

Bree snorted. "*We* are not discussing my *romantic* life."

Dana let her reading glasses drop to the end of her nose. She deadpanned over the frames. "Obviously, there isn't anything to discuss."

"How do you know?" Bree's cheeks heated.

It was Dana's turn to snort. "There's no way *that* man would leave you this . . . tense."

Bree sighed. "What about you? When's your next date?"

Dana turned off the oven. "I'm having dinner with the pharmacist next week."

"Oooooh. Is this a second date?"

"It is, but don't get too excited. We only had coffee on the first one. All a second date means is that he's reasonably normal and gainfully employed."

"I'll cross my fingers for you." Bree slid off the stool. "I'm off to work."

She took a second cappuccino in her to-go cup.

Dana handed her a paper bag. "Scones for the crew at the scene."

"Thanks." Bree's phone buzzed.

Matt's name popped onto the screen.

"What's up?" she answered.

"Are you on your way?" he asked.

"Leaving now."

"Good." Matt paused. "The doc found something you're going to want to see."

CHAPTER NINE

Bree drove out to the site. The promised rain had not materialized overnight, and humidity weighted the air. At nine in the morning, it was already past eighty degrees. The ME's vehicle was parked behind the anthropologist's SUV and Matt's Suburban. On the other side of the road, a news team was setting up to give a report. Local media was fascinated with her family's tragedy. The newly discovered graves would undoubtedly attract more reporters.

A new deputy had replaced Juarez that morning. As Bree stepped out of her vehicle, the deputy met her in the street.

"See that the press stays in the street," she ordered as she signed the crime scene log.

"Yes, ma'am," he said.

Bree headed around the side of the house, past the barn, and into the woods.

The heat was oppressive, and a mosquito buzzed past her face. By the time she emerged in the clearing, she was sweating and swatting at a bite on her neck.

Considering the early hour, the team had made an impressive amount of progress. A grid had been laid out with string. Grad students squatted in the ditch, sifting dirt. Matt, Dr. Jones, and the anthropologist conferred next to a tarp. A few dozen bones of various sizes were arranged on the tarp. Bree recognized a skull and some pelvic bones. A second skull sat in a cardboard box next to the tarp. A few students were setting up a second dig on the other side of the clearing.

Was it another body?

Dr. Jones waved, and Bree joined the ME, Matt, and the anthropologist, Dr. Sam Bernard.

Bree had met Dr. Bernard the previous day. He was tall, fit, and deeply tanned. A broad-brimmed safari-style hat shielded his face. His glasses were wire-rimmed, with clip-on sunshades. He wore dusty cargoes and even dustier boots. The back of his T-shirt was already soaked through with sweat. How Dr. Jones still looked fresh in her scrubs and sneakers, Bree did not understand.

"Morning, Dr. Bernard." Bree stepped up beside Matt and greeted everyone. "Looks like you've all been busy."

"Please call me Sam." The anthropologist rubbed his palms together. "We've gotten really lucky. But before I get into the details, a quick update on our progress. Yesterday, we took aerial photos with a drone, cleared surface debris, and marked off our grid. Serena expressed concern there could be additional graves, and we found a slight depression in the ground over there next to that tall pine tree."

Bree felt her eyebrows rise as he called the ME by her first name.

Dr. Jones blinked. Was that a blush, or was the heat finally getting to her?

Sam pointed across the clearing. "A depression can indicate a place where a body might be buried. Decomposing remains leave a void in the soil. The ground sinks or compacts into that space over time. These depressions that are formed are also called compaction sites."

Sam moved toward a wheeled machine the size of a small lawn mower with a screen mounted at waist height. "The ground is relatively flat in this clearing, so we decided ground-penetrating radar was the best tool to map this site." He tapped on the screen. "GPR data showed something is buried in that location." He motioned toward the second dig. "The depth and shape of the hole are consistent with this burial. However, the object looks too small to be adult remains, unless the victim is curled on its side—or it's a child." He indicated a blurry grayscale image on the screen.

Bree's stomach rolled. "Or a dog."

"Possibly." Sam nodded. "We're working on that excavation too, so we'll have that answer later today or tomorrow."

Bree gestured over the clearing. "How many days do you think it'll take?"

"Two, maybe three to do it properly. As far as excavating this grave"—Sam turned his attention back to the bones on the tarp—"we're just getting started, but we've been incredibly lucky to have found both skulls and pubic bones, along with some long and small bones. Let's talk about the bones first. Then I'll address the personal effects we've uncovered." He took a breath. "So far, we believe we have the remains of two victims here. From the recovered pubic bones, we've determined one is male and one is female. This skull recovered from this grave belongs to the male." He pointed to the skull in the cardboard box. "Based on age, size, and overall context of the find, the skull found in the loft likely belongs to the female skeleton. We'll confirm with DNA, but I believe it's reasonable to proceed on that assumption at this time."

Bree eyed the holes in the foreheads of both skulls. "They were both shot in the head."

"Yes." Crouching, Sam donned a glove, picked up the skull on the tarp, and turned it over to reveal a larger hole at its base. "The entry hole is smaller than the exit here in the occipital bone. Also, the hole isn't completely round. It's more of a keyhole shape, meaning the bullet struck the skull at an angle more acute than ninety degrees. I can tell that the male was facing his shooter. The entrance wound"—he pointed to the forehead—"is beveled inward, while the exit wound is beveled outward. From the location of the entry and exit, we can see a downward trajectory of the bullet."

"Can you tell how far away the shooter stood?" Bree asked.

Sam pointed to the entry wound. "Based on the fractures radiating from the entry wound, I'd say the shooter stood a few feet away. I'll be able to give you more information once we get the bones in the lab, do measurements, and run tests."

Bree could picture it easily. "He was on his knees in front of their killer."

"Most likely, yes," Sam agreed.

"An execution," Matt said.

A short pause followed his statement.

"The female was also shot in the head. But the same factors I outlined before—trajectory, fractures, beveling, et cetera—suggest she was lying on the ground when she was shot."

"Is there anything else?" Bree needed more to start trying to identify the remains.

"Yes. Quite a bit, actually." Sam pushed his glasses up to the bridge of his sweaty nose. "Based on the length of the long bones, I estimate the male was approximately five eight to six feet tall. The female was between five two and five six."

"Race?" Matt asked.

Sam frowned at the skulls one at a time. "Both were probably Caucasian."

"Ages?" Bree asked.

Sam said, "Human bones continue to grow until adulthood. The long bones grow at either end. We call these growth plates. They fully close when the skeleton is finished growing. We call this epiphyseal closure, or growth plate fusion. Just eyeballing the long bones, I know these victims were both adults." He pointed to a curved, thin bone in the center of the line. "You can also estimate age by looking at the sternal ends of the ribs, but we've only found one rib from the male victim so far. We're also still missing a good number of teeth and some fingers from both victims. The best I can do is between twenty-five and fifty for both of them. When I get them into the lab, I might be able to narrow that span based on a thorough analysis of all the bones we recover."

"I hear a *but* . . . ," Bree said.

Sam nodded. "But that might not be necessary. We have a few specific discoveries that might be very helpful." He indicated several items in an open cardboard box. "Let's start with a key piece of jewelry." He pointed to a tarnished bangle bracelet with hearts and the name *Jennifer* engraved on it. "We're assuming this bracelet belonged to the female. Most males don't wear jewelry this delicate. Plus, it's too narrow in circumference to have fit around the average male wrist. There's a date engraved on the inside of the bracelet: *6-20-1985.*"

Matt pulled out his phone and typed on the screen. "That was a Thursday."

"Maybe her birthday or wedding," Bree suggested.

Sam pointed out a smooth fissure on a piece of a jawbone lying next to the skull. "Next, the female's mandible shows a healed fracture." He squinted at the bone. "And potentially some extensive dental work to repair some sort of trauma. I'll know more if we recover the remaining piece of jaw and the molars. If we can locate her dental records, we should be able to make an identification. We have a forensic odontologist—that's a forensic dentist—available at the university."

"We need a name to locate dental X-rays," Bree said. "Do you have any indication how long the remains were in the ground?"

"Yes and no." Sam pursed his lips. "The bones have been buried for at least a year—"

"We found a wallet," Dr. Jones interrupted.

"Yes!" Sam said. "Did I forget to mention that? Sorry. Sometimes I get carried away with the bones."

The corner of Dr. Jones's mouth twitched. "The wallet was in tatters. The license was faded, but the print was readable."

"Who is it?" Bree asked.

Dr. Jones said, "Frank Evans."

The name was familiar, but Bree didn't know why.

Dr. Jones donned a glove and picked up a box full of grungy-looking odds and ends.

Bree saw a strip of elastic, buttons, a few coins, and some pieces of fabric.

Dr. Jones lifted a small plastic rectangle and displayed it in her palm. She pointed to the text. "The license says Frank was five ten, which falls in the range of Sam's height estimate. Obviously, we can't match his eye color."

"But we have a name," Bree said.

"And a date," Dr. Jones said. "The license was issued in 1988."

"One of the coins is dated 1989," Sam added.

"So, they probably weren't buried until 1989 or later." Bree scanned the items, pleasantly surprised at the amount of information they'd already gleaned from the grave excavation. "Hopefully, we can locate a missing persons report, DNA, or dental records."

"There are a few other interesting elements." Sam picked up two small bones and held them up. "These are finger bones. Distal phalanx and middle phalanx, or the first two bones of the finger when counting from the tip. If you look at the middle phalanx on the end where it connects to the distal phalanx, the edge is clean-cut." He fished around the small bones on the tarp for another that looked similar. "This is a normal phalanx."

The normal bone looked like Bree expected, more rounded with smooth edges. "What are you saying? The fingertip was cut off?" Her stomach soured.

"Yes, and we found two more like that from the male skeleton," Sam said simply. "These bones didn't separate from the skeleton naturally."

Dr. Jones leaned in to examine the bone. "No jagged saw marks. That was a very sharp edge."

Sam nodded. "Something like shears or bolt cutters would be my guess."

Next to Bree, Matt swore softly.

"We haven't found any finger bones from the female that were cut. Yet." Sam put down the finger bones and picked up two halves of a long bone. "We have a femur and several ribs from the female victim that were broken perimortem."

"So, at or around the time of death," Bree clarified.

"Correct." Sam indicated the broken ends. "Clearly, the break had no time to heal, so it didn't occur antemortem or before death. Postmortem breaks tend to be more splintered because bones dry out and get brittle after death. This break is clean. Anyway, that's all I can tell you for now." Sam removed his hat and wiped his forehead before resettling it on his head.

"Thank you for your help," Bree said.

The two doctors went back to their work. Bree and Matt turned away from the dig.

"This is going to be a complicated case." Bree led the way toward the trees. The graves unsettled her, and not just because they were in her childhood backyard. There was more to this case than murder—as if murder weren't bad enough. At least one of these victims had been tortured.

CHAPTER TEN

Matt fell into step beside Bree. He glanced sideways at her face. She was composed as usual, but under her poker face, her skin had paled. Worry lines bracketed her mouth and eyes. She was more upset by the discovery of the remains than she would admit.

"What are you thinking?" he asked.

"My father lived here until he died in 1993." Bree's voice was matter of fact.

"These bones could have been buried any time after 1989," Matt said. "Unfortunately, I agree that your father is a valid suspect, but we can't assume he did it. That property has been vacant for almost three decades."

"At least we have some information to start an investigation." Bree strode through the woods. They emerged at the barn.

"Do you want me to stay at the scene?" Matt asked.

"No. I'll leave the deputy on-site. We need to update Todd and make a game plan, and we need that damned warrant for Shawn Castillo's residence."

Bree called her chief deputy from the vehicle. After Bree and Matt arrived at the station, the three of them set up in the conference room with laptops and file folders. They ordered lunch, and Matt started two binders that would serve as the murder books. Every interview, report, and piece of evidence relating to the case would be recorded in the binders.

Bree began, "We have two initial suspects: Shawn Castillo and my father, Jake Taggert."

Todd said, "I obtained Shawn Castillo's financials. There isn't much to look at. He has a couple of bank accounts that don't see much activity. Same with his credit card."

"He lives rent-free on his brother's property," said Bree.

Matt summarized the anthropologist's findings. "We have two adult victims, one male, one female. Both were between the ages of twenty-five and fifty when they died. They were buried sometime after 1988 but before last year. The female's name could have been Jennifer, and June 20, 1985 was a significant date for her. The male's name could be Frank Evans."

Matt opened his phone. He'd taken a picture of the driver's license. He read the address and date of birth. Then Bree described the snipped fingers and the downward trajectories of the bullets. She showed Todd a photo of the bracelet she'd snapped at the scene.

"Who cuts off people's fingers?" Matt asked. "And why?"

"Maybe to keep the bodies from being identified through fingerprints," Todd suggested.

Matt shook his head. "The fingertips were buried in the grave with him."

Todd asked, "What about the mob as punishment or an interrogation technique?" He paused, his eyes widening with excitement. "Serial killers."

Bree opened her laptop. "Let's focus on identifying the remains for now."

Todd cleared his throat. "Normally, we also investigate the property owner . . ." His voice trailed off, as if he didn't know how to complete his thought—*but this time it's the sheriff's brother.*

Matt gave Bree credit. She allowed no awkward silence.

Bree nodded. "You're right, Todd. Thank you for speaking up. We need to dot all the i's and cross all the t's. Please get a background check on Adam for the file."

"The property tax records show Adam purchased the land a few years ago at auction." Todd slid a paper out of a manila file. "If you don't mind my asking, why did he buy it, considering what happened there?"

"He wanted to preserve the family property." Bree's tone said she didn't like the way Todd was zeroing in on her brother. "Adam has only owned the property a few years. Before that, it was taken by the county for back taxes."

Todd opened his mouth as if he wanted to ask another question, but then he changed his mind and closed it.

She typed on her computer. "I'll put out a press release. We will not give any names to the public until the ME officially identifies the victims. We don't want Frank Evans's family to be notified via the media. You two can tackle missing persons reports. Focus on missing women named Jennifer and a man named Frank Evans. Start local and work outward."

Matt and Todd would be spending most of the afternoon researching records and making phone calls.

Bree said, "I'll show a photo of the bracelet in the press release. Maybe we'll get lucky and someone will recognize it. It'll go out on our social media page as well."

Bree typed up the press release while Matt started a missing persons query through NamUs. The National Missing and Unidentified Persons System was a nationwide information clearinghouse used to expedite resolution of missing persons cases and identify unclaimed remains. The database was searchable by various filters.

He began with Frank Evans and got a hit immediately. The date of birth was a match to the driver's license found in the grave. "Frank

Evans disappeared from Grey's Hollow in June 1990, but his online file is incomplete. There isn't even a photo. The contact is listed as Deputy Simmons from the Randolph County Sheriff's Department. Simmons died, like, ten years ago."

"The case is thirty years old. The older cases always have less info." Bree rubbed her temple. "But there should be a physical case file."

"I'll have a deputy dig through the archives in the basement," Todd volunteered. "The file should be there."

Matt entered the known data on the female victim. "There are no missing women named Jennifer reported in Randolph County. If I expand that search to all of New York, there are four missing women named Jennifer, all adults, all under age fifty. All four of those women fit our very basic physical description."

"Any of them look promising?" Bree asked.

Matt lifted a shoulder. "Hard to say. I'm going to expand my search to include surrounding states."

On the eastern side of New York State, Randolph County was in close proximity to New Jersey, Pennsylvania, Connecticut, Massachusetts, and Vermont.

Their sandwiches arrived and they ate while they worked.

Bree checked her watch. "I have to leave for the budget meeting."

Matt said, "Todd and I will start calling contacts on the NamUs search results."

Bree nodded. "Ask about a broken jaw and extensive dental work. See if there are dental X-rays available for comparison. Also, see if any of the women went missing with a male companion. If she went missing with Frank in 1990, then she wasn't born in 1985. The anthropologist says the female victim was over twenty-five when she died."

"What if her name wasn't Jennifer?" Todd asked. "Don't women wear jewelry with their kids' names on them? Maybe Jennifer is her daughter."

"In that case, if the victim's name might not even be Jennifer, then our search just got harder." Bree picked up her laptop and the remains of her sandwich. "Hopefully, I'll be back in an hour or two. Text me if you need me." She left, taking a bite as she walked out.

Todd typed on his computer. "There are seventy missing women from New York State who meet the general physical description of our victim. If we include women from other states, we'll be searching hundreds of records. I'll work on a master list, and I'll tap into the NCIC too."

The National Crime Information Center was the lifeline of law enforcement, a national database of crime information that held records from stolen boats to missing persons to murders.

"We can run the fingertip amputations through ViCAP," Matt said. The FBI's Violent Criminal Apprehension Program collected and analyzed data on violent crimes. "Maybe we'll get a hit."

"Let's hope." Todd got up and went to the door. He summoned a deputy and sent him into the basement to look for Frank Evans's file.

Matt turned back to his computer. Without some luck, identifying Jennifer was going to be difficult, if not impossible. More than four thousand unidentified bodies turned up every year in the US, and a thousand of those remained unidentified a year later.

Skeletal remains might never be identified. Matt pictured Bree's face. She had too many tragic memories dogging her. She needed this case to be solved.

Matt pulled up his original search on the missing Jennifers from New York State. May as well start closest to home. Jennifer Swan, nickname "Jenny," was last seen in Bay Shore, New York, in March of 2011. She was forty-two years old when she went missing. Her bank account hadn't been accessed and her cell phone hadn't been used since she disappeared. She was five feet, five inches tall and weighed one hundred forty pounds in 2011.

Matt checked an online map. Bay Shore was on Long Island, about four hours from Grey's Hollow. The case contact was a detective with the Suffolk County PD. Matt picked up his phone and started dialing. Someone somewhere was missing a loved one.

Chapter Eleven

Bree felt a little sick. Todd's line of thinking was spot on. When remains were found, they always investigated the property owner. In the back of her mind, she'd considered her father as the killer. Her parents died in 1993. Frank had been killed and buried on the land while Bree's family lived there. It seemed reasonable, and not at all shocking to her, to assume her father had been involved.

But if that were true, what would that knowledge do to Adam and the kids? She hoped the other kids at school didn't tease Kayla or Luke, and she hoped just as hard that Adam could handle the possibility that their father had killed other people besides their mother. That he hadn't committed one rage-fueled act of violence, but had been a cold-blooded murderer.

Why *had* Adam bought the property? Was he keeping it as some sort of shrine? Was it a way to connect with the mother he didn't remember? Bree had thought it odd, but then the house only reminded her of the night Daddy had killed her—the night he'd almost killed them all.

A creeping sense of foreboding crawled up her spine. The press had finally stopped being obsessed with their family. Would this case refocus media attention on the Taggerts? She dreaded endless phone calls and reporters showing up on her doorstep or doing stories from the road, with Bree's farm in the background. The only way to protect Adam and the kids was to solve this murder.

Bree stopped at Marge's desk on her way out of the office.

Marge opened a drawer, withdrew a stack of files, and handed them to Bree. "I have those files you asked for."

They were heavier than she'd expected. The thick file would be her parents' case. Bree stared at the faded, frayed manila folder. Her parents' deaths would be detailed. There would be photos she did not want to see. Unfortunately, she had no choice.

But she couldn't do it this very minute. She needed to focus.

Her throat clogged. "Thank you." She slid the files into her briefcase and left the building.

In her vehicle, her phone buzzed. A glance at the screen told her the caller was Nick West, a local reporter. She answered the call as she drove out of the parking lot. "Hello, Mr. West."

"Hello, Sheriff," Nick said. "I just read your press release."

"And?"

"And I want more information. Do you have time to answer a few questions?"

"Maybe," Bree said carefully.

Nick laughed and jumped right in. "The human remains on the press release—are they the same ones that were found on your family property?"

"Yes."

"What else do you know about the remains?"

"The basic descriptions were listed in the press release." Bree had held back the information about the severed fingers.

"Are these bodies related to your parents' deaths?" Nick asked, his voice rising with excitement. "Or are they newer remains?"

"We're waiting on more information from a forensic anthropologist. These things take time, and the family deserves to be notified first. You know that." Bree turned into the municipal lot, which was only a few minutes from the sheriff's station. She shoved the SUV into park. "Why are you calling, Nick?"

"Well, your father killed your mother there."

"Yes."

"Do you think your father killed someone else?"

"I don't know," Bree answered honestly, with no bullshit. "First, I need to identify the remains. Whoever lost their loved ones deserves closure."

So did Bree.

"You must have more information," Nick said.

"The few details we have on the victims are in the press release."

"My story angle is more about the violent history of the property," he persisted. "I'd like to interview you."

Oh, joy.

"Again?" she asked.

"If you don't have time for me"—Nick's tone turned fake casual, almost smart-ass—"I can always start with your brother. He bought the property, right?"

Bree wanted to reach into the phone and give him a hard shake.

She breathed. Nick knew exactly what he was doing. She'd thought he was better than this. Instead of playing his game, Bree called him on it. "Using my family as leverage isn't all right, Nick. The Taggerts have endured enough public attention. Don't you think?"

"I'm just doing my job." Despite his denial, Nick sounded regret-ful—maybe even defensive.

"In this case, doing your job means waiting for actual evidence."

"Other reporters will be racing to post the first headline."

Bree paused. She'd sensed potential in the young reporter the first time they'd met. "I'll give you some free advice. Leave the sensational-ism to the tabloids. I'm willing to give you first dibs if you're willing to cooperate. Do you want speculation and a weak story now? Or a solid one when I have real, corroborated information? It's your choice what kind of journalist you want to be."

He laughed. "Since you framed it so delicately, I guess I'll choose the solid story."

"OK, then. Give me a day or two to work the investigation and let the anthropologist finish excavating. Then we'll set something up."

"Great!" Youthful enthusiasm bounded through his voice. "When?"

Bree gritted her molars. "If I don't call you Monday, call me and remind me."

"I will."

Of that, she had no doubt. Nick was as persistent as Ladybug tracking a squirrel.

Nick ended the call without saying goodbye. Bree called her brother. Adam didn't answer. He was probably painting. Finding the bodies would have stirred up emotions in him. Painting was how he coped.

She left him a message. "Hey, Adam. Reporters are on Mom and Dad's story again. Don't answer your phone, OK?"

As if he ever answered his phone.

"Or your door," she added. "I'll stop by this weekend."

On the way into the municipal building, she tried to put aside the community's macabre interest in her family. She mentally reviewed her points on the proposed sheriff's department operating budget.

Her conversation with Nick had set her back a few minutes, and Bree walked into the conference room three minutes late. Donovan and Keeler were already at the table. The two older men sat with their backs to the far wall, presenting a united front against Bree. Both men stood as she entered. Elias wore a frown like an accessory. Dark circles hung under his eyes. Had he been up late with his brother at the ER? The look he shot Bree was weary but less antagonistic than she'd expected. She couldn't expect him to love her after she'd arrested his brother.

A few years younger, Keeler was super fit, but extreme leanness aged his face. He'd shaved his head, and a dark shadow indicated he had a deeply receding hairline.

"We're pleased to finally have this meeting, Sheriff." Easing into his chair, Elias gave his french cuffs a tug. He wore his gray suit as if he'd been born in it.

Sitting, Keeler leaned on the table and clasped his hands together. His blue dress shirt was rolled up to his elbows to reveal bony forearms. He made a point of checking his watch. "Thank you for squeezing us into your busy schedule." His tone held just a hint of sarcasm.

Bree checked her watch. "Don't worry, gentlemen. I won't keep you long."

Keeler asked, "Have you identified the remains found on your brother's property?"

"No," Bree answered. "The anthropologist and his team are still excavating the grave."

Elias's eyes narrowed. "I heard this morning that the two victims were murdered."

Bree had not made that information public, but the leak didn't surprise her. It had happened before in critical cases. "The medical examiner has not officially declared a cause of death." She paused. "I prefer not to issue statements until the data has been confirmed, but the initial hypothesis is that both victims were shot in the head—execution style."

Elias froze, and Keeler paled. She'd surprised them. Good.

"We've had an awful lot of murders since you took over as sheriff—most of the cases are related to your family." Keeler shook his head in disbelief. "You're sure this was a homicide? It couldn't have been another murder-suicide?" His voice was hopeful. Murder was bad for business.

Bree deadpanned, "People don't bury themselves."

"I suppose not." Elias sat back. "My source says there was a driver's license found in the grave."

Bree clamped her molars together. *Damn small-town gossip.* "Yes, but we don't know for certain that it belonged to the victim."

Elias waved off her concern. "Who else would it belong to? Besides, the license belonged to a man who's been missing for thirty years."

Bree raised a brow. "And how do you know that?"

"Now, now. If I gave away my source, I wouldn't have it anymore," Elias said.

Keeler looked relieved. "If the case is that old, you probably shouldn't devote too much time to it. It's hardly a pressing matter—unless, of course, you don't have enough current cases to keep you busy." He said this as if an old murder weren't important, and as if Bree had nothing else to do. In reality, a county sheriff provided law enforcement services to unincorporated towns within the county borders, served warrants, and ran the jail. Hell, Bree was responsible for animal control.

She met their gazes over the table. Keeler looked smug, as if he'd somehow outsmarted her—how, she couldn't imagine. Elias looked tired.

"You think I shouldn't work an obvious homicide?" Bree didn't flinch from Keeler's gaze. Anger rose warm in her chest. She couldn't tamp it back down. How dare he? Had he ever lost a loved one to a violent crime? She had. "If this was your family member, wouldn't you want a thorough investigation?"

Keeler's smug smile faded, and he didn't answer.

Well done, Bree. You've pissed him off too. Excellent start to your negotiations.

The politics of this job were going to be the end of her.

She shifted her gaze to Elias. "Do you think I should work this case?"

A quick spark of anger lit his eyes but faded. "Of course I do." His voice was unexpectedly sincere. Had she misjudged him? Maybe he was trying his best to do the right thing and manage his brother. Maybe she was jaded.

She wondered if he'd mentioned his brother's arrest to Keeler. She did not bring it up. Technically, Shawn was a suspect, but only because he'd had possession of a skull and hadn't called law enforcement. His *I found it* defense was actually plausible. Until she had more facts about the murders and had identified the victims, she had no *real* suspects other than her dead father. On the bright side, if Jake Taggert was the killer, he was no longer a danger to anyone. Also, there would be no need for a trial.

Elias shifted forward, his elbows coming down on the table. He tapped the tabletop, breaking the tension. "Let's get down to business. We all have busy schedules."

"I can save us all time right now." Keeler steepled his fingers, his eyes small and superior. "There isn't any more money."

"I understand that funds are limited." Bree lifted both hands. "I'm trying to *save* the county money."

Elias's head tilted. "Save us money? Your proposal asks for more funds."

Bree nodded. "As you both know, I've recently filled five vacant deputy positions, and we're still understaffed."

"Maybe your deputies need to prioritize calls," Keeler said.

Bree gave him a level gaze. "For now, we're doing our best, but we have more issues than the number of deputies under my command."

Keeler's frown deepened the lines alongside his mouth.

Bree continued. "Three of the new hires are female. Two are currently attending the police academy and will start as soon as their training is complete. One has already started. We were lucky to hire Deputy Laurie Collins. She has six years of experience with the LAPD."

"OK." Keeler rolled a hand in the air in a *get on with it* gesture. "You hired some women. We get it."

"There are no locker-room facilities for the female deputies," Bree said. "Collins is currently using the restroom, but that isn't an acceptable long-term solution."

Keeler scowled. "You hired them. You figure out how to make it work. I'm sure they'll survive."

"Deputies need the ability to shower and change clothes," Bree said.

"Can't they change in the restroom?" Keeler asked.

"Wouldn't you want to shower immediately if a suspect vomited, urinated, or bled on you?" Bree asked. "Biohazards need to be washed off immediately."

Keeler's nose wrinkled in disgust. Elias regarded Bree with renewed interest, as if he were looking at her as an experienced cop for the first time.

Bree flattened her palms on the desk. "It happens all the time. Right now, the men have a locker room and the women don't. Frankly, the situation is a lawsuit waiting to happen."

Keeler's frown lines deepened until he looked like a marionette. "Was it necessary to hire females?"

Bree swallowed the response on the tip of her tongue. *Really? That's your takeaway?* Instead, she took a deep breath and pointed out, "Discrimination in our hiring practices would also open the county to lawsuits. This isn't the 1950s."

Keeler's expression suggested he'd preferred that decade.

"She's right." Elias surprised her with his response. "The county needs to modernize. Many of our buildings are outdated and inefficient."

Keeler shot him a *traitor* look, then shifted his gaze back to Bree. "What do you want?"

"Ideally, a new building." Bree tapped the file containing her proposal. She knew her opening bid would be rejected.

Keeler rolled his eyes. "We can't afford a new building."

"Another option is to expand and renovate our current facilities," Bree suggested.

Elias shook his head. "I understand your needs, but I honestly don't see where we can find the money for a project of that size."

Bree lifted a shoulder. "The sheriff's department used to have a larger budget. Funding was cut after Sheriff King passed away, deputies quit, and the interim sheriff didn't replace them. What happened to that money?"

Keeler's face reddened with anger. Elias looked thoughtful, as if he were thinking, *What* did *happen to all that money?*

Bree continued. "I suggest we get estimates for expanding and renovating the current building as well as new construction. If we get sued, we can at least say we recognize the inequality in our department and are making attempts to correct it. I'm sure updating the building would come with an improvement in energy efficiency. Some money would be saved in the long run."

Keeler grunted.

"Get your estimates," Elias said. "We'll take a look at our current countywide budget and see where we might find some money."

"Thank you." Bree nodded. "The next item on my list is to acquire a K-9. We've been borrowing from the state, but I've run into multiple situations when a team simply wasn't available in time to serve very immediate needs. We had a K-9 three years ago, but they weren't replaced after a shooting."

Keeler toyed with his wedding band. "Sheriff King didn't think it was necessary to replace his K-9 team. He functioned quite well without one. We know this is your first administrative position." His face turned smug. "Maybe you could ask your senior deputies—the ones who worked with King—how he managed to be so efficient."

Bree leaned back, her teeth grinding. "Efficient or corrupt?"

Keeler was working hard to not roll his eyes. "You can't believe everything you read in the papers. King was a damned good sheriff."

Bree felt her brows climbing up her forehead. The nerve of this guy . . . After King's death, dozens of accounts of corruption had come to light, from murder to excessive use of force to misappropriation of funds. The man had done everything wrong, and yet, he was still revered.

Elias held up a hand. "We must acknowledge King made mistakes. No one is perfect."

"But he kept crime under control *with* a careful eye on the budget," Keeler snapped. "This isn't the big city. You'll have to learn to work with limited resources." He lightly slapped both palms on the table. "On that note, I have another meeting."

Elias stood and leaned on his fists. "We'll confer with the other committee members and get back to you on your proposal." *No promises* was implied.

"When can I expect to hear?" Bree asked.

Keeler smiled, like a shark circling an inflatable boat. "We'll be as timely as possible, but the committee members are very busy." Then he bolted from the room, leaving Bree and Elias alone.

Bree rose, battling back irritation and frustration. She walked to the door, closed it, and returned to the table. "I need to ask you a few questions about your brother."

Elias took his time gathering his papers before making eye contact. "What do you want to know?"

Bree met his gaze over the width of the conference table. "Why does Shawn camp in the barn?"

"You'll have to ask Shawn."

"It just seems strange since he has a house . . ."

His eyes narrowed ever so slightly. "I can't speculate about someone else's motives. That said, thank you for treating him decently."

Bree froze. Where was he going with this? She considered her answer carefully before saying, "I was just doing my job." She hadn't given Shawn any special considerations. Was he implying she had? Or was he being sarcastic? The whole discussion felt uncomfortable and unprofessional.

Elias lifted a black briefcase from the floor and opened it on the table. "I'm headed to the courthouse for my brother's arraignment."

Bree stuffed her folder into her own briefcase. What was she supposed to say to that? *Good luck* didn't seem right. "I'm sure you're worried about him."

He stared at her. "I'm not worried. Not in the least."

What is that supposed to mean?

Did he have the judge in his pocket? Elias had been in local government forever. He knew everyone. Unlike Bree, who was the new player in town. She gave up deciphering his remark. The politics were out of her league. She felt like she was in over her head by a mile. Apprehension slipped over her as she walked out of the room, very well aware that she had likely made two new enemies.

CHAPTER TWELVE

Matt fueled up with a pot of fresh coffee and two bags of peanuts from the vending machine. He returned to the conference room for another round of frustrating phone calls. Over the past few hours, he'd worked his way through a list of contacts following up on the four missing Jennifers from New York State. One case was resolved. In two of the cases, the lead detectives had retired, and Matt had had to track down someone with access to the physical files. The information he'd gleaned was disappointing and often incomplete.

None of the women had any record of a broken jaw or extensive dental work in their files. There was no mention of a bracelet in any of the files either. None of the cases mentioned a male companion.

But then, the information on most of the missing women was scant. So, the absence of these conditions did not mean the remains weren't one of those women. They'd all been missing for more than ten years—one for over two decades—so the officers' memories weren't fresh. Matt promised to call back if he had anything that definitely linked his remains to the missing women.

The conference room door opened, and Todd came in, his laptop tucked under his arm.

"Anything?" Matt asked.

"Not really." Todd had been reviewing the records of all missing women in the state who fit the general physical description of their female victim. "I've narrowed down the list a little. But we don't have enough information. We might have to wait for DNA."

"Getting results with only DNA could take months or longer." Matt's coffee tasted bitter, but he drank it anyway.

The anthropologist would extract DNA from the bones or teeth, but matching DNA wasn't a quick process. State labs were always backed up, and urgent cases were given priority. Plus, DNA wouldn't be useful without something to match it to. The missing person would be in the National Missing Person DNA Database only if a family member had submitted DNA. Then there was the chance that the victims were never reported missing at all.

Needle, meet haystack.

"Is there anything else you want me to do?" Todd asked. "I have paperwork to finish."

"Keep working on the lists of missing persons when you have time. That's all we can do until we hear from the ME."

"Will do." Todd left the room.

Matt bowed his head and rubbed the back of his neck. He was not meant to sit in a chair bent over a computer all day. He checked his phone. Bree was on her way back from the budget meeting.

Someone rapped on the doorframe. Matt looked up to see Marge in the doorway.

"There's a call about the bracelet." She smiled.

"Really?" Matt was doubtful. Hotline calls were typically useless.

"He knows about the date engraved on the inside," Marge said.

"Oh." They'd held that fact out of the description in order to discern real calls from fake. Matt smiled and reached for the landline in the center of the table. He slid the phone toward him. "Put it through."

"This is a real tip." Marge turned and glanced over her shoulder. "He's a former cop."

Matt answered the phone when it rang. "Matt Flynn."

"This is Lincoln Sharp. I used to be a detective for the SFPD. Now I'm a private investigator in Scarlet Falls."

"I know your partner." When Matt had been a deputy, he'd often worked with other local law enforcement, including Sharp's partner. "He helped me out on a recent case."

"Great. Then you know where our office is."

"I do."

"I have some information about the bracelet from your press release. Can we meet?"

"Yes. Of course." Matt checked the time. "What time works for you?"

"Four?"

"Perfect."

"See you then." Sharp ended the call.

Matt packed up his gear and headed down the hall into the squad room. He spotted Bree making her way from the back door to her office. Her face was stony.

He stopped in her doorway.

She opened her desk drawer, shook two ibuprofen from a bottle, and washed them down with water. "Please come in and close the door."

He did, then perched on the edge of her desk. "Can I assume it didn't go well?"

Bree slumped into her chair. "I hate everyone."

"You did arrest a board member's brother last night. It was bound to be an issue."

She scrubbed both hands down her face, then leaned her chin in her hands. "I didn't scream at the top of my lungs or punch anyone."

"Well done?"

She snorted and looked up at him. "You look pleased. What is it?"

"We got a lead."

She sat up, her face brightening. "Really?"

"Yes." Matt explained about Sharp's call.

"Let's hope he can ID our female vic." Bree checked her watch, then scanned her desktop. Neat piles of papers and pink memo slips seemed to have multiplied during the day.

Someone knocked on her door.

"Yes," Bree called out.

The door opened and Todd stuck his head inside. "The search warrant for Shawn Castillo's house came in."

"Finally." Bree stood. "I want to get this done fast. Shawn is in court right now. He'll be out as soon as the paperwork is processed."

She ordered Oscar and Juarez to assist. Then she and Matt drove to the address. She parked on the street. There were no sidewalks. Down the road, Matt could see the much larger house owned by Elias Donovan.

Matt scanned Shawn's place, a Cape Cod–style house built of brick and decorated with black shutters. The shrubs and lawn were neatly trimmed, yet it still managed to have an air of neglect. "It's creepy, and I can't say why."

"It has a vacant feel." Next to him, Bree double-checked the house number with the search warrant.

"We don't know how long Shawn was living in the barn."

Oscar pulled his patrol car to the curb. He and Juarez exited the vehicle. Bree and Matt stepped out of the SUV and joined them in the driveway.

Bree motioned for the deputies to go around the house. "We'll enter through the front door. You watch the back."

"Let's do it." Matt rapped his knuckles on the door. "Police. We have a warrant. Open the door."

A cricket chirped in the grass.

Bree pressed the doorbell. Matt heard the muffled echo of the chime resounding through the house. They waited for a minute. They didn't expect to find anyone at home, but they followed procedure anyway.

Matt donned gloves and checked the door. "Locked."

Bree pulled a lock-bypass kit from her pocket. She inserted two tools into the lock. A minute later, the lock clicked. She opened the door. "Not anymore."

She returned her kit to her pocket and tugged on gloves. They stepped inside into a wood-floored foyer.

A foul odor assaulted Matt's nostrils. He gagged. "What's that smell?"

"Rotting food," Bree said.

Leaving the door wide open, Matt peered into a study on one side of the foyer. To his surprise bookcases overflowed, and books were stacked on every surface. He scanned the titles. Shawn's reading taste ran to memoirs and historical nonfiction. "He really likes medieval history."

"That's not something I would have predicted." Bree checked a formal dining room on the opposite side of the entrance. Both rooms were covered in a layer of dust. They proceeded down a hallway into a kitchen and adjoining living space. Flies buzzed around an overflowing garbage can. Dirty dishes filled the sink. Trash was strewn across every surface.

Bree crossed the room and opened a window. A living room adjoined the kitchen. Matt went to the french doors. Opening them, he admitted the two deputies.

"Leave those doors open," Bree ordered.

The fresh air helped, but the stench of rotting food seemed to be infused into the plaster walls.

Bree divvied up the house, assigning the deputies the bottom floor. She and Matt ascended the staircase. There were doors on either side of the landing. Both doors were open. From the mess, Matt guessed the room on the right was Shawn's. The other contained only a bed and a nightstand.

"Let's start in the spare bedroom." Bree entered.

Matt followed. Bree opened the nightstand drawers. He went into the bathroom. The medicine cabinet was empty. There were no towels or extra rolls of toilet paper under the sink. Dust coated the sink, and rust—at least he hoped it was rust—stained the toilet bowl. He emerged. "I doubt anyone has ever used this room."

"I agree." Bree closed the closet she'd been searching. "Let's do the master."

They paused at the threshold. The room stank like a locker room. Dirty clothes covered the wood floor. Up here, Shawn hadn't even bothered to direct trash to the receptacle. He'd simply left it everywhere. Fast-food wrappers and drink containers lay on the nightstand and dresser.

"I don't even know where to put my feet." Matt picked his way to the bathroom. He touched the door with a fingertip to push it open. The bathroom was a mosaic of mold and slime. The odor smelled toxic. Matt wished he'd worn full hazmat gear. "This place looks like it's never been cleaned. Ever. I wonder who takes care of the exterior. Everything outside looked well maintained."

"Elias?" Bree suggested. "He owns the property. Clearly, Shawn has some issues."

Long-term neglect suggested long-term addiction.

"You start in the bathroom. I'll work my way through this room." Bree started shifting the clothes at her feet.

Matt opened the medicine cabinet. A few prescription meds lined the shelf. He read the labels. All the medicines were in Shawn's name. Matt recognized one for depression, ear drops that had expired seven years earlier, and an old antibiotic Shawn hadn't finished. No opioids. Nothing illegal.

Something moved. Matt jumped as a small gray body darted across the floor. "Watch out for mice!"

"Great." Bree didn't sound enthusiastic.

Matt searched under the sink but found only extra rolls of toilet paper and some cleaning supplies that clearly no one used. He left the bathroom.

Bree had sorted through the clothes on the floor. She'd piled the searched items in the corner. "Find anything interesting?"

"Besides mold and mouse turds?" he asked. "No."

She turned out the pockets of a pair of jeans, then dropped the pants in the pile. "Take the dresser."

Matt scanned the top. Nothing but trash.

Moving to the nightstand, Bree opened a drawer. She pulled out a stack of papers and gasped. "Oh, my God."

Chapter Thirteen

Bree stared at a pencil sketch of a naked woman being guillotined. The blade was biting down on her neck, and her mouth was open in a scream. Bree had expected to find weirdness in Shawn's house, but this was beyond her expectation. She turned the sheet so Matt could see.

"Wow. That's disturbing."

"Right?" Bree lifted the picture to reveal the one beneath, and they stared at a sketch of a man being pulled apart by ropes and men on horseback.

Matt tilted his head. "Is that drawing and quartering?"

"I believe so." Bree flipped through several other drawings, all forms of punishment: women being burned at the stake, hangings, beheadings, disembowelment. In one, a man hung upside down and was being sawed in half vertically. The victims' faces were locked in agony, and even in grayscale, most of the pictures showed plenty of blood spatter.

Matt squinted at a picture of a man tied to a wheel, his limbs at wrong angles. "I don't even know what that is."

"I don't want to know." Bree looked up.

"He covered all the medieval torture bases."

Bree shook the pages. They rustled lightly. "These are all methods of execution."

"Our two victims were also executed, although not as creatively."

"We're definitely taking these as evidence." Bree set the drawings aside.

Matt turned back to the dresser, rooting through a drawer of socks. "Who puts a used straw in their sock drawer?" He went through each drawer from top to bottom.

Bree dropped to her knees and peered under the bed. She eyed the filthy bedding with disgust and suspicion. "I really don't want to touch the mattress."

"Can't blame you. Let me finish here, and I'll help."

"What's going on here?" someone yelled from downstairs.

"Sir, you'll have to wait outside," a deputy called. But heavy footsteps sounded on the stairs.

"That sounds like Elias," Bree said.

"I demand to know what is going on here!" Elias shouted, red-faced, from the doorway.

Juarez stood behind him, his expression chagrined. "I tried to stop him, ma'am."

"I'll handle it." Bree crossed the room and faced Elias. "We have a search warrant." She showed him the paper.

He barely scanned it. Shock dropped his jaw as he took in the room. His nose wrinkled, and his gaze moved around the space. "Was it like this when you got here?"

"It smelled worse before we opened the windows," Bree said.

Elias gaped. "I had no idea he was living like this. The house belongs to me, but I've always respected his privacy." His eyes stopped moving. He leaned over the bed and reached for one of the drawings. "I haven't been in here in years."

Bree stopped him by raising one hand. "Please don't touch anything."

But Elias had seen the drawing of the guillotined woman. His face paled and he drew back, ashen. "Are those my brother's?"

Instead of answering, Bree asked, "What are you doing here?"

"I came for clothes for Shawn." But as Elias glanced around, his face puckered as if there were no way in hell he was going to touch anything in the room.

Bree faced him fully. "Where is Shawn?"

Elias blinked at her. When he spoke, his voice sounded disconnected. "The ER doctor said he probably had a mild concussion and told me I should keep an eye on him. So, I took him to my house after his arraignment hearing."

Bree nodded. "I'd like you to wait outside while we finish our search."

But Elias seemed rooted in place by shock. His gaze kept drifting from the trash-covered surfaces to the drawings on the bed. He said nothing, but dismay and disbelief were clear in his eyes.

Finally, Juarez nudged him. "Sir, you need to go outside."

Elias sighed, and his footsteps were heavier going down the stairs than they'd been coming up.

The deputy waited for Elias to be out of earshot. "Ma'am, we found some really bizarre drawings of people being tortured." He pointed to the sketches. "Like those, but in color. The desk in the study is full of them. Are we taking those too?"

"Yes," Bree said.

Matt turned back to the dresser. He opened the bottom drawer. He cleared his throat. "Bree?"

She turned to face him.

The tone of his voice had caught her attention. "We need to call in a forensics team."

She crossed the floor. When she reached him, she peered over his shoulder and drew in a sharp breath. Inside a cigar box was a pile of dirty-white objects. Each was about an inch long. She'd seen similar objects at the burial site. "Finger bones."

Matt nodded.

"I wonder if those belong to the victims we already found. We should have a cadaver dog walk the yard in case someone is buried out back." Bree stepped aside to call a forensics team and the medical examiner. Then she joined Matt downstairs, where he and Juarez were stringing crime scene tape around the perimeter of the house. Oscar had started a crime scene log.

"Dr. Jones is on her way here to collect the bones," she said. "The search-and-rescue cadaver dog team just finished the clearing. They found no additional remains. His handler is going to come here on his way back to Albany."

She rounded up her deputies and issued new instructions. "Every square inch of this house gets videotaped and photographed." She signaled to Matt.

"Are we going to talk to Shawn?" he asked.

"Yes."

They went outside. Elias was leaning on a silver four-door Mercedes. He straightened when Bree and Matt walked out of the house.

"We need to talk to Shawn," Bree said.

Elias searched her face. "What did you find?"

Bree paused. She wanted Shawn off guard when she confronted him with their gruesome discoveries. "I'd prefer to have this discussion with Shawn. It's his property and his privacy."

"Fine." Elias gnashed his teeth. "I'll phone my lawyer." He slid behind the wheel of his car and headed down the road.

Even if she couldn't question Shawn without his attorney, she was still hoping to see his reaction. Bree hurried to her vehicle, Matt keeping pace beside her. They stepped into the SUV. She drove to the large house and parked in the circular driveway behind Elias's sedan. Elias stood on his front step. Bree hustled to catch up with him. Matt followed her as she strode up the brick path to the front door.

Elias shot them an annoyed look over his shoulder. "Please wait out here."

Bree stood still, her thumbs hooked over her duty belt, frustrated that she couldn't demand entry to Elias's house. Just as impatient, Matt paced the front walk. The house loomed over them, blocking out the light. The combo of brick and black shutters matched Shawn's small guesthouse, but this place was huge. Bree roughly guessed the floor plan encompassed at least six thousand square feet of living space.

Ten minutes later, Elias appeared at the door.

He looked shaken. "He's gone."

"Gone?" Bree asked.

"Yes." Elias moved backward, holding the door for them. They walked into a huge foyer. A staircase curved up one wall. "I checked every room."

He led the way back to an enormous white kitchen that opened to a great room with a cathedral ceiling. In the middle of the room, a sectional couch faced a stone fireplace. On either side, french doors opened onto a patio. "He was resting on the couch when I left."

Matt went to the doors and opened one. "Are these usually unlocked?"

"No," Elias said. "Since I'd been out, all the doors should have been locked."

"Do you own any other vehicles?" Matt asked.

"Yes. There's a Jeep in the garage." Elias exited through a french door. Bree and Matt followed him across the paver patio, down several steps, and along a walkway that led to a detached four-car garage. Elias punched four numbers into an electronic keypad and opened one of the overhead doors.

The garage was just as organized as the house. One bay held lawn machinery, a snowblower, cans of gasoline, and an ATV on a trailer. Tools hung on pegs over a small workbench. On the back wall, racks stored two mountain bikes, tennis rackets, and a pair of kayaks with oars. A roof rack for transporting kayaks and bikes hung from the ceiling.

But there was no Jeep.

"Let me guess," Bree said. "He took your vehicle?"

"Yes." Elias still looked shocked. "He knows where the keys are. He's borrowed it before. He doesn't have a vehicle of his own. But he seemed so sick when I left him. He could barely keep his eyes open. His face was black and blue and swollen."

"I'll put out a BOLO." Bree took the Jeep's information from Elias. "Would you walk around and see if anything else is missing?"

Elias wandered off.

Bree turned to Matt. "Could you call Sharp and move our meeting back an hour or so?"

Matt nodded. "Of course."

"I'll call the deputy on guard at the excavation in case Shawn shows up there." By the time she'd finished her call, Elias was back, his face drawn. He placed a hand on the top of his head. "My shower was wet, and my closet was open. I think he changed clothes."

"Do you know what he took?" Matt asked.

"A pair of khaki slacks and a blue polo shirt are missing." Elias smoothed his hair. "I usually keep some cash in my top drawer. That's also missing."

"How much?" Bree asked.

"I don't know exactly," Elias answered. "Maybe five or six hundred dollars. I can't believe he left, or that he stole from me. I *give* him money."

Bree believed it because Shawn was a manipulative liar. Also, drug addicts would do anything for their fix. "Where would he go? Do you know where he obtained his drugs?"

"No." Elias gave his scalp a rigorous rub. "I don't know why he isn't here. I gave him his house to keep him off the streets, and he still wanders."

"Shawn doesn't have a job. Who covers his living expenses?"

"I do." Elias dropped both hands to his hips. "He usually comes to the house once a week for groceries, and I give him cash when he needs it."

Which he probably uses to buy drugs, thought Bree.

"Shawn wasn't always like this," Elias said. "He became addicted to drugs in college. He tried to fight addiction for the first few years. I sent him to rehab twice, but the drugs changed him. His whole personality changed. He became a different person. He's erratic and depressed. I've been accused of enabling him by covering his bills and giving him a place to live, but I love my brother. He's the only family I have left. I can't give up on him."

"Drugs are hard." Matt's best friend had been battling them for years.

Elias nodded. "But I still don't believe my brother would hurt anyone."

Bree wasn't sure at all. Drugs did change people. Was the new Shawn capable of murder?

CHAPTER FOURTEEN

Matt sat in the passenger seat while Bree drove the SUV. The medical examiner had collected the finger bones. The forensics techs were crawling over Shawn's house, and Todd was questioning Elias about his brother's habits. Matt thought it was pretty clear that Elias didn't know much about his brother.

"Shit. It's six o'clock already." Bree called home and let them know she'd be late. She turned down a side street in the business district of Scarlet Falls and parked in front of Sharp Investigations. The office occupied the first floor of an up-and-down duplex. Matt followed Bree up the front walk. Despite beginning to drop in the sky, the sun blasted them like a heat lamp. By the time they reached the front door, Matt's shirt was stuck to his back.

The office had clearly once been an apartment, and they entered into the former foyer. The air-conditioning was a relief.

A man appeared in a doorway. "Sheriff Taggert. Matt Flynn?"

"Yes," Bree said.

Matt held out a hand. "That's us."

"I'm Sharp." He was in his mid- to late fifties, with the lean body of a runner. He wore jeans and a T-shirt emblazoned with a globe and the words THERE IS NO PLANET B.

He led them into his office, and they sat in two guest chairs facing his desk.

"Can I get you some green tea? I just made a fresh pot." He went behind his desk and raised a mug that read PRIVATE DICK. "We have coffee too."

Bree and Matt declined.

Sharp eased into his chair. "In June 1990, I was a patrol officer for the SFPD. I took the initial report for a missing persons case. Jane Parson went to a party at her parents' country club and was never seen again." He set down the mug. "Jane had a history. From the very beginning, finding her seemed like it was going to be a challenge. The case got referred to a detective, but he let me work the case with him."

"Did either of you ever suspect foul play?" Bree asked.

"We talked about various scenarios, but our biggest concern at the time was suicide," Sharp said. "Jane suffered from depression. On June 20, 1985, at the age of twenty-three, she had a baby she named Jennifer. When the baby was about one, she drowned in the bathtub. According to the family, Jane blamed herself. She'd stepped away for a minute to answer the phone." Silence hung as Sharp drank more of his tea.

"That's horrible." Bree's voice was hoarse with emotion.

Sharp continued. "After the baby's death, Jane was never the same."

"I'm sure she wasn't," Matt said.

Sharp nodded. "Jane married young because she was pregnant. They divorced shortly after the baby died. Jane's parents had nothing bad to say about him, just that the marriage had never been strong and it couldn't withstand the tragedy."

"So, the ex was never a suspect?" Bree asked.

"No." Sharp shook his head. "He died in an auto accident in '88."

"I'll officially request the information from the SFPD, but that will take time. I'd love to get a head start on reviewing your reports. Do you have copies of your file?"

"Not everything. It wasn't officially my case. The detective who handled it died years ago." Sharp removed a manila file from his bottom drawer and tossed it on the desk. He opened the file, thumbed through a few pages, and produced a photograph. He slid the picture across the desk. "But I have copies of my own reports, and I found this photo of Jane taken a few weeks before she disappeared. Is this the bracelet you found?"

Matt picked up the photo. In it, a woman sat at a table on a patio. The unmistakable green of a golf course fairway filled the background. The woman was in her late twenties, but she looked older. Her hair was shoulder-length platinum blonde. Her skin looked dry and sallow. Tight creases framed her mouth and eyes. "Yes. That's it."

Sharp shifted back in his chair, and the springs squeaked. "Jane's parents had money. She never had to work, and she'd quit college when she married. Her parents tried to get her involved in the family busi-ness—they owned car dealerships—but she had no interest. She had no hobbies. She spent most of her time partying. She drank too much. A close friend said Jane also abused pills, and she was known to fre-quent local bars and hook up with strangers. We canvassed the local nightclubs. Several bartenders recognized her as a regular, and we found footage of her on the surveillance video from about a week before she was last seen. She left with an unidentified man." Sharp pulled a second image from the file and set it on the desk.

Matt leaned forward to examine the image. It showed Jane and a man walking across a dark parking lot. The glow of a streetlamp shone on her. The man remained in darkness. Matt passed the picture to Bree.

"We never identified him." Sharp lifted one hand off the desk, then let it drop. "I'm not sure it mattered. Everything pointed to Jane being depressed and in a yearslong downward spiral."

Bree studied the two photos. "What happened the night she disappeared?"

"Jane was last seen at a charity event along with two hundred other people. She parked her own car, a 1989 BMW convertible. The club had security cameras on the parking lot, the front entrance, and the rear patio. We collected a video of Jane leaving the building, alone. She was stumbling and weaving as if heavily intoxicated. We questioned the valets. They both denied noticing her leave. I called bullshit on that, because she walked right past their stand, but I couldn't budge them on their statements."

"Why do you think they lied?" Bree asked.

Sharp shrugged. "Their statements were oddly similar. I got the feeling they'd been coached, possibly by the club management. We also interviewed waitstaff. A few remembered seeing Jane at the event. None would admit she was hammered."

Matt said, "So the country club didn't want to admit any liability for serving her too much alcohol and allowing her to leave intoxicated."

"That was my take," Sharp agreed. "The video of Jane leaving that event is the last time anyone saw her—or admitted to seeing her." He swept a hand over his salt-and-pepper buzz cut. "The event was on a Saturday night. The anniversary of the baby's death was the following Monday. Jane lived in a guest cottage behind her parents' house. Her mother noticed her car wasn't there the next morning, which was Sunday. But since Jane had a habit of hooking up with strangers, her mom didn't get upset until Jane was still missing on Monday morning. She'd never stayed out that long before. Given the date, the mother called us. She was very worried about suicide."

"Understandable," Matt said.

"Yes. We issued BOLOs, knocked on doors, dragged a pond at the back of the family's property. There was no activity on her bank accounts or credit cards. Her phone was never used again. Her parents put up fliers."

"What about her car?"

"We never found it," Sharp said. "We worked the case for about a month before the chief pulled us off it. If her parents hadn't been rich, we probably would have only been allowed a week or so. There was no sign of foul play. My partner thought she drove off a bridge or something like that."

"It's plausible. What did *you* think?" Matt asked.

Sharp gave him a slow headshake. "She was self-destructive. If she went off a bridge, I thought it would have been intentional." He breathed. "My chief said she could have just driven away to start over. I didn't buy it, but there was no evidence to disagree. It's not a crime for an adult to just up and leave. But her suitcases and toiletry kit were still in her closet, and her mother said it didn't appear Jane had taken any clothing."

Bree asked, "But you didn't believe that's what happened?"

"No." Sharp sighed. "When I had free time, I'd make calls. Every time remains turned up in the state, I checked. Now, it seems she might have finally turned up."

"Do you know if her parents are still alive?" Bree asked.

"Her father died of a heart attack a couple of years ago." Sharp checked his file. "But her mother is still alive."

"Poor woman," Matt said.

"Gloria is OK." Sharp's smile was bittersweet. "Jane had a younger brother, Bradley. He's married with kids and grandkids. They live on the estate, and Gloria is really close to them. So, she still has family around her."

"*Is?*" Bree sounded surprised. "You still talk to her?"

Sharp nodded. "We keep in touch, though I haven't talked to her in a while."

"Does she think her daughter is still alive?" Matt asked.

Sharp considered the question with a tilt of his head. "No. Gloria has her feet on the ground. The news will be hard, but it won't be a shock to learn Jane is dead. She'll finally have closure. How did Jane die?"

"She was shot in the head," Bree said.

"No." Sharp came forward. His hands curled around the edge of his desk. "*That* will be a shock to Gloria." His gray eyes tightened. "Could the shot have been self-inflicted?"

Matt visualized the skull. "The medical examiner thinks she was lying on the ground when she was shot."

Sharp inhaled. "OK, then. Definitely murder."

"Plus," Matt added, "she didn't bury herself."

Sharp exhaled hard. "She was buried?"

Bree nodded. "Her remains were found with the bones of a male, who also died of a gunshot to the head. Did Jane have a companion? Anyone in her life who also disappeared?"

"Not that I know of," Sharp said. "According to people who knew her, Jane preferred one-night stands. She never hooked up with the same man twice. She once told her friend she didn't want any emotional entanglements."

Bree nodded. "I'll give the ME Jane's name. Are her dental records on file?"

"Yes," Sharp said. "Jane was in a car accident in '87, a DUI. She broke her jaw and had some dental surgery. Her X-rays are unique."

"Then the ME should be able to make a quick comparison," Bree said. "I'll call you as soon as I know."

"OK," Sharp said. "Gloria's son will want to be home when you notify her. She's had some heart issues in the past few years."

"All right." Bree stood. "Thanks for your time. Can we take these photos with us?"

Sharp gestured toward it. "Please. Take the reports too. The main file should be in the SFPD archives. Let me know if there's anything else I can do. I'd like to see the case closed."

Matt and Bree returned to the SUV. Inside, the vehicle was stifling. Matt slid into the passenger seat, where the hot vinyl burned his back. "Now that we have a name, we can get a dental X-ray comparison."

"Yes." But Bree seemed distracted.

"Is something wrong?" he asked. "Aren't you excited to have our first real lead?"

She started the engine. Hot air blasted from the vents. "Yes. Of course I am." But instead of driving, she put both hands on the wheel and stared out the windshield, her face troubled.

With a glance back at the house, Matt reached over and grabbed her hand. "What is it?"

She shook her head, her lips pressed into a flat, bloodless line.

"Bree, you can tell me anything."

When she lifted her chin, her eyes were conflicted. "This is going to sound callous, but I'm grateful both sets of remains are so old. Adam is cleared. He wasn't even born in 1990."

"I doubt Adam is capable of killing someone."

"I agree." Bree's voice went hoarse. "Let's be honest. If one of us was going to be a killer, it would be me, not Adam. He's the quiet, calm one."

Killers could be quiet and calm, but Matt didn't mention that.

"You're calm." His attempt at levity fell flat.

Bree continued as if he hadn't spoken. "Cops who have shot suspects have told me they have nightmares forever. That those dead men stayed with them. That hasn't happened with me. Sure, I've had a few bad dreams, but the men I killed in the past six months haven't weighed on me like they should have. Maybe there's something wrong with me. Maybe it's genetic. Maybe it's too easy for Taggerts to kill."

Matt had killed a man a few months ago. That man's face haunted him on nights when he couldn't sleep, but he didn't tell Bree.

Worry deepened the crow's-feet around her eyes. Her voice trailed off for a few seconds. "Most cops go their entire careers without drawing their weapons. But I didn't even hesitate when I pulled the trigger."

"You're trained to stop the threat, and that's exactly what you did. If you had hesitated, you'd be dead. Instead, your training kicked in, and you did what you needed to do." The same had happened to Matt.

Bree's nod was tight. "Todd asked about Adam. Clearly, he had nothing to do with the murders, but the press will still call. One reporter already called me. He wants to interview Adam."

"Which reporter?"

"Nick West."

Matt squeezed her hand. "Nick seems like a decent guy. He's not known for publishing speculation."

"I know," Bree agreed. "But my family has endured more than enough. I don't want them dragged into another murder. Maybe I made a mistake accepting the job of sheriff. The position is very public. And there's a decent chance my father killed those people."

"Taking the job wasn't a mistake. You're a damned good sheriff. But the sooner we solve the case, the sooner the attention on your family history will die down."

"You're right. We need to get back to work." Bree picked up her phone. "I'll call the ME."

CHAPTER FIFTEEN

Bree waited while her phone rang, one hand resting on the steering wheel.

Dr. Jones answered on the third ring. "Sheriff, I'm glad you called. I just spoke with Sam."

"I'm going to put you on speaker, Dr. Jones. Matt Flynn is here with me." Bree set the phone on the console. "We have a probable identity for the female victim based on a former police detective recognizing the bracelet." Bree gave the ME Jane Parson's information. "She disappeared in 1990."

"That matches what the team has found so far," said Dr. Jones. "This grave has been heavily scavenged, and recent rains might have washed away evidence. Sam's team is still excavating, and they've expanded their ground search to include the recently flooded area. They've recovered a belt, the wallet, and an elastic waistband likely associated with the male victim, and remnants of a dress, one high-heeled shoe, and the bracelet from the female. All of these items show several decades of degradation. These are not recent burials."

"Can Sam estimate the postmortem interval for the victims?" Matt shifted in the passenger seat.

"Yes, but keep in mind these are rough estimates. Laboratory confirmation will take time. On visual inspection, he estimates the PMI for both victims to be between twenty and forty years. He will conduct tests to confirm these estimates, but I've worked with Sam before. He's rarely wrong."

Bree said, "So 1990 would match Sam's estimation?"

"Yes," Dr. Jones confirmed. "Now that we have a probable identification of the female, we'll attempt to confirm with dental records or DNA."

"What about the additional compaction site the anthropology team was excavating?" Bree asked. Maybe there were even more bodies in the clearing.

"Those remains are canine," Dr. Jones answered.

Bree closed her eyes for one split second. *The dog.* Then she shook her head to block the memory. "Any idea when the excavation will be complete?"

"Tomorrow morning, I think," Dr. Jones said.

"Thank you." Bree ended the call. "We need to regroup with this new information." She put the SUV in gear and headed back toward the station.

"Bree."

Bree glanced over. "What?"

"It's late."

She glanced at the dashboard clock. "It's only six forty-five."

Matt gave her a look.

"You're right," she said. "I should go home. Dana is holding dinner until Luke gets home from a friend's house. I should be there to eat with them." She called Todd.

Her chief deputy answered on the first ring. "Harvey."

Bree asked him to assign a deputy to dig up any and all information on Jane Parson. "It sounds like the Scarlet Falls PD conducted a thorough investigation. See if you can get ahold of their records. Get whatever other personal information you can as well."

"Yes, ma'am," Todd said before he ended the call.

Matt shot Bree a look. "You're going to work after Kayla goes to bed, aren't you?"

Yes. "Maybe a little. I'll review the reports Sharp gave us. Other than that, we don't have that much information yet." She smiled at him. "Do you want to have dinner with us? Dana always cooks enough for three families, and the kids would love to see you."

He tilted his head and gave her a cocky grin. "What's she making?"

Bree dictated a text. Dana answered in a few seconds. The digitized voice said, "Shrimp and lemon risotto."

"With garlic bread?" Matt asked.

Bree shook her head. "Of course with garlic bread, and probably some kind of homemade dessert. This is Dana we're talking about."

"Then I'm in." Matt patted his washboard abs. "I could use the calories."

Bree voice-texted Dana again, then tugged at her own snug waistband. She needed to run more. Riding was fun, but it didn't burn the same number of calories. Or she could eat fewer scones. Who was she kidding? Dana's scones were irresistible. Bree would have to add some miles to her weekly workout routine or buy bigger uniform pants.

She dropped off Matt at the sheriff's station so he could stop home and feed his dogs.

A short while later, Bree pulled into her own driveway. The barn doors were open. Through the windshield she could see Luke mucking stalls. He pushed the wheelbarrow to the manure pile and dumped it. Kayla followed him in and out of the barn, her lips moving constantly, no doubt chattering nonstop. In the background, yellow wildflowers dotted the green of the pasture. Ladybug chased a squirrel to the base of a tree and sat, focused on the branches over her head. Luke patted his leg, and the dog ran to his side.

Bree let the peace of the scene wash over her. The tension of the day eased, sliding off her shoulders.

The previous summer, she never would have predicted this would be her life. Now that it was, she loved it so much, she almost felt guilty. This was the life Erin had made for herself. Her sister hadn't always made good choices, but building a homelife for her family was something she'd done very, very well.

Bree grabbed her briefcase, making sure it was securely closed, and stepped out of her SUV. She didn't want either kid to see any of the photos inside. Ladybug raced across the lawn. Bree braced herself so the dog didn't knock her flat. Ladybug loved hard. After an enthusiastic greeting, the dog pranced at her side as she jogged up the back-porch steps. She shed her boots on the tray at the back door. She hadn't lived on a farm since she was a kid, but the habit of not tracking muck into the house had returned immediately. Bree stopped to wash her hands at the kitchen sink.

Dana looked up from stirring a pot on the stove. "Dinner will be ready in twenty minutes."

The dog sat at attention at Dana's feet, watching her cook. Bree went to her office and locked the files in her desk drawer. Then she climbed the stairs to her bedroom, took a quick shower, and changed into jeans and a T-shirt. She put her duty belt out of reach on the top shelf in the closet and locked her sidearm in its gun vault. But she restrapped her backup piece to her ankle. With the way her life had changed over the past six months, she liked to be armed at all times.

Downstairs, Dana was slicing a loaf of Italian bread.

"How was the day?" Bree plucked a piece of bread off the cutting board.

"Good. Kayla cleaned tack most of the day. Then we went to the craft store for ribbon she wanted for Cowboy's mane. Good luck with that." Dana lifted the board. Using the blade, she scraped the sliced bread into a basket.

"I'll be praying to the gods of YouTube tonight." Bree poured some olive oil into a shallow dish and dipped her bread.

"Then we stopped at the library. Kayla checked out a joke book." Dana pointed to a stack of cookbooks on the counter with the knife. "I've been wanting to perfect a basic chocolate cake."

The book on the top of the stack had a cake the size of a barn on the cover.

Bree's waistband felt tighter. She stared at the bread in her hand and ate it anyway.

"Fair warning, though," Dana said. "Her excitement has reached an all-time high."

"Good." Bree smiled. "The horse show is the first event she's been excited about since Erin died."

"I know. Watch the risotto. I'll be right back." Dana wiped her hands on a dish towel draped over her shoulder and left the kitchen.

"Watch it do what?" Bree crossed the room and peered into the pot.

"Just don't let it burn!" Dana yelled from the other room.

"You're going to have to be more specific!" Bree called back.

Matt knocked on the door and entered the kitchen. He'd changed his clothes, and his hair was damp. He walked closer and leaned over her shoulder. "That smells good."

Bree turned her head and kissed him. "So do you."

He kissed her back. "I like off-duty Bree." He lifted a hand. "Though I totally understand why Sheriff Taggert can't kiss me in uniform."

"She wishes she could," Bree said.

"It would be hot." He grinned, his blue eyes sparkling.

Dana walked in. "Hi, Matt."

"Hey, Dana." Matt backed up a step and plucked a piece of bread from the basket.

Dana nudged Bree away from the stove, where she wasn't being very useful anyway.

"Why don't you call the kids?" Dana asked.

Bree headed for the back door. After opening it, she called their names. A minute later, Kayla raced up the back-porch steps. Luke followed. They washed their hands and dropped into chairs at the table. Ladybug drank her entire bowl of water and flopped down under Kayla's chair, ever hopeful for stray crumbs.

Dana's shrimp risotto was full of garlic, lemon, and butter. Bree mentally added two more miles to her morning run. At this rate, she'd be running all the way to Philadelphia.

Kayla bounced in her seat. "We got red, white, and blue ribbons for Cowboy's mane. He's going to look so pretty." She clapped her hands together. "Maddie's mom said Mommy would be watching from heaven. I want her to see Cowboy looking beautiful. You're going to wear your fancy sheriff hat, right, Aunt Bree?"

Grief welled in Bree's throat, and her risotto turned to sawdust. She cleared her throat and drank some water. "Of course." Her face felt like it was going to crack, but she smiled anyway. Kayla was talking about her mother without getting sad. Bree would not ruin it, but she spotted a tear in the corner of Luke's eye too.

A minute of silence passed.

Luke cleared his throat. "Kayla. Tell them those jokes you told me in the barn."

"I got a joke book at the library today." She grinned and zeroed in on Matt. "Matt, why didn't the teddy bear finish her dinner?"

"I don't know, why not?" Matt asked.

"Because she was stuffed." Kayla giggled.

Matt leaned closer to her. "How do you make a tissue dance?"

"How?" Kayla asked.

Matt grinned. "Put a little boogie in it."

Kayla exploded into laughter.

They told corny jokes back and forth for the rest of dinner. Then Luke retreated to his room, and Kayla went upstairs to get ready for bed. Bree was clearing the table when her phone buzzed. "It's the ME."

Matt followed her as she took the phone into her office and pressed "Answer." "Sheriff Taggert."

"This is Dr. Jones," the ME began. "Jane Parson's dental records were on file. They're a match, so her ID is official. There aren't any dental records or DNA on file for Frank Evans, but his case details match. We're going to issue a presumptive ID. Do you want to perform the next-of-kin notification?"

"Yes," Bree said.

"We'll need a family member to submit DNA. Then we can run a familial match."

"I'll do the death notifications in the morning." Bree ended the call and relayed the details to Matt. Then she unlocked her desk drawer and removed her files.

Matt said, "They both went missing in June 1990."

"Yes." Bree tossed files onto her desk. "We need to establish if they knew each other."

"Agreed." He stroked his beard. "Shawn is our only living suspect."

"He was eighteen in 1990. That's old enough to have killed them." Bree lifted the file Sharp had given them earlier, and they spent the next hour reviewing his reports.

Rubbing his eye, Matt set down the page he was reading. "We need the main case file, but Sharp's reports don't indicate any foul play." He closed the file.

"But we have the advantage of *knowing* she was murdered and having a second victim to work with." Bree took a legal pad from her top drawer and started a list.

"What's your schedule tomorrow?" Matt asked.

"We'll do death notifications and question both victims' next of kin in the morning. In the afternoon, I'm helping Kayla get the horses ready for the fair."

Matt picked up the top file on Bree's desk. "What's this?"

"Those are my father's criminal records."

Matt just stared at her for a minute.

"I remember him being arrested at least once," she said. "But I haven't looked at his file yet."

Matt opened it. "He was arrested a few times. Do you want the details?"

"Yes." Bree didn't fear her father's criminal record. But the murder file beneath it was intimidating as hell.

Matt flipped pages. "B and E, burglary, simple assault, unlawful possession of a firearm. He served six months in jail for the burglary when you were a baby."

"Not a surprise."

"His file is thin." He set it on her desk. His hand paused over the second, much thicker file. "What's this?"

"Nothing." She reached for it, but she wasn't fast enough.

He picked it up and read the tab. "Bree, is this your parents' case file?"

"Yes."

"Have you looked at it?"

She shook her head.

"Good. Don't."

"There could be valuable information in there," Bree protested.

Matt walked around the desk and perched a hip on its surface, facing her. "You trust me, right?"

"I do." That fact still surprised her. They'd barely been dating for a couple of months, and Bree did not trust easily. Her childhood had taught her she could depend on only herself, and that the people you loved had the potential to hurt you the most.

"Then I'll take this with me." He set the file on the other side of the desk. "If there's anything relevant inside, I'll let you know."

"But—"

"But what?" he challenged. "There's no reason you need to see what's in there. It's not reasonable for anyone to expect that of you." He reached forward and took her hands in his. "And it's not healthy."

"To look away feels . . ." She searched for the word. "Cowardly."

"Cowardly?" His eyes studied hers, and as always, it felt as if he could see right into her soul. "You're braver than anyone I know." He stopped her before she could argue. "But this is needless. You're too close to effectively evaluate the information. You'll see it through the filter of your own experience."

She swallowed her protest.

Matt continued. "And if you can't effectively evaluate the information, what's the point in tormenting yourself? There are some things once seen that cannot be unseen."

"My father could be our killer." Conflicted, she sighed. "I still feel like I'm passing the buck."

Matt shook his head. "You're delegating."

"I don't like that word."

He squeezed her fingers. "I know you don't, but you're not a detective in charge of a case anymore. You're the sheriff. You have too many responsibilities to do everything yourself. You're the boss. Bosses delegate."

"You're right," she admitted. As much as she hated to give up control, part of her was relieved. She didn't know how she would handle photos of her dead parents. Her memories of her mother were tainted enough.

Matt grinned, and his blue eyes shone. He pulled her to her feet, then tugged her closer until she stood between his thighs. With him perched on the edge of her desk, their faces were nearly level. Bree leaned into his chest and pressed her forehead to his. He released her hands and wrapped his arms around her. He was solid and strong, and for a long minute, she let herself accept his comfort.

She lifted her head and studied his face. His eyes were dark with intensity.

"I'm not used to having someone to lean on," she said. Ironically, having support made her feel stronger. She'd expected the opposite.

"I know." He lifted a hand and cupped her cheek. "It's my honor."

She wrapped her arms around his neck and kissed him. As always, the bone-deep connection between them stunned her for a few seconds. How could this have happened so quickly? She'd only really known him for six months. She pulled back, letting her hands rest on his chest. "Thank you."

He rested his hands on her lower back. "Anytime."

"I wish I could go home with you."

He inhaled deeply. "So do I." He slid his hand beneath the hem of the back of her shirt. He splayed his fingers across the bare skin of her lower back. Heat radiated from his touch.

"That's not fair." She kissed him again, then pushed away. "See you in the morning."

When they would inform two families that their missing loved ones had been murdered.

CHAPTER SIXTEEN

Matt stood next to Bree at the base of a circular driveway worthy of a resort and studied the big property. The Parsons owned a hundred-acre estate outside of town. There was nothing in sight but lush grass, mature trees, and flowers in bloom. "Sharp said the Parsons had money. He wasn't kidding."

The main house was the size of a hotel.

Bree checked her watch.

"We're a few minutes early," Matt said. "Sharp will be here soon."

"I know." Without taking her eyes off the house, she asked, "Did you look at my parents' file?"

"Yes." It hadn't taken as long as he'd expected—not as long as it should have. The thickness of the file belied the thinness of the investigation. Sure, there were plenty of crime scene photos and full autopsy reports. But the actual investigation had been almost cursory. He'd found one heartbreaking picture of the three children in the police station. The younger two had been asleep, but Bree had been awake, her hazel eyes wide open over deep, dark undereye circles, as if she'd had no intention of ever sleeping again. Even at the age of eight, she'd known what had happened. Those eyes had processed everything and understood that her entire world had imploded.

He'd reviewed the photos of her dead mother. Blood had matted her hair and pooled around her head. Bruises had marred her delicate face and throat. Jake Taggert had been sprawled on his back several feet away. His bullet wound had been in his temple. His eyes had stared at the ceiling.

Bree had inherited her mother's narrow face and thick brown hair. But her hazel eyes had come from her father. He'd been a vile human being. After reviewing the file, Matt wondered how she ever trusted another person in her life. The strength of her humbled him.

"Did you find anything relevant?" she asked.

"To this case?" Matt shook his head. "No." He hesitated.

"What?"

"To be honest, there wasn't much to investigate in your parents' case. The scene was clear. There's no question what happened."

She sighed and nodded. "I know. I thought maybe there'd be background info on my father."

He shook his head. "They noted statements from your grandparents and other family members that the marriage had been rocky, but your mother never called the police."

"Rocky?" She huffed. "My grandparents lived in the great state of denial, and my mother didn't call the police because she was terrified of him, with good reason."

So, eight-year-old Bree had been the one to do it. The sheriff had included a transcript of Bree's 911 call and had taken her statement as well. She'd been clear and incredibly articulate for a child. Matt supposed she'd learned to compartmentalize early on. The kindness of that sheriff had influenced her decision to pursue a career in law enforcement.

"Yeah." He took her hand in his and gave it a squeeze. She tightened her fingers around his for a few seconds. Tires crunched on gravel, and she pulled her hand away. A Prius pulled to the curb, and Sharp stepped out. He wore jeans and running shoes, but he'd upgraded his T-shirt for a blue button-down.

Sharp led the way to the front door. "Thanks for letting me come along. I feel like I owe the family to be here."

"We understand," Bree said.

The door opened. A maid in uniform stood at the entry. She clearly recognized Sharp.

"We're here to see Mrs. Parson," he said.

She led them across a marble foyer, down a hall, and into a sunroom. The glass walls overlooked a paver patio and sparkling pool. The air had to be eighty-five degrees. Matt started to sweat ten paces into the room.

Three people turned to face them. Gloria Parson was a thin, well-dressed older woman with a sleek bob of white hair. She wore a white cardigan sweater and navy blue slacks. Despite her age, her posture was straight. Her eyes were clear and measuring. Matt knew her to be in her eighties, but she could have passed for ten years younger.

The man was about sixty years old, tall and thin, with stooped shoulders. A woman stood at his elbow. She was about the same age, petite, with dark hair and eyes.

"This is Gloria Parson, her son, Bradley, and his wife, Nancy." Sharp introduced Matt and Bree.

Gloria's gaze passed over Bree and Matt and settled on Sharp. In a second, realization dawned in her eyes. She knew why they were there. She eased her body into a cushioned patio chair. When she spoke, her voice was flat. "So, you've finally found her."

Bradley walked to a cart in the corner and poured a glass of water from a pitcher. He brought it to his mother. She took it but didn't drink. Her hands shook as she set the glass on the table.

"I'm so sorry, Gloria. The medical examiner officially identified her remains." Sharp gestured to Bree and Matt. "Sheriff Taggert and Investigator Flynn will give you the details." He moved aside so Bree could address Jane's mother.

"I'm sorry for your loss, Mrs. Parson." Bree sat in the chair next to the older woman and angled her body to face her.

Matt remained standing, keeping his eye on Bradley and Nancy. They stood side by side, holding hands in a touching way.

The older woman stared down at her blue-veined hands folded neatly in her lap as if she couldn't process the information. "I knew she was dead. If she'd been alive all these years, she would have used her bank account or her credit cards. Jane didn't rough it." She looked up. The sharpness had faded from her eyes, and her face had paled. "This isn't a surprise, but it's still a shock to learn your daughter is dead."

"What can you tell us about the night Jane disappeared?" Bree asked.

"We went to an event at the country club, and Jane drank too much." Mrs. Parson heaved a long sigh. "I intended to get her keys and force her to drive home with me, but she left without saying goodbye. I never saw her again."

Bree tilted her head. "Was she upset that night?"

Mrs. Parson wet her lips. "Jane had issues. She suffered from depression all her life, but when she lost her baby, something broke inside of her. She stopped trying. All she wanted to do was forget, but she couldn't. When she went missing, we all thought she'd been in an accident somewhere remote or she'd hurt herself." She paused for another breath. "Where did you find her?"

"Her body was found in a shallow grave on a vacant farm in Grey's Hollow." Bree hesitated. "That farm is owned by my brother. He and I are the ones who found her."

"Shallow grave?" Mrs. Parson sounded confused. She twisted a huge blue-stone ring on her forefinger. "Do you know how she died?"

Bree nodded. "She was shot."

Mrs. Parson stiffened. "Shot?"

"Yes, ma'am," Bree said.

"Suicide?" Mrs. Parson asked.

"No, ma'am." Bree's eyes reflected the older woman's pain. "It was murder."

Bradley gasped. "What?"

Confusion clouded Mrs. Parson's eyes. "She was murdered?" She blinked and turned toward the window. But her eyes were unfocused, as if she were looking within.

Bradley poured himself a glass of water and drank deeply. "I can't believe it."

"Do you know of any reason someone would have wanted to hurt Jane?" Bree asked.

Mrs. Parson shook her head.

"You're positive she was shot?" Bradley interrupted. "She's been gone for thirty years. How can you tell?"

Matt gave him a traffic-stop stare. Did he really want his mother to hear the grisly details?

Nancy tugged on her husband's hand and gave him a look. "Honey, I'm sure the sheriff knows what she's talking about. Let's not distress your mother."

But Mrs. Parson inhaled deeply. "No. I want to know what happened to my daughter."

Bree's jaw shifted, as if she were grinding her molars. "There is a bullet hole in Jane's skull."

Mrs. Parson flinched and squeezed her eyes shut for a few seconds. Nancy pressed a hand to the base of her throat. Bradley merely frowned. Maybe he hadn't been so close to his sister? Even if that had been true, Matt still wanted to smack him for being insensitive to his mother.

Matt zeroed in on Bradley. "Where were you the night she disappeared? Did you attend the party?"

Bradley shook his head. "No. The kids were sick. I stayed home." A sheen of sweat covered his forehead, and he drank more water. Was he hot or nervous?

Nancy cleared her throat. "Both of our kids had a stomach bug. It was more than one parent could handle."

Matt remembered reading her statement in Sharp's file. Wives lied for their husbands, didn't they?

"Did Jane know a man named Frank Evans?" Bree reached into her pocket. She'd brought photos of Frank and Jane. She turned the headshot to face them.

No one reacted.

Bradley finished his glass. "Who is Frank Evans?"

Matt searched their faces. "His remains were buried with your sister's."

Shock widened Mrs. Parson's eyes. Nancy cast a nervous glance at her husband. Bradley cocked his head, his brows drawn together.

Mrs. Parson put her hands on the arms of her chair and pushed to her feet, the motion seeming to take all her energy. She hadn't looked frail when they'd come in, but she did now. "I need to lie down. Please excuse me."

"Of course." Bree stood.

Mrs. Parson paused next to Bree. "You'll keep me informed of your investigation?"

"Yes, ma'am." Bree nodded.

Bradley went to the doorway and called a name. The maid appeared and waited for her employer. Mrs. Parson walked slowly out of the room. By mutual, unspoken agreement, they waited for her to be out of earshot.

Matt skewered the brother with his gaze. "Did Jane have a boyfriend?"

Bradley pursed his lips in disapproval. "No. Jane liked variety. Every weekend it was a different man." He returned to the drink cart and refilled his glass of water. "It's possible this Frank was one of her flings."

"Was there anything unusual about your sister's activities in the weeks before her disappearance?" Bree asked. "Did she argue with anyone?"

Bradley stared into his water. When he spoke, his words sounded hollow. "Not that I recall. It's been a long time."

Matt's instincts waved a red flag. Bradley sounded like a politician on trial. Thirty years might have passed, but surely your sister's disappearance would make the events of that night stick with you.

Matt pressed harder. "Did your sister date married men?"

"I have no idea." Bradley set down his glass. "I have to check on my mother. Excuse me." He hurried from the room.

Nancy wrung her hands. Something was eating at her.

"Nancy." Matt squared off to face her directly. "What do you remember about the week Jane disappeared?"

She offered a weak smile and looked like she wanted to follow her husband. "Not much. It was so long ago. Everything is a blur when you have young children at home."

"Were you close to Jane?" Matt asked.

She shook her head. "We didn't spend much time together. I didn't have time for country club lunches every day." Her statement was matter of fact, with no jealousy in her voice.

"Surely you could have afforded childcare," Matt said.

Her shoulders shifted back. "I wanted to be with my kids, not pass them off to some nanny."

Bree said, "That's admirable."

Nancy lifted a thin shoulder. "It's just what I wanted. I enjoyed my kids. Not everyone does."

"Did Jane spend any time with your kids?" Matt asked. "They were her only niece and nephew."

A bright spot of anger flared in Nancy's eyes. "No."

Hot topic? Matt tilted his head but said nothing.

Nancy wasn't a very good liar. She had no poker face. She twisted her fingers through a few heartbeats of silence before filling it. "I would never say this in front of Bradley or his mother. I wouldn't taint Jane's memory for them. But she could be cruel. Sometimes it felt as if she wanted to make me as unhappy as she was." Nancy met Matt's eyes. "When Bradley and I first got married, we wanted children right away. I had a hard time getting pregnant. Every time Jane saw us, she asked us if we were pregnant yet. This went on for years."

"She wasn't genuinely concerned?" Bree asked.

"No." Nancy shook her head. "Her reminders were pointed. She would say things like, 'It's a shame you're barren. Bradley so wanted children.'"

"That must have made you feel awful. Who uses the word *barren*?" Bree's voice was sympathetic.

"Right?" Nancy rolled her eyes. "Jane was being dramatic."

Bree dropped her voice conspiratorially. "You must have been angry with her."

Nancy mashed her lips flat. "Picking on my kids was not acceptable."

Matt asked, "Was Jane like this with Bradley too?"

"No. She never said anything when he was present." She studied her thumbnail. "Later, our son was born with a cleft palate. You'd never know now, but it was disconcerting at the time. The surgery had to wait until he was about ten months old. Every time we saw Jane, she would say how ugly he was. She implied the birth defect was my fault." She folded her hands, the knuckles white. "Those days were so horrible. Just getting the baby to feed was a nightmare. I had no energy left for her meanness."

"I'll bet you didn't," Bree said.

Nancy sniffed. "Bradley thought that once we had children, Jane would dote on them. After all, she'd loved her own baby. But that's not what happened. Her bitterness couldn't let her love our children. Eventually, I stopped bringing the kids here when Jane was home."

Until she was gone . . .

"Did Bradley believe you?" Matt asked.

"Yes. He's good that way." Nancy nodded. "She picked on him when he was young. He agreed that she shouldn't be around the children. I hate to speak ill of the dead, but I'm glad she's gone. My grandchildren are free to visit whenever they like."

Sharp's eyes narrowed. "You didn't mention this when she disappeared."

Nancy picked at a thread on the hem of her blouse. "Jane hurt other people. She might even have hurt herself, either accidentally or intentionally, but it never occurred to me that anyone would have hurt her. But now . . . I wonder." Her eyes shifted to the doorway where her husband had disappeared. "I wonder if there were other people she treated poorly."

"When did you and Bradley move in here?" Matt asked.

"After Jane went missing," Nancy said. "Gloria didn't handle it well. Bradley thought it would be best if she didn't live alone." She glanced at her Rolex. "I have to go. I promised to babysit our grandchildren today."

"Thank you for your time," Bree said. "And your honesty."

Nancy nodded, but her eyes were uncertain. "Please don't tell Gloria. It would hurt her to have Jane's memory tarnished."

The maid escorted them out the front door.

Sharp followed Matt and Bree to her vehicle. "Nancy's assumption that she killed herself, either intentionally or by accident, was the general consensus when Jane disappeared."

"Did anyone else say she was mean?" Bree opened her vehicle door.

"No," he said. "But I always felt people were holding back. Gloria didn't fool herself about the probability Jane was dead, but she is the matriarch of a wealthy and powerful family. People might have feared backlash if they were honest about Jane's personality."

He held out his hand to Bree, then Matt.

Matt shook Sharp's hand. "Maybe people will be more willing to talk now that we know Jane was murdered."

"The fact that thirty years have passed might help too. Bradley has taken over the family businesses. He doesn't have the ruthlessness that Gloria did back in the day. You might not run into as much fear of reprisal." Sharp lifted both hands in a surrender gesture. "I'm going to back away now. Thank you for letting me come with you today, but I think it would be best if you looked at the investigation with fresh eyes. Let me know if you need anything else." As he opened his vehicle door, Sharp glanced back at the house. "Clearly, the family has some secrets."

CHAPTER SEVENTEEN

Bree stepped into her SUV and turned to Matt in the passenger seat. "What do you think of Bradley and Nancy Parson?"

Matt clicked his seat belt. "I think we should add them both to our list of suspects."

"Agreed. They held back information from the original investigation."

"Nancy was very nervous. Was she upset over Jane's treatment of her child or lying about it?"

Bree shrugged. "We need to find out more about her and Bradley."

"Another possibility: Jane slept with a married man and his wife found out."

"Which would explain Jane's murder but not Frank's." Bree started the engine. "Do we have an address for Frank Evans's next of kin?"

"Yes." Matt pulled out his phone and opened the email Todd had sent him that morning. "Frank Evans also has a brother, Curtis. Back in 1990, Frank's mother was listed as next of kin, but Todd couldn't locate her."

"It's been thirty years. She could be dead."

"Curtis is a partial owner of A Cut Above Landscaping." Matt plugged the address into the GPS. "Curtis did time for robbery when he was young. He was released in 1988. His record since then is clean."

"Maybe he learned his lesson." Bree drove away from the mansion. "What do we know about Frank?"

"He also had a record," Matt said. "A couple of arrests for assault. One for theft. He did two short stretches in jail. Nothing hard core. But then, he died young."

Ten minutes later, Bree pulled into a dirt driveway that led through thick woods. They bumped down the lane and emerged in a shadowy clearing. Compared to the estate they'd just left, Curtis's place couldn't have been more different. He lived in a tiny one-story home. Cinder blocks formed the front stoop. An ancient pickup truck was parked outside. Rust was eating through the front fenders.

Bree and Matt climbed out of the SUV. She joined him in the rutted dirt. A fluffy black-and-white mutt came rushing around the corner, barking. It stopped and considered them, tongue lolling and tail wagging. Fear lifted the hairs on Bree's nape. Her heart jumpstarted, banging against her ribs. Sweat broke out between her shoulder blades. But she held her ground. She had learned the hard way not to run from charging dogs. Fleeing made them see you as prey. Then you became prey. The scar on her shoulder began to ache with the memory. She blocked it out. She wasn't five years old. She wasn't helpless.

And the dog wasn't charging, she realized, almost surprised that she could control her panic.

Breathe.

"He looks friendly," Matt said in a calm voice.

Bree couldn't take her eyes off the dog. "How do you know?"

"Its eyes are soft, and its body posture isn't stiff. The tail is wagging in a loose and relaxed way."

"So, what do I do?"

"First of all, don't stare directly at its eyes. Dogs perceive staring as a threat. If the dog is aggressive, it won't like it."

"Then where do I look?"

"Just look in the direction of the animal without making eye contact."

"OK." Bree shifted her gaze to the dog's feet.

"Most dogs bite out of fear, not aggression. They're defending themselves." He glanced at her. "Your case was unusual."

In every way.

When she was a child, one of her father's dogs had mauled her. Her father had blamed five-year-old Bree, though he'd bred and conditioned his dogs to be aggressive. Her father had been cruel. She had no doubt his dogs had been as mistreated as his family had been.

Matt continued. "Signs of nervousness are licking the lips, shaking, averting their gaze."

"But I thought that was good?" Bree was confused.

"When it's fear-based, they look like they're cringing."

"I guess that makes sense." *Sort of.*

"The more time you spend with dogs, the easier it gets to read their body language."

"Then that's what I need to do." Bree needed to get over her fear of dogs. It was the last legacy of her father's abuse that she was determined to shake.

"You can work with Brody and Greta."

"Yes. I want to."

Matt crouched and held out his hand. The dog jumped closer, lowered his front end to the ground, and barked. "That's a play bow. It's a very good sign."

The dog wiggled closer. When it reached Matt's feet, it flopped over on its back. "Generally, wanting belly rubs is a good sign." He rubbed her belly. "This is a female. Hello, pretty girl."

Bree moved closer and crouched beside him. "Can I pet her?"

"Sure." Matt moved aside.

In protest, the dog rolled onto her belly and army-crawled toward him.

"Let her sniff your hand," he said.

Bree held out her hand. The dog licked it, then flipped it with her nose. "She wants me to pet her." Bree stroked the dog's shoulder. "It feels stupid to be this happy over doing something most toddlers can do."

The front door bounced open. "Digger! What was all that barking about?" A tall man stepped outside. He wore faded jeans, a gray T-shirt, and Timberlands. His head was shaved. Over his shoulder, he hefted a chain saw. In his midfifties, he was the kind of fit that came from hard, physical work, not a weight bench.

The dog jumped to her feet and raced to the man. On the way, she snatched a tennis ball from the dirt. Stopping at her owner's feet, the dog spit the ball at his shoes and barked.

The man stared at Bree and Matt, then his gaze took in her official vehicle. "I didn't do anything wrong." He lowered the chain saw to the ground, picked up the ball, and tossed it across the clearing. Digger tore off after it. She was back in less than a minute, expelling the ball with force at the man's feet. The dog dropped into another play bow and barked at him, her feathery tail wagging hard. The man scooped up the ball and heaved it harder. The dog shot off into the woods.

"Beautiful dog," Matt said.

"She's a good girl." The man crossed his arms, his spine rigid. The tattoo of an eagle decorated his forearm. His eyes were wary. "What do you want?"

Bree straightened. "We're looking for Curtis Evans."

"I'm him." Curtis shifted his weight, and his tone grew downright suspicious. "But I don't have to talk to you."

"This isn't about you." Bree didn't move out of the driveway. "It's about your brother, Frank."

Curtis's head drew back. "Frank?" The dog rushed back to his side but seemed to sense her owner's shock. She dropped the ball and put her front paws on his thigh. He scratched her head absently.

"Is there somewhere we can sit down?" Bree asked. "I'm afraid we have bad news."

Curtis cast a worried glance over his shoulder at the house, then shook his head. "Just say what you have to say. I have to go to work. I'm already late."

"You work for yourself," Matt pointed out.

"We have a big job and we're behind schedule," Curtis said.

Bree nodded. "The remains of a man were found in a shallow grave in Grey's Hollow. Your brother's wallet and driver's license were found in the grave."

Curtis didn't respond. He just stared at them as if he couldn't comprehend what Bree had said. She watched emotions play over his face. Disbelief faded to understanding and grief.

The door opened again, and a white head poked out. "Curtis? What's going on out there?"

"Nothing, Mom," Curtis replied. "I'll be in in a minute."

"Nothing, my ass. That's a cop." The elderly woman held the doorknob as she carefully navigated the cinder block steps. She was about five feet tall. Extraordinarily skinny, with a pouf of white hair, she looked like a cotton swab. She walked toward them gingerly, as if her entire body hurt with every step. When she reached them, she swayed slightly. Her son reached out to catch her elbow, but she waved him off with an angry gesture. She eyed Bree and Matt. "What do you want with my son?"

Curtis said, "Mom, the sheriff is here about Frank."

"You're here about my Frankie?" She took a step closer to Bree and squinted. The old woman's eyes were opaque blue, as if she had cataracts that needed to be removed. Her face was as wrinkled as an elephant's hide.

"Are you Frank Evans's mother?" Bree asked.

"Yeah. I'm Wanda Evans." Suspicion filled the old woman's voice, and her eyes narrowed.

Sympathy filled Bree. "Is there somewhere we can sit down?"

"Just spit it out," Mrs. Evans said. "You found him, didn't you?"

"We think so." Bree repeated what she told Curtis. "I'm sorry for your loss." The words felt hollow. They always did. "The medical examiner has issued a presumptive ID. Curtis should call her office to arrange to give a DNA sample. Then Frank's ID can be officially confirmed with a familial match."

Curtis nodded. "I'll take care of it today."

The old woman froze for a few seconds. Then she moved faster than Bree would have thought possible. Her hand snaked out and slapped Bree right across the face. She didn't have much strength, and the slap surprised Bree more than it hurt.

On reflex, Bree grabbed the woman's wrist. Matt had shifted closer, but Bree shook her head to stop him. She was fine, and she wasn't going to throw an eighty-year-old woman to the ground regardless of what she did. Mrs. Evans looked like her body would shatter with any rough treatment.

"Mom!" Curtis yelled. "You can't do that."

Bree's fingers completely encircled Mrs. Evans's wrist. Her skin was stretched tightly over her bones, and Bree kept her grip gentle but firm. "Don't worry. It won't happen again, right?" Bree stared her down.

"Right," Mrs. Evans agreed between clenched dentures. But she didn't look sorry. Not at all.

Bree released her wrist anyway. When she was eighty, maybe she wouldn't have any fucks left to give either.

Mrs. Evans spit in the dirt at Bree's feet. "The damned cops wouldn't even look for my Frankie. They didn't do anything. Lazy SOBs."

Frankie. The name triggered a flash of déjà vu. Bree dug around in her brain but couldn't find the reference.

"Mom," Curtis said. "This sheriff was only a kid when Frank went missing."

Mrs. Evans didn't appear to care. She vibrated with anger and grief.

"Mom, why don't you go inside?" Curtis put his hands on his mother's arms.

"I will not!" She shook him off but nearly lost her balance.

"We'll all go inside." Curtis steered her toward the house.

Bree and Matt followed them. The house was cramped but cleaner than Bree had expected. The small living room and kitchen were attached. A basket on the kitchen table held more medications than anyone could possibly keep track of. A short hall likely led to the bedrooms. The dog raced into the kitchen and drank from a stainless-steel water bowl.

Curtis guided his mother to an old chair and eased her into it. The house was dark. Trees blocked the light from the small windows. Curtis turned on a lamp on an end table. Tears shone in Mrs. Evans's eyes. Two women had learned of their children's deaths today. Both were over eighty. They couldn't have been from more different circumstances, but their devastating grief over losing their children was universal.

Images of Kayla and Luke popped into Bree's head, and the fleeting thought of something happening to either one of them was almost crippling. Nausea rose in her throat.

"You're not going to arrest my mom for hitting you, are you?" Curtis asked.

"No." Bree swallowed.

"Thank you." Curtis sank into the chair next to his mother. "She had a stroke two years ago and went into a nursing home. I just got her out last winter. I don't think she could physically handle being arrested."

Bree and Matt took the love seat facing them over a dark-pine coffee table.

Mrs. Evans shifted in her chair as if she couldn't get comfortable. "Now I have cancer, and Curtis doesn't want me to die there." She shuddered. "Awful place."

"They tried, Mom," Curtis said.

His mother crossed her arms and gave him an insolent glare.

"I'm sorry to hear that, ma'am." Bree pulled a notepad from her pocket. "I wish I could have brought you better news today."

"I knew he was dead." Mrs. Evans hunched her shoulders. "He wouldn't have left us. My husband died when the boys were little. It was just the three of us for a long time. We were close."

Bree leaned forward, her notepad on her knee. "Tell me about Frank's disappearance."

"The deputy didn't bother to look for my Frankie. He had a record, so the cops didn't care what happened to him."

Bree didn't argue with her. When adults went missing, unless there were indications of foul play, there wasn't much law enforcement could do. There was no law against walking away from your home and your family. It was hard to find someone if they wanted to disappear.

Thirty years ago, there was no E-ZPass to track. There weren't as many security cameras. People still used cash. Not everyone carried a cell phone, and even if they did, the devices hadn't been equipped with GPS. Smartphones hadn't existed. Hell, the internet hadn't even gone live until 1991.

"When was the last time you saw your son?" Bree asked.

"Before I went to work. That was back in June 1990. I used to waitress at a bar in town. It's closed now." Mrs. Evans wiped a tear from her cheek. "Frank made me dinner before I went to work. He was good like that."

Bree asked, "Did he say where he was going that night?"

"No," Mrs. Evans said in a weary voice. All the fight seemed to have left her, like air from a slashed tire. "He was a grown man. He was only living with me temporarily because he'd lost his job. When he didn't come home the next day, I called the sheriff. They said it was too soon to report him missing. He was an adult. He could come and go as he pleased." She drew in a shaky breath. "A few days later, they finally took a missing persons report. They never did much about it, though. Frankie had a record, but he was a good man. He'd just gotten involved with the wrong people."

Curtis looked away, his eyes misty.

"Where did you live at the time?" Matt asked Curtis.

"I rented an apartment over a friend's parents' garage," Curtis said. "Place was so small, I couldn't even have a bed."

His mother gave him a soft look. "Curtis was helping me pay my rent. My boys might not have been perfect, but they always looked after me."

Bree leaned forward and rested her clasped hands on her knees. "Had Frank gotten into any fights? Was anyone angry at him?"

"Frank wasn't an angel," Mrs. Evans said. "He'd been in trouble before, which is why he was sleeping on my couch. I didn't want him doing nothing illegal because he was desperate for money. Family sticks together." She reached across to give Curtis's hand a quick squeeze. "We've never had many material possessions, but we have each other."

Staring at his work boots, Curtis blinked away a tear.

"Do either of you recognize the name Jane Parson?" Bree pulled a photo from her pocket and showed it to them.

Curtis glanced at it, then swiped a hand under one eye. He shook his head.

Mrs. Evans squinted and studied the photo for a few seconds. "I don't think so. She doesn't look familiar."

"Could Frank have had a relationship with her?" Matt asked.

"Not that I remember," Mrs. Evans said.

Curtis said, "Frank didn't have a steady girlfriend. Said he couldn't afford one."

"Did he spend time with women?" Bree asked.

Curtis's shoulder jerked. "He'd go to a bar now and then, but he wasn't a dog, if you know what I mean."

"Were there any places that Frank used to frequent? Bars?" Matt asked.

Curtis scratched his head. "He worked as a bouncer at McNary's on Fifth sometimes. They closed about ten years ago."

Matt dopped his hands between his knees. "Did Frank have a trade?"

"He was a mechanic," Curtis said. "But he'd lost his job when the shop closed. He'd been out of work for a couple of months."

"But you have no idea where he went the night he disappeared?" Bree asked.

"None," Mrs. Evans said. "I went to work. I thought he was staying home. He didn't have any money."

Matt speared Curtis with a long gaze. "Where were you that night?"

"Home," Curtis answered.

"Alone?" Matt pressed.

"Yeah." Curtis's chin came up.

"Not hanging with a girlfriend or a buddy?"

"No. I didn't have a girlfriend." His tone was wry.

Bree glanced at the row of snapshots on the table. There were two of Curtis and his mom. In another picture, a blond man posed with them in front of a birthday cake loaded with candles.

"Now you have your own business?" Bree made a note to ask Todd to run a full background check, including financials, on Curtis.

"I have a business partner," he answered, pointing to the blond man. "We bought the company almost ten years ago, and it's still growing."

"You have a record, don't you, Curtis?" Matt asked. "Tell us about that."

Curtis didn't say anything for a full minute. His face flushed, and his jaw shifted back and forth. He wouldn't make eye contact and talked to the floor. "I made plenty of mistakes when I was young. I'm not proud of some of the things I did back then, but I haven't been in any trouble since. I learned my lesson the hard way, by spending time in jail." He glanced at his mother. "I'm a different man now."

Chapter Eighteen

Matt stepped out of Bree's official vehicle in the fenced-in parking lot behind the sheriff's station. The late-morning sun roasted the top of his head as they walked toward the back door.

Bree glanced at her phone. "I only have a few hours before I need to be home. Also, I scheduled the press conference to start in thirty minutes."

Matt caught her gaze. "Don't feel guilty. You have the right to a personal life. That's why you run a whole department. You do not have to do everything by yourself."

Bree was getting better at delegating, but she still fought her desire to be in control of every aspect of the case.

Her nod lacked enthusiasm. "I don't like leaving investigations hanging, and I'm tied up all day tomorrow."

"The case is thirty years old. Whatever we don't accomplish today will keep until Monday." Matt followed Bree through the rear entrance. Two deputies were typing reports in the squad room. Matt could hear the dispatcher in the communications room down the hall. Todd looked up from his computer.

Bree tapped her watch. "Conference room, five minutes."

She headed for her office. Matt carried their files into the conference room and jotted down notes from the morning's interviews for his reports. Bree and Todd arrived a couple of minutes later, lugging their own files. Todd brought his laptop and a box.

Bree sipped on a cup of coffee while Matt summarized their interviews for Todd.

Todd shoved a faded manila file across the table. "This is the SFPD file for Jane Parson's missing persons case."

Bree lifted a brow. "It's thick."

Todd nodded. "They covered all the bases." He pulled out a stack of stapled pages. "Here's the guest list from the country club charity event where she was last seen. Everyone in town was there, including Shawn Castillo."

"Seriously?" Bree leaned over to scan the list. "Shawn was there?"

"He's on the list." Todd pointed to his name.

"So are Elias Donovan and Richard Keeler." Bree skimmed over the names of Gloria and Jane Parson. "The mayor, the old sheriff, and the police chief of Scarlet Falls were invited. Mr. and Mrs. Bradley Parson are on the guest list too, though their names are noted as no-shows. Keeler's wife is also on the no-show list."

Todd thumbed through the file and found an envelope of photos. "Publicity and private photos from the event. The SFPD identified everyone who appeared in pictures with her." He dealt them out on the table like playing cards.

Matt picked up a photo of Jane with her mother. Thirty years ago, Gloria had been an attractive fiftysomething, with sleek dark-blonde hair and pricey-looking but tasteful jewelry. Her dress was a floor-length navy gown that subtly hugged her in all the right places but remained classy. In contrast, Jane flaunted a set of long, lean legs in a little black dress with an emphasis on *little*. Her nails and lips were painted fire-engine red. Her smile and bleached hair looked equally brittle. She was smoking hot, but with a self-destructive edge.

Bree held a photo in her hand. "Here she is with Elias and Shawn. Shawn is really young in this picture." The tuxedo-clad men flanked

Jane. Elias and Jane smiled for the camera, their faces on automatic pilot. Shawn's eyes were riveted on Jane's cleavage. "He's holding what looks like a beer. At eighteen, he would have been underage, not that anyone there would have cared."

"Would Jane have been interested in someone that young?" Matt asked.

"He was a good-looking young man before he started using drugs," Bree said. "Years of addiction have clearly taken their toll."

"They always do," Matt agreed.

"We need to talk to Elias about Jane." Bree lifted the photo. "We haven't seen him since we ID'd her, but clearly they knew each other."

"Small towns," Matt said. "The rich people always know each other."

"But was Elias rich then?" Bree asked. "Marge said he made most of his money in the '80s and '90s."

Matt tapped the picture. "His family's been around here for ages. They were never poor, but he definitely increased the family wealth." He read the back of another photo. "Here's Jane with Richard Keeler." Keeler had his arm around Jane's waist. His hand rested on her hip in an intimate gesture.

"The event was the who's who of Randolph County." Bree peered at the picture. "They look cozy. Who was interviewed back in '90?"

Todd pulled out several reports. "Interview summary report for Keeler. Here's one for Elias Donovan. The event ended at midnight. Keeler left around eleven forty-five. Elias stayed until just before midnight. These times were confirmed by security camera footage."

"Is there one for Shawn Castillo?" Bree asked.

Todd shook his head. "Not a whole interview, but he confirmed that Elias was home before twelve thirty. Shawn was just a kid."

"Interesting," Bree said. "Eighteen is an adult." She pointed at the picture of Shawn looking down Jane's dress. "He doesn't look very innocent here. What time did he leave the club?"

Todd checked his notes. "About ten minutes after Jane. Most of the guests left between eleven and midnight."

"Did anyone confirm what time Keeler got home?" Matt asked.

Todd scanned a page. "Yes. His wife said he was home around midnight."

"We need to question Richard Keeler and Elias Donovan about that night and their relationships with Jane," Matt said. "Do you want to do drop-ins or play nice?"

Bree chewed on her lip. "I'm tempted to play nice . . ." She laughed. "Just kidding. I don't want anyone to lawyer up before we get to them."

"Drop-ins it is." Matt approved.

Bree checked the time. "We'll swing by their houses after the press conference."

Matt turned to Todd. "Any sign of Shawn?"

"No." Todd shook his head. "Deputies have tried all the usual places homeless people hide out: the park by the river, underpasses, the beach at the lake. So far, no luck."

"He doesn't mind camping." Matt touched his beard. "Have a deputy run by the state park facilities."

"Also, have them check with the local campgrounds," Bree said.

"Yes, ma'am." Todd made a note.

Matt gestured to a stack of photos that Todd had set aside. "Who's in those?"

"People who are no longer alive or didn't look physically capable of the crime in these pictures," Todd said.

Matt skimmed through them. Jane posed with two elderly women sitting at a table. Jane leaning over an elderly man's wheelchair. He was staring at her cleavage much like Shawn had done. *Old creep.* "These people look too old to dig shallow graves. We'll put these aside for now."

Todd patted a cardboard box next to the file. "We have VHS tapes of the country club security camera feeds and the bar surveillance videos. Also, the video of the search of Jane's home."

"Great," Bree said. "Have you watched the vids?"

Todd nodded. "I didn't catch anything useful. The images are dark and grainy. Video surveillance technology in 1990 wasn't what it is today."

"Send the videos over to forensics," Matt said. "They might be able to make them clearer or brighter."

"Did you find Frank Evans's missing persons file?" Bree glanced at her watch.

"Yes, ma'am." Todd shifted his paperwork around to bring a skinny file forward. "There isn't much to it. They took a few statements and declared that he probably left town. He was a low-life, petty criminal. He didn't have a job. He'd been evicted from his apartment. He'd been sleeping on his mother's couch. Frank had no real reason to stay in town."

"His mother and brother say otherwise." Bree reached for the file.

The wealthy woman had earned a thorough investigation by virtue of her social status. Frank had been written off. Ironically, both had ended up in the same shallow grave.

A few photos fell onto the table.

Bree stopped and stared at a faded snapshot that had been tucked inside the file. Her face paled. Matt moved closer. In the photo, four men sat on the porch steps of her childhood home. They held cans of beer and smoked cigarettes. Curtis Evans hadn't aged well. Matt had to look closely to recognize him. He sat next to his brother, Frank. Bree pointed to the man on the right. His face was partially in shadow.

"Is that who I think it is?" Matt recognized him from his arrest record.

"That's my father." Bree adjusted the photo under the lights. "With Frank and Curtis Evans. I thought Frank's name sounded familiar the first time we heard it."

Matt craned his neck for a better view of the photo. "Curtis didn't mention knowing your father."

"Maybe he didn't make the connection." Bree frowned. "Not everyone in town is obsessed with the Taggerts."

"But most people know your backstory. Of course, you didn't recognize Curtis either."

"I avoided my father as much as possible." Her tone was unemotional. "I used to disappear when men came over."

"So, Frank came to your house?" Matt stared at the image. The men sat apart from one another, and there was no sense of camaraderie in the photo. Every man for himself rather than all for one and one for all.

"I can't be one hundred percent positive, but I think he did." Bree looked thoughtful. "I remember my father talking to someone named Frankie."

"What about Curtis?" Matt pointed to his face.

"I can't be sure." Her tone was detached, as if she needed to separate herself from her father's image. "His name doesn't feel familiar, and I didn't have any sense of recognition when we talked to him. Like I said, I did my best to stay out of sight."

"You were a smart kid." *A survivor,* he thought. "Who is this fourth man?" Matt pointed to the man on the left.

"I don't know." Bree stared at the image. "But he looks a little familiar too. Obviously, he knew my father. He was at the house."

"We'll ask Curtis who he is," Matt said.

"But how did Frank end up buried in the yard." Bree's question was rhetorical.

"Frank was your father's friend?" Matt asked.

"My father didn't have friends." Her voice went flat. "Frank, Curtis, and the mystery man must have worked with him."

Matt checked Jake Taggert's file. "Your father's background info says he was unemployed much of the time."

Bree nodded. "I actually don't know what he did for money. I assume a variety of illegal activities. I suspect the dogs he kept were for fighting."

Matt flattened a palm on the file. "Maybe Curtis knows."

"Todd, get Curtis's financial and cell phone records. Let's see what he's been up to recently." Bree stood and gathered her files. "I'll go give the press conference. Both of you come stand with me." Bree disliked being in the media spotlight and would attribute credit to her team whenever possible.

She went outside, where a half dozen reporters had gathered in front of the sheriff's station. A thirty-year-old crime didn't generate the same level of interest as a fresh murder. Bree began by identifying the victims. She gave their dates of disappearance, and then introduced Matt and Todd as part of her investigative team.

"Is it true the remains were found on your family's property?" one reporter shouted.

"Yes," Bree admitted.

"Your father killed your mother," another reporter pointed out. "Do you think he could have killed these people too?"

Bree didn't even blink. "This is an active investigation. We aren't making any assumptions, but we are considering that possibility." She concluded by asking anyone who had pertinent information on the crime or victims to contact the sheriff's department.

After she had finished the press conference, she and Matt drove to Richard Keeler's address, a restored hundred-year-old farmhouse on a sizable chunk of land. A large red barn sat behind the house, and sleek horses grazed in several pastures. In one field, horse jumps had been set up. In contrast to the Parsons' estate, this house exuded quiet money.

Old money that didn't have anything to prove to anyone.

No one answered the front door. Bree and Matt walked across the grass to the barn. A young man braided the mane of a gorgeous chestnut mare. The horse tossed her head, jangling the snaps on the cross ties.

"That's a nice animal." Bree eyed the horse with appreciation. "Is she competing tomorrow?"

"Yes." The groom's voice held a slight Irish lilt. "Miss Becca rides her in the hunt seat division."

"She's beautiful," Bree said.

The groom smiled and rubbed the horse's shoulder. The mare nuzzled him. "That she is."

"Is Mr. Keeler at home?" Matt asked the groom.

"I don't know." The man tied off a braid and stroked the sleek neck. "He's not much for the horses. Try the batting cage on the other side of the house."

Bree and Matt retraced their steps. As they walked by a patio and pool, Matt could hear the sound of a mechanical pitcher and the regular whack of a bat hitting a ball. They walked behind a tall hedge to see a thin man standing inside a caged-in batter's box. A machine pitched baseballs at him, and he hit them into the nets.

They stopped just short of the space. Matt caught Keeler's side-eye, so the man knew they were there. Still, he hit several more balls before lowering his bat. He picked up a remote control and hit a button to turn off the machine.

"Pitches balls at ninety miles per hour." Keeler turned to them and leaned on his bat. His head tilted back at an arrogant angle.

"That's nice," Matt said with just a hint of *don't care*. "We've come to talk with you about Jane Parson."

For a second, Matt thought he might have a chance to practice his CPR training. Keeler's face went as white as the baseballs on the ground, and he made a choking sound, as if he'd swallowed one.

He wheezed a few times. "Jane Parson?"

"We've identified the remains." Bree's smile was ice cold. "The female is Jane Parson. The male is Frank Evans. Did you know him?"

"No," Keeler said.

"How did you know Jane?" Bree asked rapid-fire, not letting him get his bearings.

"We were in the same social circle," Keeler stammered. "But I didn't know her that well."

Liar, liar.

Bree pulled the photo of Keeler and Jane out of her pocket. "You look pretty cozy in this picture."

"She was drunk." Keeler's face turned cardinal red. "I don't have to answer any of your questions. Get the hell off my property."

"We could do this interview at the station," Bree suggested.

"I won't be intimidated, Sheriff." Keeler spit in the dirt. "Unlike most of the lowlifes you arrest, I know my rights."

"No one understands their legal rights better than a criminal," Bree said with a bland expression.

Keeler's nostrils flared. "Are you here to arrest me for something?"

"What would I arrest you for?" Bree asked.

"Just answer the question," Keeler snapped. "Am I under arrest?"

"Not at this time." Bree held eye contact.

Keeler broke it. "Then go away. I didn't know the man. Jane and I were no more than social acquaintances. I have nothing more to say."

"What are you afraid of?" Matt asked.

Keeler stepped back into the batting box, restarted the pitching machine, and lifted the bat over his shoulder. A ball whizzed out. Clearly trying and failing to ignore them, he swung hard. The wooden bat broke in half.

"Maybe he should slow down the pitches," Bree said as they turned away. "Seems like the speed is too much for him."

"Definitely overkill," Matt agreed.

Keeler swore behind them as they walked back to her SUV.

Matt slid into the passenger seat. "That went well."

Bree snorted. "He is the definition of an asshat."

"His picture should be in the dictionary under *asshat*," Matt agreed. "If you were trying to soften him up regarding your budget, you failed."

"I told you I sucked at politics," Bree said. "Did we go too hard?"

"No." Matt shook his head. "Once he heard Jane's name, he shut down. It freaked him out."

"He has something to hide." Bree started the engine. The smile she cast at Matt was cagey. "We need to talk to his wife. Marge said he didn't make money. He married it."

"So, the provider of all this"—Matt waved a hand at the windshield and the beautiful grounds visible through it—"might not be thrilled if her husband was cheating."

"Most wives wouldn't like it."

"So maybe he killed Jane to keep her quiet."

"It's possible." Bree drove to Elias Donovan's house.

Elias answered his door. He wore a sweat-soaked T-shirt and athletic shorts. His face went pale, and he put a steadying hand on the doorjamb. "Are you here to tell me my brother is dead?"

"No," Bree assured him. "We just have a few follow-up questions. May we come in?"

"Sure." Elias stepped back and admitted them into the fancy foyer, then led the way to the kitchen.

Matt began. "Have you heard from Shawn?"

Elias shook his head. "No, and I've been driving all over town looking for him."

Bree pulled out the photo of the four men on the porch. "Do you recognize any of these men?"

Elias reached for a pair of reading glasses on the counter. He perched them on his nose and picked up the photo to scrutinize it. "I don't think so."

Matt pointed to Frank's face. "This is one of the victims found in the shallow grave. His name was Frank Evans. Did you know him?"

"No. Have you identified the second victim?" Elias removed his glasses.

"Yes." Matt paused. "Jane Parson."

Elias's head snapped back as if he'd been struck. "Jane?"

"You knew her," Bree said.

"Yes. She belonged to the country club. I know her family as well." Elias pinched the bridge of his nose. "I still see her brother and his family there occasionally."

Bree set the photo of Elias, Shawn, and Jane on the counter.

Elias stared at it, then eased onto a stool. "I don't know why this is a shock. Jane has been missing for a long time, but we all thought . . ." He paused. "Jane was self-destructive, but why would anyone kill her? The only person she ever hurt was herself."

"What was the nature of Shawn's relationship with Jane?" Matt asked.

"Shawn and Jane?" Elias gave a shocked laugh. "In that photo, he was barely out of high school. Jane was much older. They knew each other enough to say hello in passing. That's all. Our families don't have a close relationship. We're acquaintances. We see each other at community and social events. That's about it."

"He looks plenty interested in her," Bree pointed out. "Younger men like older women. Sometimes that goes both ways."

Elias shot her an irritated look. "He was eighteen, and she was an attractive woman. But I assure you, Jane would not have given Shawn more than a pat on the head. She was . . . experienced. She treated him like a child."

Matt dealt out the photo of Jane with Richard Keeler like an ace. He said nothing, just waited.

Elias straightened. "You'll have to ask Richard about that."

"Was there any country club gossip about them?" Matt asked, his tone encouraging.

Elias looked down his nose at him. "I don't engage in gossip."

Frustrated, Matt backpedaled. "We don't want gossip. We want to know if you ever saw them together."

"Richard and his family belong to the same club. Of course they saw each other." Scowling, Elias pointed to the photo. "This photo was taken in the middle of a charity event. There's nothing secretive going on here."

Everyone has secrets.

Matt collected the photos. "And yet, this is the last time Jane was seen alive."

CHAPTER NINETEEN

Bree's saddle creaked as Cowboy tossed his head. It was eight a.m. and she was already sweating under her uniform. Her horse's white-and-brown coat gleamed in the morning sun. People lined the street, waving. Ahead of her, a half dozen local veterans formed the color guard. Behind her, classic convertibles carried the mayor, this year's Miss Scarlet Falls, and the oldest veteran in the county, Rich Bartlett, age 102. The Scarlet Falls High marching band played a surprisingly good cover of "Bad Romance" a block back.

"Easy, boy." Bree touched her horse's sweaty neck. Generally a calm horse, Cowboy snorted. The crowd and noise excited him. The crowd thickened as they approached the fairgrounds. Children held flags. Bree waved to a little boy sitting on a tricycle. Ribbons had been woven into the spokes of his front wheel. Here and there, she spotted a deputy among the crowd. She'd approved overtime to make sure crowd control was adequately covered.

A cheer went up as the color guard turned into the entrance and started up the grass aisle that ran between rows of tents and temporary food stands. They topped a slight rise in elevation. In the near distance, Bree could see the grassy parking areas already filling. A large field held stock trailers parked in neat rows. Larger tents to the south held live-stock for judging. Cowboy arched his neck and pranced. Grateful for all the hours she'd spent riding over the past six months, Bree dropped her butt deeper into the saddle and moved with him. The red, white, and blue ribbons braided into his mane fluttered in the warm morning breeze.

Bree spotted her family near the funnel cake stand. Dana and Luke waved. Kayla jumped up and down. Powdered sugar smeared her face. Bree passed the sheriff's tent. Marge and Matt's sister, Cady, were collecting donations for Greta's training and equipment and selling tickets to the black-tie fundraiser being held in September. Deputy Oscar handed out gold star "Sheriff" stickers to kids.

Matt waved at her from his place in front of the table. Brody sat at his side, playing ambassador. As a former K-9 shot in the line of duty, the big dog was a local celebrity. The mayor was making a special announcement midday, and Matt would bring Greta into the ring to show her off.

In the stall next to the K-9 booth, a few of Bree's deputies had volunteered to be "dunked" to raise additional money. Five dollars bought three tries. Todd was first in line. A few more hours in this heat and Bree would gladly sign up to be dunked.

Fifty feet away, the grandstand and show ring, the end of the parade route, appeared ahead. The fairgrounds were packed, and everyone crushed forward to see the parade. The marching band launched into "Uptown Funk." The band was close enough that Bree could barely hear herself think. The thought made her feel incredibly old.

Just outside the entrance to the show ring, Cowboy startled, shot sideways, and bucked twice. Bree held tight, holding his head up so he couldn't dump her and trying to keep him in the center of the space. She couldn't allow him to slam into the crush of people on either side of the parade route.

"Easy, boy," she said in a low voice.

But the normally sensible horse was having none of it. He sounded off with a thin, plaintive whinny, then reared straight up. Bree pitched her weight forward and prayed he didn't go over backward. Her duty belt dug into her stomach. Her hat flew off her head. Cowboy came down and stood still, blowing hard and pawing the ground. She waited for him to settle, aware that the parade had come to a halt because of her.

A few minutes later, the horse calmed, and Bree moved forward. She could feel the weight of hundreds of eyes on her. The color guard had scattered for fear of being trampled. At the entrance to the show ring, she exited the parade.

Todd rushed to her side as she brought her mount to a full stop twenty feet away. "Is he OK?"

"I don't know what spooked him." Bree dismounted. She wanted to check every inch of her horse. She started with his shoulders, running her hands down his forelegs. "He's not flighty, and he's been in parades before without issue."

"I know what it was." Todd pointed to the horse's flank. Two splotches of paint the size of tennis balls decorated his rump.

"What the hell? Is that a paintball?" Bree pointed to the spots.

"That had to hurt." Todd surveyed the crowd. "But we'll never find who did it."

"Probably not," Bree agreed. She scanned the area. "The crowd is thick, and the band would have drowned out the sound of a paint gun."

"Probably some stupid kid's idea of a prank." Todd shook his head.

"Maybe someone saw the paintball gun. Aren't they big?"

"They make pistol-size ones now," Todd said.

Bree touched Cowboy's hindquarters, and he flinched. Anger bubbled in her throat. She had no patience for anyone who hurt kids or animals.

"Come with me," she said to Todd. She turned to the ring, where the mayor was giving the opening remarks. When he'd finished, she signaled to him that she'd like to speak.

The mayor looked startled. "It looks like Sheriff Taggert would like to say something."

She led Cowboy right up to the stage. Handing Todd the reins, she jogged up the steps and moved behind the microphone. "Hello, everyone. Welcome to the Randolph County Fair. I'm sure this is going to be the best year yet. Unfortunately, a few minutes ago, someone shot my horse with a paintball." She paused while angry murmurs spread through the audience. "This was a very dangerous prank. Not only was my horse frightened and potentially hurt, but someone could have been seriously injured. If anyone saw someone with a paintball gun or has any information regarding this incident, please come to the sheriff's tent. This type of behavior will not be tolerated." Bree waved. "Thank you!"

Bree jumped off the stage, collected her horse, and led him from the ring to a standing ovation. She walked Cowboy back to their horse trailer. She untacked him and gave him fresh water and hay.

Kayla, Luke, and Dana rushed back and fussed over him. Luke fetched a bucket of water and attempted to wash off the paint, but blue stains remained on Cowboy's white rump.

Matt came by to make sure she and the horse were both OK. The local large animal vet stopped to check on him and declared Cowboy bruised. The mayor's daughter brought him an apple. A teenage boy brought Bree her hat.

The next two hours saw a steady stream of visitors. Cowboy enjoyed every moment—and every carrot.

At eleven o'clock, Bree saddled Pumpkin, and Kayla warmed him up in the practice ring. She wore jeans, a western shirt, and boots. Under her cowboy hat, her hair was in pigtails. The effect was almost too adorable.

Adam arrived. His jeans and T-shirt were liberally smeared with paint. Even his sneakers were splattered.

Bree hugged him. "How are you?"

"Good." He leaned on the fence. "I saw your press conference."

"I tried to call you to give you an update."

"I'm sorry I didn't return your call," Adam said. "I've been working."

"That's what I thought." She took in the distraction in his gaze and the exhaustion that shadowed his eyes. "Almost done?"

When he immersed himself in a painting, he thought of little else until it was complete. As the piece progressed, his focus tightened until even sleep and food were secondary. But since their sister had been killed, he'd forced himself to emerge from those artistic fugue states to maintain regular contact with the family. He'd clearly dragged himself away from his studio to see Kayla compete today.

"I'm that transparent?" Adam laughed.

Bree cocked her head. "Your shirt is on inside out, and your socks don't match."

Adam's careless shrug said he didn't care. He might have other faults, but Adam wasn't the least bit superficial. He didn't care about clothes or appearances. "Do you think Dad killed those people?"

"I don't know yet, but I won't lie to you. It's possible."

He turned to watch Kayla. "I know. He was a violent man."

"He was." Bree wrapped one arm around his shoulders. "His guilt or innocence changes nothing. We already knew he was a killer." As much as she wanted to soften the impact of bad news for him, she couldn't. He needed to be prepared to handle the truth.

Kayla rode over to him. "Uncle Adam, you came!"

"Of course I came." Adam stepped up onto the lowest rail of the fence and hugged her. "I wouldn't miss my favorite niece's horse show debut."

Kayla grinned and rolled her eyes as if she were eighteen instead of eight. "I'm your only niece."

Adam grinned back at her. They all trooped to the show ring for her walk/trot class. Bree, Dana, Adam, and Luke leaned on the fence and watched the little girl win third place. Pride rushed in Bree's heart as the judge pinned the yellow ribbon on Pumpkin's bridle. Kayla beamed, and Bree was filled with a rare moment of pure joy.

Adam leaned sideways and spoke to Dana. "Someday, you're going to break down and ride a horse."

Dana laughed. "Nope. I'm a city girl. I'm fine patting noses."

Kayla rode out of the ring, and they returned to the trailer. She changed out of her riding clothes in the trailer but insisted on wearing her hat and boots with her shorts. Then Luke loaded the horses. He climbed into the passenger seat, and Dana slid behind the wheel. He had an evening shift at the grocery store, but he would settle the horses at home before he left. Bree watched the truck and trailer roll away.

"Come for dinner tonight?" Bree asked Adam.

He blew an overgrown curl off his forehead. "Not today. I want to get back to work."

She and Kayla hugged him goodbye, then Bree took Kayla's hand and they walked back to the sheriff's tent just in time to see Todd fall into the water in the dunk tank. Cady sold tickets from behind the table. Like all the Flynns, Cady was tall and athletic. Today, she wore denim shorts, a tank top, and white sneakers. Her strawberry blonde hair was tied back in a long ponytail. Todd climbed out of the tank, his wet T-shirt clinging to his chest, and Bree watched in amusement as Cady tried not to stare at him.

Brody lay in the shady grass at Cady's feet. Air from a box fan ruffled his fur. Kayla dropped onto the ground and hugged him. The big dog shifted to rest his head in her lap. Bree reached down and gave his head a scratch. His tail thumped on the ground. Once upon a time, she would have been afraid of him, but he'd proven himself to her. Brody had once been a big bad police dog, but now he loved tiny humans and belly rubs. He was utterly devoted to Kayla, and Bree trusted him completely with the child. She also swore the dog understood plain English. When she spoke to him, he always acted as if he knew exactly what she was saying.

"Kayla!" A dark-haired girl raced to the sheriff's tent. Emma was Kayla's current best friend.

Her mother, a short woman with a wide smile and one thick gray streak in her nearly black hair, offered Bree a smile. "Hi, Sheriff."

"Hi, Cathy." Bree smiled. "Please call me Bree."

Kayla and Emma had regular playdates. Bree often felt out of her element with the moms of Kayla's friends. They were all normal; some stayed at home, others worked outside their households. Bree was the only one who carried two Glocks, an expandable baton, and a Taser.

"Emma would love Kayla to come to the food tent with us." Cathy lowered her voice. "I'd like to promise I'll make them eat something healthy, but honestly, I'm going to let them eat whatever they want."

Bree laughed. "If you can't eat hot dogs and funnel cake at the county fair, when can you?"

"Exactly," Cathy said. "It won't come again until next summer." She smiled, her expression wistful. "I still remember running these fairgrounds as a kid, covered in cotton candy, insect bites, and sunburn."

Bree had no such wholesome, happy memories, but she very much wanted Kayla to have them.

Kayla jumped up and grabbed Bree's hand. "Can I go eat with Emma?"

"Sure." Bree gave her a quick hug. "You remember the rules?"

"Stay close to Emma's mom, don't wander off, stay alert." Kayla spoke in the monotone of a child who received frequent lectures on personal safety.

"What do you do if you get lost?"

"Stay put. Ask a mommy with kids to call you," Kayla said without hesitation. Then she recited Bree's cell phone number. She squirmed. "Can I go now?"

Bree nodded. "Have fun. I love you. Be safe."

Just before she raced off, Kayla pulled off her hat and shoved it at Bree. "Aunt Bree, would you hold this?"

"OK." Bree waved.

"She's having a good time?" Matt came out from behind the table. He held Greta on a short leash. She sat utterly and almost eerily still, her attention on Matt as sharp as a brand-new razor blade.

"I think she is." Bree watched her skip away hand in hand with Emma. "I don't think I've ever seen her this happy."

"That's awesome." Matt smiled. Greta fidgeted, and Matt spoke to her in German.

"Is she ready for her public debut?" Bree watched the sleek, young dog snap to attention at a single command.

"She's gorgeous," Matt insisted. "The crowd is going to get one look at her and . . ." He brushed the fingers of one hand across the other in a money-flowing gesture.

"I hope you're right." Bree's department really needed a K-9. Importing a dog from Germany or Poland, where most police K-9s originated, would cost additional money they didn't have. Heck, they didn't even have the basic training fees and necessary K-9 equipment. She hoped they would by the end of the month.

"I am." Matt knew what he was doing, and he was right. Greta was gorgeous. Sleek and black, with huge ears she hadn't quite grown into. "She's smarter than most humans too."

Bree stroked Brody's head one last time, then stood and brushed wrinkles out of her dress uniform pants. "Then let's do this."

She stashed Kayla's hat in the sheriff's tent. She and Matt walked back to the show ring together. The mayor once again took the stage. "Hello, Randolph County!" The mayor waved his hand toward Matt and Greta. "This is Matt Flynn. Many of you might remember Matt from his K-9 days with the sheriff's department. The beautiful dog with Matt is Greta. Who would love to see Greta as our sheriff's department's new K-9 officer?"

The crowd cheered. Matt paraded Greta around in a circle. She heeled and sat and lay down on command. When he held a tug toy over her head, she leaped for it, and Matt held her suspended a foot off the ground. The audience clapped wildly.

The mayor continued. "If you'd like to contribute to Greta's training and equipment costs, please visit the sheriff's tent or go online and contribute directly. You can make a straight donation, buy a ticket to their fundraiser, or purchase a chance to dunk a deputy. Every dollar raised goes toward making Greta one of ours. Seriously, folks, we need Greta on our team! Loosen up those wallets and make it happen!"

Matt led Greta from the ring and walked a short distance to stand in the shade of a tree. The dog pranced.

Bree stepped back as the dog spun on the end of her leash.

"Fuss," Matt commanded her in German. The dog moved to his heel obediently, her tongue lolling. In another minute, she sat on command.

"She really did well." Bree reached out a hand. Greta's tail thumped and she shifted forward so Bree could stroke her head.

"I told you." Matt grinned. "She's a rock star. For a young dog, she was incredibly focused in front of hundreds of people. Training will only make her better."

Bree scratched under Greta's ears.

Matt shortened the leash. "I'm going to take her home. She did great, but she's had enough excitement for one day. Would you let Cady know? Tell her I'll be back in about an hour."

"Sure." Bree met his eyes. She wanted to kiss him goodbye but settled for a smile.

He led Greta away toward the parking areas.

Bree turned and walked back toward the sheriff's tent. The crowd in front of the table was so thick, Bree had to elbow her way through the throng. The line in front of the dunk tank reached for three stalls. Dressed in academy-blue shorts and a T-shirt, Collins sat on the ledge while a grade-schooler tossed baseballs at the target.

Smiling, Bree felt the wholesomeness of the day to her bones.

Behind the sheriff's table, Marge and Cady were working hard. Bree reached for a roll of gold-star stickers and started offering them to the kids in line.

"Sheriff!" a woman shouted.

The panicked pitch of her voice grabbed Bree's attention. She swiveled her head, seeking the source. It was Emma's mother, Cathy. Her face was white and stricken. She dragged her small daughter through the crowd by the hand.

Where's Kayla?

Panic grabbed Bree by the lungs. "What happened?"

Out of breath, Cathy panted. "Both girls were right behind me at the hot dog stall. I paid for our food. When I turned around, Kayla was gone."

CHAPTER TWENTY

Terror blinded Bree for a breath. She exhaled hard.

Focus.

Get your shit together.

Find Kayla.

Bree was a champion compartmentalizer, but a threat to Kayla overrode her coping mechanism.

"You last saw her in front of the hot dog stand?" Bree asked Cathy while simultaneously signaling for Todd, who was behind the table helping Cady.

"Yes." Cathy nodded. "I'm so sorry. The girls were holding hands. I don't know how this happened."

Todd muscled his way around the table and through the crowd. "Sheriff?"

"Put out a lost-child announcement over the PA." Bree gave him a description of Kayla's clothing. "I want everyone looking for her."

Todd, once again wearing his uniform, reached for the radio mic on his shoulder. "I'll post a deputy at either end of the parking area too. We'll lock down the exits." He raised a hand and summoned the other deputies at the tent.

Bree went down on one knee so she would be at Emma's eye level. Tears streamed down the little girl's face.

"Emma, what happened?" Bree asked.

Emma's lower lip trembled. "I don't know. There was a clown. He grabbed Kayla."

Kayla had been abducted.

Fear turned Bree's stomach inside out. She took Emma's hands. Bree needed this child to have more information. Kayla's life literally depended on it. "I want you to picture him in your mind. What do you see?"

Emma's face screwed up. "A clown."

"Was he wearing a clown suit?" Bree tried.

The little girl looked down at her own pants and shook her head. "Jeans."

"What about his shirt? What color was it?"

"Red," Emma said.

"Was his clown face painted on?" Bree asked.

Emma frowned. "It was like a Halloween mask."

Bree used her cell to relay the information to Todd, who was already on his way to the judge's stand to use the PA system.

"I'm so sorry," Cathy cried.

"I know. I'm sure it wasn't your fault." Bree set her aside. "Right now, we have to find her."

Bree rushed to the sheriff's table, where she quickly explained to Cady and Marge. She had to fight the irrational urge to run wildly through the crowd screaming Kayla's name. She had a whole team of deputies on-site, and they knew what to do.

Something cold and wet nudged her hand. Brody sat at Bree's side and whined, as if he could sense her distress.

"Do you think Brody could find her?" Bree asked Cady.

"Yes!" Cady grabbed the dog's leash. "We don't have his working harness, but I think he'll figure it out."

Bree retrieved Kayla's cowboy hat from the tent. "We should take him to the hot dog stand. That's where Kayla was last seen."

They jogged across the grass. Brody knew something was up. His ears were forward, and his attitude had shifted from pet to police dog. At the stand, she offered the hat to the dog and repeated the command Matt used to ask him to *search*. She expected him to put his nose to the ground, but the big dog stood stock still. His head swiveled and he sniffed the air.

Bree kept the leash slack. "Am I doing this right?" she asked Cady.

Cady bit her lip. "I don't know if he'll work for anyone but Matt. Every dog is different, but Brody is in a class by himself."

Watching the dog, Bree pulled out her phone and called Matt. "Where are you?"

"Home," Matt said. "What's wrong?"

"Kayla's been abducted." Bree's voice caught as she said the words out loud. "I've given Brody her hat. Will he search for her?"

Before Matt could answer, Brody set off between the tents. The leash went taut, and Bree hurried to keep up with the dog. "He's going somewhere. I'll call you back."

She heard Matt shout, "I'm on my way," as she hit "End" and shoved the phone into her pocket.

Brody weaved in and out of the stalls, pulling Bree as she struggled to keep pace. Stranger abductions were rare, but when they occurred, the children were typically killed within three hours. Because she was a cop, Bree's brain automatically conjured the worst-case scenario, and fear balled under her breastbone like a cancer. She was vaguely aware of Cady jogging behind them. Hope gathered in her heart, but she was afraid to give it a voice. *Please, please let him find her.*

The dog stopped behind the funnel cake stand. Bree waited while he sniffed the air.

"Did he lose the scent?" *Please say no.*

"I don't know," Cady said. "Give him time."

They didn't have time.

"How can he smell her with all these competing odors?" All Bree could smell was hot dogs and popcorn.

The dog started off again. He leaned into the collar, pulling hard. Bree jogged behind him. The tents ended. A strip of weeds and grass separated the fairgrounds from the parking areas. Deputy vehicles blocked both exits. Brody made a hard right and traveled behind the tents. Bree ducked under a rope and struggled to keep up. The German shepherd made a beeline for a storage building, picking up his pace as they neared it. Bree tripped. The leash slipped out of her hand, and Brody shot off. Cady steadied Bree, and both women sprinted forward.

Brody hit the door of the building with both front paws and barked. He was agitated, whining and pacing. The metal door was padlocked. Bree and Cady circled the building. There were no windows and no back door. Cement slab. Metal walls and roof. She either needed to open the door or find a blowtorch.

The dog faced the door, then looked back at Bree and barked as if to tell her to open it. Banging sounded from inside the building.

Bree pounded a fist on the door in the same rhythm as she heard pounded against the inside of her ribs. "Kayla, are you in there?"

"Aunt Bree!" a high-pitched voice cried out.

Relief, gratitude, and fury flooded Bree. The combination was so extreme, her legs wobbled. "Are you OK?"

"Let me out!" Kayla screamed, her voice wild.

"I'll have you out of there in a few minutes." Bree used her radio to call for a deputy. She gave her location. "I need bolt cutters."

Brody barked. He stood at the front door and pawed at the metal. Cady picked up his leash and tried to calm him, but he ignored her. His entire focus was on the metal door.

Todd pulled up in his vehicle. He jumped out and used bolt cutters to snip the padlock. Bree yanked open the door. The building was empty. In the middle of a space the size of a basketball court, Kayla stood on the concrete facing the door. Her braids were disheveled, and her T-shirt ripped. A stuffed pink teddy bear lay on the floor next to her boots. Bree dropped to one knee, and Kayla ran into her arms. Her face was red, her cheeks wet with tears.

As she registered Kayla's safety—and her panicked state—anger replaced fear in Bree's heart. Rage rose like a phoenix, a blistering surge of emotion that obliterated every ounce of reason, like a red-hot poker had pierced her soul and stirred her fury to a boiling point. The power of it both shocked and emboldened her. A man had frightened, endangered, and attempted to kidnap Kayla.

He put his hands on her.

On the outside, Bree's body was as still as stone. Inside, her anger bubbled and popped like magma beneath a volcano. Never in her life had she felt an overwhelming urge to hurt someone. The emotion and drive were primal.

The violence of anger would have shocked her if she'd been capable of rational thought. She took several deep breaths. She inhaled the reassuring smell of sweat, hay, and kids' shampoo. Kayla was OK. Bree let herself absorb the news.

Bree held her tightly against her body until the desire to rip off a head passed. Brody barked and nudged Kayla.

Bree loosened her grip on the child. "Brody is the one who found you."

Kayla wrapped one arm around the big dog's neck and kissed him. "I love him. He's the best boy."

"He is," Bree agreed.

Kayla leaned back and wiped her face with the back of her forearm. "I did what you told me. I kicked and fought. I even kicked him where you told me to. I scratched him too."

"I'm proud of you." Bree released the child and scanned her from head to toe. "Are you hurt?"

"I was scared before." Kayla shook her head and stomped her booted foot. "Now I'm mad."

Good for you.

"Me too, honey. Me too." Bree gently took both her niece's hands in hers and examined her fingernails, but it was hard to tell if the debris under them was dirt, or blood, or a combination of both. Kayla was not a prissy little girl. She lived on a farm, spent hours and hours in the barn with her horse, and was usually downright filthy by the end of the day.

Bree looked up. "Todd? We need to, um . . ." She didn't want to use the word *scrape.* "Clean under her nails."

"I keep a kit in my car," Todd said. Rural policing meant being more autonomous. It wasn't always practical to call out a crime scene tech. Todd brought an evidence-collection kit from the back of his vehicle. He set Kayla on the hood of his car. "I'm going to clip your fingernails, OK?"

She nodded. "OK."

Todd walked her through the process and collected the samples. Then Bree used sanitizing wipes to clean her niece's hands. The thought of her harboring a predator's biological material made Bree want to use bleach. But she realized the temptation was irrational, and she resisted.

Deputies Oscar and Collins arrived. Bree asked them to search the immediate area for clues while she questioned Kayla.

"Can you tell me everything that happened?" Bree asked.

"I was waiting with Emma. Her mom was getting us hot dogs. I stayed right with her. I promise." Kayla's eyes brimmed with tears.

Bree lifted her niece's chin. "Kayla, you did everything right. This is not your fault, but I want to catch the man who did this."

Kayla nodded and gave the same description of the man's clothes as Emma: jeans and a red shirt. "He was pretending to be a clown, but he wasn't a real one. They wear makeup, and he had a mask. He picked me up and ran away. I kicked him and yelled. Then he stuffed me in there." Her small mouth toughened. "I screamed for a while. Then I heard Brody barking, and I knew it was OK." She smiled, slid off the

car hood, and knelt on the grass to hug the big dog again. Brody's tail thumped.

Bree rested her hand on the shepherd's head. Her eyes stung, and she blinked away a tear.

"Did you see the man's hair?" Bree asked.

Kayla shook her head. "He was wearing a baseball hat. A black one."

Bree added *black baseball hat* to the description. "What about his eyes? What color were they?"

Kayla shrugged. "I couldn't see. I'm sorry."

"You did great," Bree said.

Todd asked, "Do you want to put out a BOLO?"

"Yes. Even if we don't have enough of a description to identify him, I want neighboring jurisdictions to be aware that we had an attempted child abduction."

Todd returned to his vehicle to issue the BOLO.

Bree's mind began to settle. Was Kayla's abduction a crime of opportunity? Did a predator simply see her and decide to grab her? Or had this been planned?

The thought of someone watching Kayla and waiting for an opportunity to kidnap her sent ice through Bree's veins.

"Ma'am?" Oscar called from inside the building.

Bree hesitated. She didn't want to leave Kayla's side.

Still holding Brody's leash, Cady stepped forward. "Brody and I will stay with her."

Bree crouched. "Kayla, I'm going inside the building for a few minutes. You stay right here with Cady and Brody, OK?"

Kayla gave her a solemn nod, her eyes open wide, arm still slung around the dog's neck. Cady was standing right behind the child, and Bree's deputies were all around. But she had to force herself to walk away. She entered the building. Oscar was squatting next to the teddy bear. It was a small and cheaply made carnival prize.

"It probably came from one of the game stalls." Wearing gloves, Oscar handed Bree a small envelope with a gold elastic band that ran through a hole in the corner. Her name was written in block print on the outside. "This was attached to the bear."

Bree accepted the envelope, touching only the edges. The envelope flap wasn't sealed, and she slid out the small card. More block print spelled out a message. Her hands shook as she read the card.

DON'T MAKE ME HURT YOU. LET SLEEPING DOGS LIE.

Though she knew he was dead, her mind automatically read the message in her father's voice. She'd heard him say *don't make me hurt you* over and over to her mother throughout her childhood. Whoever had kidnapped Kayla had known Bree's father well enough to know that. Bree's blood went ice cold. Goose bumps rose on her arms. She knew in her gut that the second half of the message was a reference to her father's dogs. The abductor had also known that the grave site was near the dog yard.

Twenty-seven years after his death, her father still haunted her.

CHAPTER
TWENTY-ONE

Matt jogged across the parking lot toward the storage building. Two sheriff's deputy vehicles blocked access to the area. He waved to the deputy controlling the scene and threaded his way between the cars. Bree had let him know that Kayla was safe, but Matt wanted to be with them.

Brody's bark alerted Matt, and he spotted Kayla and his dog on the grass next to a deputy. Brody appeared calm, but Matt recognized the signs of heightened alertness. Brody's ears were forward, his nose in the air, and his posture was far from relaxed. The leash trailed on the grass, but the dog didn't leave the child's side as Matt approached. Brody had put himself on guard duty.

Bree exited the storage building, holding two evidence bags. Their eyes met over a span of thirty feet, and it took effort for Matt to restrain himself. He wanted to hold her. Instead, he crouched and hugged Kayla.

"Brody rescued me," she said in his ear, her voice a little shaky.

"He's a very good boy." Matt moved her at arm's length. Her clothes and hair were disheveled, but he didn't spot any bruises or other injuries. Her eyes were dry but red around the edges, and her face was puffy, as if she'd been crying. Anger filled Matt to the brim. "Are you OK?"

She nodded. "I was scared."

"I would've been scared too," Matt said.

"Really?"

"You bet." He nodded. "Everyone gets scared sometimes. But you fought back anyway. That was brave."

She sniffed, seeming to feel better.

"I'm going to talk to Aunt Bree for a minute, OK?" Matt asked.

"OK." She plopped down on the grass next to Brody.

Matt scratched his dog behind the ear. "Thanks, buddy."

Brody's tail thumped on the grass twice.

Matt made sure Deputy Collins was focused on Kayla before he turned and walked across the grass to Bree.

"We'll find him." Bree's words were measured and level, but underneath they hummed with fury. He saw the same cold resolve in her eyes that he felt deep in his own chest. She paced back and forth across the ground. Usually, Matt was the pacer, and Bree was the cool one. Clearly a threat to the kids went above and beyond her ability to keep calm.

Matt nodded once. "We will."

"I've called Dana. She's running a complete diagnostic on the security system." Bree had a state-of-the-art alarm. She'd even wired the barn. "I don't have a spare deputy to put a guard outside, but Dana will be there." As a former cop, Dana was usually armed. "But I still don't want to leave them. Kayla was already targeted. Luke is at risk too. But to find Kayla's abductor, I have to investigate. I can't do that from inside my house." Bree shoved a hair off her forehead and pressed her palm to her scalp. Rage and vulnerability simultaneously filled her eyes. She looked like she wanted to lock Kayla in a bunker but also tear someone to pieces.

"I can ask Nolan to help." Matt pulled out his phone. "He has a concealed carry permit, and no one is better at hand to hand."

"He's better than you?"

Matt snorted. "He's been beating the hell out of me since I was born. Sometimes, I think that's why my parents had me." He paused. "Seriously, Nolan used to do personal security work. Between him and Dana, the kids will be safe. Should I call him?"

Bree nodded. "Yes, and thank you."

Matt stepped away to make the call. When Nolan answered, Matt explained what had happened.

Nolan's answer was one sentence: "I'll be at Bree's place in an hour."

Matt walked back to Bree. "He's in. Do we have any evidence?"

"The descriptions both kids gave matched, but neither of them saw his face. We might have his DNA from under Kayla's nails, and he left this note." Bree held up one of the evidence bags and spit out some words. "A threat with a fucking carnival toy."

Matt read it. "'Don't make me hurt you. Let sleeping dogs lie.'" A fresh burst of anger warmed him. "That does sound like a threat."

"A very specific threat." Bree's eyes drifted to Kayla, then back to Matt. "I believe he's referencing my father." Her nostrils flared as she exhaled. "My father used to say *don't make me hurt you* or *you always make me hurt you* to my mother right before he beat the hell out of her. I believe *Let sleeping dogs lie* refers to the grave in the dogs' area of our property."

Matt glanced at the note again. "Maybe we can get fingerprints from the note."

"Maybe. But the connection is definitely to my father."

"We have one suspect who knew him."

"Curtis." Bree blew a stray hair off her face. "We'll get Kayla settled at home, then go see Curtis."

"Is there anything else to do here?" Matt scanned the scene.

"No. I'll have a deputy pull prints from the doorknob. We'll try to get a match. If there was biological material under Kayla's nails, then we could get a match in CODIS." The Combined DNA Index System stored DNA profiles from crime scenes and offenders.

"That takes time." First, the lab would have to determine whether the material even contained DNA. If it did, then samples had to be prepared. Backlogs were the rule, not the exception. This was not TV, and they would not have the answer before the next commercial.

"Let's get Kayla home." Bree collected her niece. "Considering the circumstances, I'll ask the mayor to cover for me at the closing ceremony. I want to get Kayla out of here." She pursed her lips, thoughtful. "Something else just occurred to me. At first, I thought the paintball incident was a prank, but now I'm not so sure."

"The note specifically referred to hurting you." Matt picked up Brody's leash, but the big dog was already on Kayla's heels. He and the dog escorted them to Bree's SUV before returning to their own vehicle. Then Matt followed them back to the farm.

Dana greeted them in the driveway. She hugged Kayla hard. She was wearing her sidearm and Matt noticed the bulge of an additional weapon at her ankle.

"Can we have macaroni and cheese for dinner?" Kayla asked.

"We can have anything you want." Dana took her hand and led her toward the house. She paused and looked back over her shoulder at Bree and Matt. "I didn't let Luke drive to work. I dropped him off. He'll need a pickup when his shift is over at ten."

"Was he OK with that?" Bree asked.

"He wasn't happy," Dana said.

A black F-150 pulled into the driveway and parked next to Bree's SUV. Nolan Flynn stepped out. He wore jeans and a gray T-shirt. He was still fighter lean. His head was shaved, and two full sleeves of tats decorated his arms. He wore a shoulder holster as if he were comfortable in it. He did not look like someone anyone would want to mess with.

He slapped Matt on the shoulder and gave Bree a quick hug. "You go do what you have to do. Dana and I can handle business here."

Gratitude filled Matt. "Thank you, brother."

"No need to thank me." Nolan smiled. "We take care of family, right?"

They went inside. Bree went upstairs to exchange her dress uniform for her preferred working attire: tactical cargoes and a uniform shirt. Matt could tell by the fit of her shirt that she wore her body armor underneath. Kayla went into the family room to watch TV. Ladybug curled on the couch next to her. Brody stretched out on the floor in front of her. Vader walked along the back of the sofa and perched just over Kayla's shoulder. Animals just knew when they were needed.

"Can Brody stay with me, Matt?" Kayla rested her feet on the big dog's shoulders. Her hazel eyes were wide and serious. The day's events had traumatized her, but she was trying to be brave.

"Of course he can." Matt met his dog's gaze. Brody didn't need a command. He'd lay down his life for that little girl without hesitation—and so would everyone else in that house. "Nolan's going to hang out with you too."

She nodded. "I like Nolan."

Matt dropped to the seat next to her. "Brody, Nolan, and Dana will keep you safe. You can trust them."

"I know." But her voice was heartbreakingly soft.

Matt gave her a one-armed hug. Before January, he'd barely known her, but today he felt like she was his own. How did people carve their way into one's heart so fast?

Matt and Bree waited until Dana had given Nolan a tour of the property and a rundown of the alarm system before Bree said goodbye to her niece. "Are you OK with me leaving?"

"You have to go," Kayla said. "You need to catch the bad man."

"I love you." Bree kissed her on the head.

"I love you too." Kayla wrapped her arms around Bree's neck and gave her a hard squeeze.

Watching them, Matt felt his heart break.

Bree's eyes were misty and fierce when she turned away, and Matt appreciated the strength she was summoning in leaving the house—in trusting others to keep her kids safe when she'd probably rather barricade them all inside and light a moat filled with tar all around the property.

In a hoarse voice, she said, "Let's go."

They left through the kitchen door. They heard the deadbolt slide home as they walked down the back-porch steps. Matt stopped at his Suburban for his Kevlar vest. He donned it over his polo shirt. By silent, mutual agreement, he and Bree were taking no chances.

Bree had her phone in her hand and a worried frown on her face. "I'd like to swing by Adam's place first. I called him twice and texted him. He isn't responding."

"That's not unusual," Matt said.

Bree's brother often disconnected from the world when he was working. His art had the potential to consume him.

"I know. But considering what happened to Kayla, I need to make sure he's safe."

A car pulled into Bree's driveway. Matt went on alert, and Bree's hand settled on her weapon. The car door opened, and Deputy Laurie Collins stepped out. She wore jeans and a black T-shirt, but she carried her sidearm.

Bree stopped short. "Collins? Is something wrong?"

"No, ma'am," Collins said. "The other deputies and I agreed that one of us will be here at all times until this perp is caught."

Confusion creased the corners of Bree's eyes. "There's no money for overtime in the budget."

"No matter, ma'am." Collins turned back to her vehicle. "We have your back."

Chapter Twenty-Two

"I can't believe my deputies are guarding my house off duty." Bree adjusted her grip on the steering wheel. Her deputies' support still overwhelmed her as she turned down the quiet country road where her brother lived.

"I'm not surprised at all. You're a good sheriff. You've earned your deputies' respect."

Except for one or two exceptions, Bree's department was starting to come together. They were beginning to feel cohesive in a way that only developed from working together and relying on each other in dangerous situations.

Ten minutes later, Bree knocked on her brother's door. Adam lived in a converted barn. Nothing but meadow surrounded it. In the winter, it was forlorn and lonely. But on a bright summer day, wildflowers bloomed in a sea of color.

He had no neighbors within sight—or earshot. He didn't answer, and anxiety ticked up her heart rate. His beat-up Ford Bronco sat outside, so she knew he was home. She knocked again, harder, but heard no movement inside. "He tunes everything out when he's working."

Nothing.

With no shade, the summer sun beat on her relentlessly. The screech of a hawk carried across the fields, and sweat dripped under Bree's body armor.

Matt pounded his fist on the door.

She held her breath. The door opened, and a bleary-eyed Adam stood in the doorway. He was still dressed in the same clothes, but with additional paint spatter. She wasn't prepared for the surge of relief at seeing him. She exhaled hard, the tension leaving her body with a rush of air.

Adam rubbed an eye. "Is something wrong?"

"Can we come in?" Bree asked.

"Yeah, of course." He stepped back. "I finished the painting and crashed pretty hard."

Adam's house was essentially one giant room, with the space divided by function and furniture. A partial wall separated his studio from the sleeping and living spaces. Pizza boxes, empty seltzer cans, and discarded clothes covered almost every surface. He didn't apologize for the mess. He didn't care. When he finished his painting, he'd sleep, eat, and clean for a week or two, then start all over again.

Bree walked to the studio area. A picture window flooded a huge canvas with light. Bree drew back. Adam had been born into a family filled with grief, anger, and abuse. Like Bree, he'd carried that burden into adulthood. Darkness always filled his work, and this piece was no different. Dark reds, bold blues, and stormy grays dominated the canvas. Bree saw sadness and anger and lack of control in the turbulent brushstrokes. But in one corner, a shaft of light blue with just the slightest hint of pale-yellow shadow pierced the darkness. The darker colors surged toward it but were held at bay. Despite being a minute portion of the overall work, the small sliver of brightness drew and held the eye. It was a spark of hope at the edge of overwhelming despair.

She scanned the overall painting again, and that tiny ribbon of light pulled her in.

Hope won.

She heard Matt draw in a sharp breath and realized he was standing next to her. Bree had been so transfixed by the painting, she hadn't noticed that he'd followed her.

She looked for her brother and spotted him leaning on the far wall. "Adam, this is . . . amazing. I don't even have words for it."

"Is it?" His gaze was critical as he examined his own work. "I don't know. It felt a little different."

And that was the whole point.

"Adam, it's incredible," Matt said without taking his eyes off the painting.

"It's my second favorite painting of yours." Bree smiled. The painting he'd done of their sister hung on her living room wall.

Adam squinted at his painting. "Maybe it's *not* done."

"Do not change a thing. It's stunning." Bree pinned him with a look.

"OK. You win. I promise." The corner of his mouth turned up. "But I know you didn't come here to see this." He gestured toward his art.

"No." Bree hated to break the moment, but Adam needed to know. "I'll start by saying that Kayla is fine." She told him what had happened at the fair after he'd left.

His face went pale. "Who's with her now?"

"Dana and my brother," Matt said.

"But I would feel better if you were there too," Bree added. "Kayla is upset. She needs you."

"Yeah, of course. I'll stay with the kids." Adam brushed a hand through his unruly hair.

With one last glance at the painting, Bree followed him out of the studio area. Her brother grabbed a duffel bag from under the bed, then stuffed some clothes into it. He disappeared into the bathroom, emerging in a minute with a small travel case. He shoved it into the duffel bag. "I'll head over there now."

He slung the straps over his shoulder.

"Text me when you get there." Bree hugged him.

"I will." He walked out of the house and climbed into his ancient vehicle. "You worry too much."

"It's my superpower." Bree would not breathe easy until she knew he was safe, but she had to trust him to take care of himself. He wasn't the baby she'd protected all those years ago. He was a grown man.

She and Matt climbed back into her vehicle and headed for the main road. Stopping at a traffic light, Bree tapped her fingertips on the steering wheel. "After Curtis, we visit Bradley Parson."

"We spooked someone with our investigation."

"Big time." Bree drove to Curtis's address and parked on the street. Trees blocked the view of the house. "We're here. I don't want him to see us and run."

They exited the vehicle and walked to the driveway. Digger greeted them with a flurry of barking, then ran in a circle around them before letting Matt give her a few pats.

"His truck isn't here," Bree said.

They went to the front door and flanked it. Matt knocked on the wood. The sound of shuffling feet approached the door. A curtain moved aside, and Mrs. Evans peered out.

She opened the door. "What do you want?"

"We have some follow-up questions for Curtis," Bree said. "Do you know where he is?"

From her distrustful expression, Mrs. Evans clearly didn't buy the casual tone. "He went to work."

"On a Sunday?" Matt asked.

"They work when they have jobs," Mrs. Evans said. "My Curtis works hard. He hasn't done anything wrong. You can call his cell, and he'll answer you when he has time. He has rights. We don't even have to talk to you at all." She tried to shut the door, but Bree's boot was blocking it. "Move it or lose it, Sheriff. You're trespassing."

Bree had to give her credit—and respect. She was so old and frail. She had the bones of a sparrow. Yet she was ready to brawl for her son. Now that Bree had the kids, she understood the term *mama bear*. She wanted to find the man who'd scared Kayla, and she wasn't proud of the violent thoughts popping into her head.

Bree pulled her foot free and stepped off the cinder block. Mrs. Evans firmly closed the door.

"It's five o'clock. The company should be finishing up for the day." Matt pulled his phone from his pocket. "Let's swing by the landscaping company's office." He plugged the address into the GPS. They got into the vehicle, and Bree followed the directions. A Cut Above's official address was in an old industrial complex. The company rented a row of garages. When Bree pulled the SUV into the parking lot, employees were cleaning up and stowing equipment for the day.

Matt stopped next to a guy oiling a hedge trimmer. "Where's your boss?"

The guy pointed to one of the garages. Matt and Bree walked to the open overhead door. The air inside smelled like oil and gasoline. Curtis wasn't in sight. A blond man in his midfifties was stretched out on the ground, looking under a riding mower. He saw them and got to his feet. "Can I help you?"

"We're looking for Curtis." Bree introduced Matt. "Can I ask your name?"

"I'm Anders Nilsen, Curtis's business partner." He pulled a bandana from his back pocket and wiped his hands. A worker brought a Weedwacker into the garage and stored it on a rack. Anders frowned. "Let's go into the office."

He led the way into a dirty room with a concrete floor, a few filing cabinets, and a dented metal desk from the '70s. The only chair was behind the desk. Anders didn't sit, nor did he invite Matt or Bree to make themselves comfortable. He merely turned, folded his arms over his chest, and waited. From his posture, Bree expected him to be uncooperative.

She squared off with him, but she kept her voice casual. "Where's Curtis?"

Instead of answering, Anders cocked his head. "What's this about?"

Bree gave him a sad smile. "Curtis's brother."

Relief relaxed Anders's posture. "Did you find Frank?"

"Yes," Bree said.

"Is he dead?" Anders asked.

"Yes." She nodded.

"Ah, shit." Anders lowered his chin and shook his head. "I know they say closure helps, but it would have been better for his mom to go to her grave still hoping Frank was alive. Hope is hope, and dead is final, you know? How'd he die?"

"Frank was murdered," Matt said. "We're trying to solve his case."

"Murdered?" Anders whistled. "I guess it's not a huge surprise. Frank was rough."

"How well did you know him?" Matt asked.

Anders perched on the edge of the desk, as if the story might take a while. "Me and Curtis have been friends since high school. Frank was older. We looked up to him. Thought he was a badass, which is how me and Curtis ended up in jail."

Bree's eyebrow crept up. "How was that Frank's fault?"

"It was indirect. Frank had disreputable friends and wads of cash. Me and Curtis were young and dumb. We thought they were cool, so we experimented with the theory that crime pays." He sighed. "It didn't, at least not for us. Sadly, I guess it didn't pay for Frank in the end either."

"Do you know where we can find Curtis?" Matt asked.

"I don't know where he is. He called me this morning and said he had something he had to do today and couldn't come in. Curtis only takes off if he has to take his mom to the doctor. She's dying."

"When was the last time you saw him?"

"Yesterday," Anders said. "He was late because she had some problem with her medication. I assumed today's callout was for her too. Our current job is big, a complete redesign. The weather for the last couple of weeks has set us behind schedule. We're working seven days a week to catch up. He knows this, so I assume whatever he needed to do was important. I can't blame him for taking care of his mom. She doesn't have much time left."

"Hold on a minute." Bree left the garage to retrieve the photograph of the four men. She showed it to Anders. "Can you identify these men?"

"There's Curtis and Frank." Anders tapped their faces. "I forget this guy's name." His brows dipped into a V as he pointed to Bree's father. "But this other guy was his cousin."

Bree touched her father's picture. "This is Jake Taggert."

"Jake." Anders snapped his fingers. "Yeah. That was his name. This guy was . . ." He circled his hand in the air. "I think his name began with an *H*. Hank, Henry."

Harley. A memory hit Bree with no warning, like a bucket of cold water or a slap across the face. She pictured her father and his cousin out back, drinking beer and throwing horseshoes. It was a slice of time, a minute of her past she hadn't known she could remember. What else had she forgotten? Probably a lot. She'd spent most of her life actively suppressing her past, but this memory popped up and bobbed like a decomposing body.

"This man's name was Harley," she said.

"That's it." Anders pumped a fist.

Matt pointed to Harley's image. "Are you sure he was Jake's cousin?"

Anders nodded. "I remember thinking it was strange because Frank and Curtis were brothers, and these other two guys were cousins, like they were from two crime families." He lifted a hand. "I know it's weird, but I was just a dumb kid back then. I was impressed by the stupidest things. I was poor, and they had cash. That's all I wanted. It sucks to watch your mom bust her ass to make the rent and feed you. It sucks to be hungry literally all the time. I remember my mom using food stamps a few times she was out of work, the dirty looks people gave her, and her trying to hold her head up."

"I'm sorry your family experienced that," Bree said.

He dropped his chin. "Thanks."

"Was Harley's last name Taggert?" Bree lowered the photo. Her childhood memories didn't include last names, just faces and snippets of action too brief to understand.

"I think so." Anders shrugged. "It's been a really long time."

Matt asked, "How did knowing Jake and his cousin lead to you and Curtis going to jail?"

"As I said, we were all broke. My dad left us early on. My mom worked two jobs, and we were still always behind on bills. Frank and Curtis's dad died. They were in the same situation. You know what? You get real tired of government cheese-and-ketchup sandwiches." His face flushed. "Anyway, Curtis didn't have details, but he knew Jake, Harley, and Frank were up to illegal shit. Frank didn't have a job. Yet he'd come home with a roll of cash. He had a cell phone. Back then, I wanted one so bad, but we couldn't afford it. Frank would take me and Curtis out for pizza. He'd buy us beer. We thought he was a big shot. So, one day, me and Curtis talked about a quick way to make some money. We had the not-so-brilliant idea of robbing a convenience store. We were the dumbest motherfuckers alive. We barely planned anything, just stuck our fingers in the pockets of our jackets and demanded money from the clerk. We deserved to go to jail for sheer stupidity. We both did time and decided we didn't want to repeat the experience."

Bree wrote in her notepad. "When did Frank disappear?"

"A year or two after we got out," Anders said.

Matt asked, "You have no idea what kind of illegal activity Jake, Harley, and Frank participated in?"

Anders stared at the ceiling for a few seconds. "With thirty years' hindsight, I think they were hired thugs. These men were not criminal masterminds. They were low-level thugs. I remember Frank saying shit like they had to go bust a head. It all felt very *Goodfellas*, if you know what I mean."

Bree lifted her pen. "Who did they work for?"

"That I can't tell you." Anders shook his head. "Once I got out, I avoided all of them. I went to work for a landscaping company. I didn't even see Curtis until his brother disappeared and he needed money. Jail changed me. Frank's disappearance knocked the sense into Curtis. He came to work here. There aren't a lot of job opportunities when you have a record, but the guy who used to own this business"—Anders waved—"was an ex-con. He hired us, but we were warned: one fuckup and we were history. We worked hard and stayed out of trouble. When he was ready to sell the business, he let us pay him in installments. He was a really good guy."

Bree took Anders's contact information, and he went back to work. Bree and Matt returned to the SUV. Bree put out a BOLO on Curtis and his pickup truck.

She started the engine and gripped the wheel with both hands. "What now? We have two potential murder suspects and no idea where either of them is."

"Door number three?" Matt suggested.

Bree steered the SUV out of the parking lot. "Let's hope we can actually find Bradley Parson."

CHAPTER TWENTY-THREE

Matt stepped out of the vehicle at the Parson estate. On the drive, they'd called Todd and asked him to track down Harley Taggert. Matt used the dashboard computer to check motor vehicle records. Harley didn't have a driver's license or vehicle registered in the state of New York.

Matt joined Bree in the long driveway. "Do you remember anything about Harley?"

"I don't know." The V between her eyebrows deepened. "Maybe. The word *cousin* jogged a memory I didn't even know I had."

The sounds of splashing and children's voices floated on the hot breeze, and the air smelled like barbecue.

On the way to the front door, Matt inhaled. "I'm hungry."

They rang the bell. The maid opened the door and raised her brows at them.

"We're here to see Mr. Parson," Bree said.

"Do you have an appointment?" The maid's tone indicated they should.

"No." Bree pointed to her badge. "But I need to speak with him."

The maid frowned and glanced over her shoulder, as if uncertain what to do. Then she stepped back and opened the door wider. "Come in."

She showed them into a large study. An antique desk held a blotter, a small globe, and a pen in a brass holder. Bookshelves lined the walls. Two leather chairs and a love seat formed a conversation area. The room had an overall unused feel.

"Wait here." The maid withdrew.

Bradley kept them waiting twenty minutes. When he walked in, a scowl darkened his face. He didn't bother with a greeting. "I hope this is important."

"It is."

"I'm sorry for keeping you waiting. I was in the pool with my grandsons. I had to change clothes." Bradley wore khaki trousers and a navy blue polo shirt. His hair was damp, and his face was flushed from heat and sun. He sat in one of the leather chairs and gestured for them to take the love seat. "What is this about?"

Matt and Bree eased onto the cushions.

"Where were you earlier today?" Bree asked.

Bradley leaned back and crossed his legs. "Nancy and I took our grandsons to the fair this morning, just like every year. We brought them here afterward, and they took a nap. Why?"

"There was an incident that might be tied to your sister's murder case." Bree watched his eyes.

Bradley hesitated. "I don't understand. How could that be? My sister has been dead for thirty years."

"Someone threatened my niece." Bree quelled a quick surge of anger. "The note he left with her indicated it might be related."

To his credit, Bradley acted concerned. He shifted forward, planting both feet on the wood floor. "Is your niece all right?"

"Yes." Bree nodded. "Thank you for asking."

He studied the picture. "None of them look familiar." He handed it back.

She turned the picture to face Bradley and pointed to Frank's face. "This is Frank Evans, the man who was buried with your sister."

"Jane didn't bring her male friends to family or social events." Bradley turned up a palm in a *who knows* gesture. He didn't even try to look at the photo again, which Matt found odd. Wouldn't he want more information on the man who had died with his sister?

"You assume Frank had a relationship with your sister?" Matt asked.

"I really have no idea." Bradley motioned toward the photo. "He could have slept with Jane. He could have worked on her car. They could have had no relationship whatsoever. My sister didn't keep me apprised of her life in any way."

"Do the following names sound familiar?" Bree began. "Curtis Evans, Jake Taggert, Harley Taggert."

"No." Bradley didn't blink. "I've never heard of any of those men, but two of them share *your* last name."

"Yes," Bree admitted. "Jake Taggert was my father."

Bradley's gaze went cold. "And my sister's remains were found on your father's land. Maybe he killed them both. Maybe you should be interrogating your own family instead of mine, or are you too close to the case?"

"My father *is* a suspect in your sister's murder," Bree said. "But he's been dead for twenty-seven years. He didn't threaten my niece today."

"And we have no indication that he even knew Jane," Matt added.

"That is your problem." Bradley stood and smoothed the wrinkles from his slacks. "I'd like to go back to my family now. My son and his wife are on their way over for a barbecue."

Bree stood and faced him. "I'd like to ask your mother if she recognizes these men."

"She doesn't," Bradley said.

"I'd like to hear that from her," Bree insisted.

Bradley dismissed her with a shake of his head. "My mother hasn't been feeling well since she learned of Jane's death. I won't allow you to upset her again. In fact, none of us will be speaking with you again without our attorney. I don't want to make your job difficult, but I will protect my family."

"We're done," Bree conceded. "For now."

They were given the boot without seeing anyone else in the house. The door closed behind them, and they started down the walkway.

Matt turned and tried to look at his own back. "Do I have a shoe print on my ass?"

"Right?" Back in the SUV, Bree said, "His concern for Kayla and his own family seemed sincere, but I don't trust him."

"I don't trust anybody," Matt agreed. "What do we do now?"

"We should go home and get some sleep." Bree rubbed a hand down her face. "Before the stunt with Kayla, I could easily have believed my father was the killer, but now . . ."

"Our investigation clearly triggered someone to threaten you, and why get triggered if you aren't guilty?"

"That's how it feels to me." Bree thumped the wheel with a fist. "Our killer overplayed his hand."

Matt had no doubt they would eventually solve the case. Bree focused like Brody on a scent. She would never let up until she'd figured it out.

If the killer was willing to target a child this early in the investigation, what would he do as they drew closer?

CHAPTER TWENTY-FOUR

Bree was parked in front of the grocery store. Luke emerged just after ten o'clock, his black apron tossed over his shoulder. Bree pulled up to the curb, and he stepped into the vehicle.

"How was your shift?" she asked as he buckled his seat belt.

"OK." Luke leaned back and stared out the passenger window. His attitude was so cold, Bree could almost feel frost in the middle of July.

She fumbled for words. "I'm sorry the case has intruded on your life."

"Are you?" he snapped. Luke was usually even tempered, so the outburst surprised Bree.

"Yes. I am."

He sulked, also not typical for him.

Bree often stumbled with parenting. She had no experience, and taking on the job with two half-grown kids often felt like being tossed into the ocean without knowing how to swim. The only lesson she'd learned from her own parents was what not to do. She'd survived most of her adult life by compartmentalizing her feelings and locking them away. Now that she needed to connect on an emotional level, she floundered.

Instead of circling around Luke's feelings, Bree plowed straight through. "What's going on?"

He chewed on a thumbnail. "Nothing."

"Luke, I can't read your mind. I'm sorry I'm not better at this communication thing, but you need to tell me what's happening with you." She glanced at him.

His jaw jutted forward in a very Taggert way. Bree could see Erin in him, but she also saw herself. He was kind like his mother, but also stubborn like Bree. Where did that trait originate? Jake? Bree hoped not. She knew half her DNA came from her father. She and both the kids had inherited his hazel eyes, but she didn't want any of his personal characteristics. And she didn't wish them on Luke either.

"Talk to me, Luke."

"You still treat me like I'm a kid." He balled up his hands into fists and rested them on his thighs.

"I'm sorry. It's a hard balance for me."

"I could have driven myself to work."

"Maybe, but I appreciate your cooperation," Bree said. "The fact is, I don't know if you're in any danger or not, but I can't take any chances. Not with you or Kayla. You're too important to me."

Luke didn't look at her, which meant he had more to say. Bree pulled away from the curb and started home in the dark. She'd learned that he often opened up better if they weren't staring at each other.

He dropped his head and stared at his clenched fists. "How long is this going to last?"

"I don't know. I'm trying to catch him."

"What if you don't? Will I ever be able to drive by myself again?"

Bree swallowed a pat answer. "Yes. This won't last."

"But how long?" Luke nearly whined, which was not like him at all.

"Luke, what is really going on? This isn't like you."

He looked to the window. "I have plans for next weekend."

"OK. I'm sure we can work something out. What are your plans?"

He hesitated. "There's this girl . . ."

"Do you have a date?"

"Not exactly. A bunch of us were just going to hang out."

"OK. So, you have plans to hang out with your friends next weekend, and a girl you like is going to be there."

"I think."

Bree did not miss being a teenager. Not one bit. Poor Luke had to navigate his most difficult years around his mother's violent death, his father going to jail, and his aunt's new job as the county sheriff. The kid had more strikes against him than a minor league team. "What are your plans?"

He gave her a jerky shrug. "Maybe a movie. Maybe the diner."

"OK. I'll tell you what. I will do everything I can to make sure you can go next week, but I can't make any absolute promises."

He flushed, but his chin came up. "OK."

Bree reached across the SUV and squeezed his forearm. "I love you, and I won't let anything happen to you, even if that makes you mad." Her eyes turned hot with tears. "There is absolutely nothing I wouldn't do for you." *Including kill or die.*

She might not have given birth to Luke and Kayla, but they'd become her kids. The love she had for them was fierce and also terrifying.

"I'm sorry if I'm being a pain."

"You're never a pain, Luke. I want you to talk to me. There is no topic that's off limits. You're getting older. You'll be off to college in two years." The thought of him leaving made her a little sick. "I'm not going to be able to fix all your problems, but I'll do what I can. And I'll always be here to listen. Sometimes, just talking to someone helps."

Luke turned and looked at her for the first time since he'd gotten into the car. "Who do you talk to?"

Bree had to think. "Last year, I would have said Vader. I could have talked to Dana, but I probably wouldn't have. I kept things bottled up."

She paused. "I don't have to tell you how hard it is to trust or open up after you've lost someone."

Luke sniffed and swallowed.

"But I'm learning that's not the best way to live. Honestly, I was missing out. Life is much better if you have people to share it with you."

"Are you happy with us?" Luke asked, his tone completely serious.

"I'm not even sure how to answer that question." Bree stopped at a traffic light and turned right. "I'm happier than I knew I could be."

"You didn't answer my question about who you talk to." Luke circled back to his previous question like a seasoned interrogator.

"I said Dana."

"You also said you probably wouldn't talk to her."

"You're tough," Bree said. "Now I have you, Kayla, and Adam."

"Matt?" Luke's tone turned teasing.

"Yes. And Matt." Bree laughed. "Having people to talk to isn't just about sharing problems. When good things happen, they aren't as good if you're all alone." Bree searched for the right words. "Everything is better with family, whether it's the family you're born into or one you form by choice. That's something I'm learning late in life. I wish I'd figured it out sooner. I missed out."

"Good." Luke nodded. "I like Matt."

Violence had damaged her in childhood. Growing up, she'd protected her heart by walling it off. She'd always thought her scars were permanent, but maybe she could heal. When she'd assumed the job of raising the kids, she'd been forced out of her emotional comfort zone. Their needs had outweighed her own fears.

But Luke had a point about Matt. He was the person outside the family who Bree reached out to when she had news to share, good or bad. Her feelings for him were growing more complicated, but underneath it all, she *liked* him. She enjoyed spending time with him, which was something she should give more consideration. But tonight, she was focused on Luke.

"So, what's her name?" she asked.

"Paris." Luke's wistful tone said it all.

"Is she fun?"

"Yeah. Sometimes we just talk for hours." His voice brightened. "She's really smart."

"When you're ready, she can always come out to the farm. Does she like horses?"

"She's never ridden one, but she's always wanted to."

"I'm sure Kayla would loan her Pumpkin."

"Yeah. That could work. Anybody can ride him." Luke perked up and was his normal self the rest of the way home.

At the house, Bree parked and scanned the yard.

"Did you check the horses?" Luke asked.

"Not yet." Bree almost told him to go into the house but changed her mind. He was nearly an adult, the barn had its own security system—and she was armed. Together, they tucked in the horses for the night, then went to the house.

Nolan let them inside and reset the alarm. "Dana went to bed early. She'll be up at four to take over."

Ladybug greeted them at the door. Vader sat on the island and waited for them to come to him. Bree scratched his head on her way through the kitchen. Luke and his bottomless appetite beelined to the pantry for a snack. Adam was asleep on the living room couch. Bree tiptoed past him. She went upstairs, showered, and changed into jeans and a T-shirt. She usually locked up her weapons at night, but tonight, she wore her sidearm in a hip holster and her backup piece on her ankle. Kayla's bedroom door stood open a few inches. Bree peered through the gap. The light slanted across the little girl's innocent face. She was sprawled on her back, her legs pushed to one side by the German shepherd that occupied the entire foot of the bed. Brody's ears pricked in Bree's direction. Then, seemingly satisfied it was only her, he settled his head on the blanket.

196

Bree's heart filled as she stared at the sleeping child and protective dog, imagining how different the night could have been if Brody hadn't found Kayla. Bree pressed a fist to an ache in her chest. The love she felt for the kids was almost painful. She had survived numerous tragedies in her life, but she could not even contemplate anything happening to Luke or Kayla. She blocked that train of thought and walked downstairs. She tapped her brother on the shoulder. When he lifted his head, she said, "Go sleep upstairs."

Half-asleep, he nodded, rolled to his feet, and trudged up the steps.

Nolan was in the kitchen doorway, a cup of coffee in his hand. "Not tired?"

"Not sure if I can sleep. No point in wasting a perfectly good bed."

He nodded. "Sounds sensible." He turned and went back into the kitchen.

Bree followed him. Through the windows, she could see the backyard was lit with floodlights.

"Everything is fine." Nolan sat at the island in front of an open laptop. He'd pulled the stool around to the wrong side, so he was facing the windows and door. "I've done this before. Brody is on the job too. He'll let us know if anyone is within fifty feet of this house."

"I know. I have control issues." Bree walked aimlessly around the kitchen, debating on coffee. She really should try to catch a nap at least.

"I respect that." He worked on his laptop.

Bree tilted her head to see his screen. "What's that?"

"I installed a few cameras outside." He turned the machine to face her. Four small windows lined up on the top of his screen. A larger one occupied most of the space. "I have a view of each side of the house, and one of the barn. No one is sneaking up on us." He clicked on a small window, and it changed places with the main one.

"Thank you for your help." Bree went to the fridge and opened it. She stared at the neat piles of leftover containers.

"Happy to do it." Nolan didn't take his eyes off his laptop. "I brought broiled chicken and broccoli. Help yourself."

Nolan's diet and exercise program were the reason he still had the body fat of a professional athlete.

Fuck it.

She didn't need the body fat of a professional athlete, right? She could still clock seven-minute miles. She reached for the pasta and scooped a large helping onto a plate. "No judging."

Nolan lifted one hand. "Nope."

She warmed the bowl in the microwave. Tortellini with prosciutto and peas in a cream sauce was not light fare, but she didn't care. Ladybug followed her into the living room and watched her eat every bite. Then Bree stretched out on the couch. Images of Kayla in the storage shed at the fair tormented her every time she closed her eyes.

Kayla was fine. She was asleep in her bed.

Safe.

And there was nothing Bree wouldn't do to keep her that way.

Nothing.

CHAPTER TWENTY-FIVE

"Knock it off, Jake."

Huddled under the porch, Bree watched her dad's eyes go small and mean. She knew that look. Something bad always happened when he looked like that.

She pulled back into the shadows, hoping no one saw her. The cold began to work its way through her worn-thin coat and settle into her bones, but it was fear that made her knees shake.

Mommy winced as Daddy tightened his grip on her arm. "Mind your own business, Harley. Please," she begged.

"Yeah," Daddy said. "Fuck off, Harley."

"Why don't you go fuck yourself, Jake?" Harley shot back. "Or are you too busy beating up on women and children? Some man you are."

Bree shuddered. Harley was about the only person who dared stand up to her daddy. But if Daddy got mad, it didn't matter who made him that way. After they left, he hit Mommy. Bree used to pray to God to keep Mommy safe, but she'd given up. No matter how much she prayed, no one came. Daddy did whatever he wanted. No one ever made him stop. She touched her sore cheek, where the back of his hand had knocked her off her feet the day before.

Melinda Leigh

"You stay out of my business, Harley." Daddy's voice dropped to the tone that made Bree feel sick.

"You're a disgrace, Jake." Harley spit in the dirt of the backyard.

Mommy was trying hard not to cry. "Harley, please go home. You're not helping."

"Why do you stay with him?" Harley yelled. "Grab your kids and get out of here."

Bree's mom shook her head. Harley was making everything worse. Bree was just a kid, but she knew that Daddy would never let them go. She also knew that Mommy would never leave. There was an invisible rope that bound her to Daddy. Bree had never understood, but she knew it was there.

Besides, if they tried to leave, Daddy would kill them.

"Please, Harley. Just go," Mommy begged.

Sadness filled Bree, and something else she didn't have a name for. Her life would never change. She was trapped here.

"Go!" she whispered at Harley, even while she wished she belonged to him instead of her own daddy. For a second, she wanted to run and hide in his truck. Daddy wouldn't miss her. But that would leave Mommy and Erin and baby Adam alone. Bree couldn't do it. As much as she wanted to, she couldn't.

"Are you sure, Mary? It doesn't have to be this way." Harley sounded sad.

"Yes. Go. Please." Silent tears slid down Mommy's face.

"Yeah, Harley. Go." Daddy grinned like the wolf in Bree's fairy-tale book.

Harley turned and walked toward his truck. He glanced back over his shoulder. "You can call me anytime, Mary. I'll take you and the kids away from this asshole."

Bree had spent many nights wanting just that very thing to happen, but she knew it wouldn't. No matter where they went, Daddy would always find them.

Mommy's head went sideways. Daddy had a handful of her hair in his fist.

"I won't call," Mommy shouted. "You're making it worse, Harley."

"You heard her. Don't come back here, Harley." Daddy's tone held more weight than his words.

Harley's truck drove away. Bree's heart hurt.

Mommy yelped as Daddy dragged her inside by the hair. Bree shivered and drew farther back under the porch. She wanted to be invisible. Bree knew she couldn't stay under the porch forever, but she couldn't make herself go back inside either. She tucked her knees under her coat.

Over Bree's head, something thudded, her mother cried, and Bree crawled out from her hiding place. She knew what was coming, how the rest of that horrible day and night would play out, and that there wasn't anything she could do to stop it.

◆　◆　◆

"Bree!"

A male voice woke Bree. She bolted upright. Sweat plastered her T-shirt to her chest. Nolan stood in the doorway to the kitchen. His face was wary, as if he didn't know what to do.

She scanned the room, slowly recognizing the furniture and placing herself in the living room. She was not a child. She was not at her parents' house. Sorrow clutched at her heart. In the dream, her mother and little sister had still been alive. Waking was like losing them all over again.

She breathed and tried to slow her scrambling pulse. This wasn't the first time she'd dreamed of that night. She'd experienced the reminder of her tragedy countless times. But it was the first time she'd relived that particular moment.

It was the first time Harley had made an appearance.

"You were having a bad dream," Nolan said.

"Yeah." She shoved her sweaty hair off her forehead. "Thanks. I'm OK now."

Nolan nodded. "Let me know if you need anything." As if he knew and respected that she wanted to be alone, he retreated to the kitchen.

Unable to sit still, she jumped off the sofa. Her skin felt too tight, and her heart fluttered like a moth trapped in a lantern. Bree's normal response to stress was to compartmentalize her emotions and divert her attention, usually to a case. Typically, she didn't fidget. Instead of wasting stress energy, she diverted it to something productive. But tonight, she couldn't clear her head. Her memories wouldn't fall back no matter how hard she beat at them.

Bree paced, the dream still lingering like a foul odor. Even with the details hazy in her mind, she knew that was the night her mother had died.

And Harley had been there.

Bree snatched her phone off the coffee table and rushed through the kitchen. She couldn't be in the house for another minute. She was suffocating. "I'm going to take a drive."

"You OK?" Nolan looked over his laptop, concern in his eyes.

"I need some air." She fought to keep her voice steady.

His nod was respectful. "Be careful."

"I will." Bree stepped into her running shoes and went out onto the porch. She used her app to reset the alarm. Then she stood still for a few seconds, just breathing. After the cool air-conditioning in the house, outside felt warm and sticky. The humidity settled in a damp layer on the bare skin of her arms. Nighttime in the country was typically dark. There were no streetlamps. Porch lights were often miles away from each other. The moon shone in a cloudless sky, casting an eerie glow over the landscape. A symphony of crickets chirped in the meadow, and a bat flapped its way over the pasture.

Being outside wasn't enough. Bree needed to move. She jogged to her SUV and headed out of the driveway. She lowered the window and let the night air flood the vehicle. She passed a cow-dotted field and inhaled the scents of manure and grass. Every sight, every sound, every smell brought her rural childhood back in a barrage of images and emotions.

When she'd moved back to Grey's Hollow, she'd known she was returning to the past she'd avoided most of her adult life. But she hadn't fully realized she'd mentally buried so many memories. How could she have blocked an entire person from her consciousness?

She drove on autopilot with no conscious thought of her route, but a short while later, she stood on Matt's doorstep. How she'd gotten there was almost scary. Inside, Greta barked, setting off an answering chorus from the kennels out back. Seconds later, Matt opened the door. He wore gym shorts, an old T-shirt, and a worried frown. His hair was mussed, and his bleary eyes told her she'd woken him. Greta stood at his side, her ears pricked forward, her expression curious.

He blinked the sleepiness from his eyes. "Is everything all right? Did I miss your call?"

"Everything's fine." Emotions lodged in her throat. "Can I come in?"

"Yeah. Of course." He stood aside.

Bree walked past him. Greta followed, her tail wagging as if she were enjoying the unusual nighttime activity.

Matt closed the door and led the way into the kitchen. He turned on the pendant lights over the island. Bree paced. She'd driven to Matt's house, but the unyielding restlessness had followed her. She paced the gray tiles in front of the island.

"What's wrong?" Matt leaned a hip on the island.

Bree didn't know where to start. Her emotions were a hot, jumbled mess she couldn't sort out.

"Bree." Matt stepped in front of her and stilled her with firm hands on her biceps. "Stop."

When her body stopped moving, her thoughts seemed to pick up their pace, whirling through her mind. She felt lost, numb, and disconnected. She stared up into Matt's worried eyes. Standing next to Bree, Greta whined and pawed at her sneaker, as if the dog also sensed Bree's distress.

"What happened?" he asked.

Still choked up, she shook her head.

He pulled her close, wrapping his arms around her. After a few seconds of automatically resisting, she leaned into his broad chest. Her body was shaking, and it felt as if his arms were holding her together. It wasn't fear roiling inside her, but an overwhelming onslaught of suppressed memories and emotions. They stood like that for a few minutes until she was reasonably certain she'd stopped trembling.

"Are you all right?" he said into her ear.

"I think so." She leaned back to look up at him.

"Want to talk about it?"

"No. Not yet." But being with him made all the difference. It sounded sappy, but she felt like they were in sync, as if she didn't need to talk to be understood. And all that made her want to be even closer to him.

Heat sparked and caught. She stood on her toes and pressed her mouth to his. He kissed her back, his arms around her tightening. Bree jumped, wrapping her legs around his waist.

Matt hooked his hands under her thighs to support her. Then he strode across the kitchen floor and pressed her back against the wall. His body was hard and solid against hers, and his hands were everywhere. His mouth trailed down her neck. Cool air hit her skin as he pulled at her clothes. His hands were warm on her rib cage. Bree returned the favor, tugging at the hem of his shirt and stroking his rippled abs. Heat rushed through her. She couldn't get enough of him.

Leaning into her, Matt ripped his shirt over his head and dropped it on the floor. Then he lifted her again and headed down a hallway.

He exhaled. "We don't know each other very well, but I would never threaten a child."

"Were you with your wife and grandsons the entire day?" Bree thought it convenient that Bradley was at the same event where Kayla had been nabbed.

Bradley's eyes locked on hers. "I wouldn't hurt a child," he said in a snooty tone, as if he expected her to simply take his word for it. But then, he came from a wealthy family. Being challenged was likely a rare occurrence for him.

Bree ignored his attitude and enunciated each word of her next question. "So, you were with your wife and grandsons the entire time you were at the fair?"

"Yes." He bit off the word.

"You didn't go to the restroom or run back to your vehicle for anything?" Matt jumped in, pushing Bradley harder.

"No." He blinked and broke eye contact. "Wait. I went for food alone. Nancy watched the boys' pony rides while I went to the food tent. The boys don't have much patience for lines yet."

"How long were you apart from them?" Matt persisted.

Bradley tugged at a crease in his slacks. "I don't know. Not long."

"How long is not long?" Matt asked.

Bradley's face flushed. "I don't know. Maybe twenty minutes."

From the way he was resisting giving them a time, it was probably longer.

Bree made a note. "What did you do after you returned home?"

Matt was suspicious. Was he reading too much into Bradley's arrogance or the way he conveniently forgot he'd separated from his wife and grandsons for a short time?

"I also took a nap." Bradley gave them a wry smile. "Running after two little boys is exhausting. My wife has more energy than I do."

Bree pulled out the photo of the four men on the porch and handed it to Bradley. "Do you recognize any of these men?"

She didn't notice they were in his bedroom until he pressed her down onto his mattress.

As her desire grew, the painful turmoil inside her quieted. Had she ever wanted a man like this?

Not *want*, she corrected herself. What she felt for Matt went way beyond sex. She'd wanted and enjoyed sex before. This was different. It was all consuming. It was . . .

Need.

The word gave her just a split second of pause. Needing people was an adjustment. It left her vulnerable. People you needed had the power to hurt you. Her entire world had shifted on its axis over the past six months. She'd made more connections with people in that short period of time than in her first thirty-five years.

With him, she would never be able to separate sex from intimacy. They were intertwined. He made her happy. He made her laugh. He brought her peace.

It was high time she stopped being a fucking coward. She needed to be grateful for being offered a full and rich life instead of turning her back on the chance for real happiness that was literally right in front of her.

Some people were never so lucky.

Matt lifted his mouth from hers. His eyes were dark. "Are you sure?"

With a push to his shoulder, Bree rolled him onto his back and straddled him. She took off her sidearm and her ankle holster and set both weapons on the nightstand, along with her cell phone. Then she pulled her T-shirt over her head and tossed it over her shoulder. "I'm all in."

Chapter Twenty-Six

Matt spooned Bree's naked body. Above them, the ceiling fan turned in a lazy circle. Moonlight streamed through the window and onto the bed.

He stroked the dragonfly tattoo that covered Bree's shoulder. It was a gorgeous piece of work, done in brilliant blues and greens he'd never seen in a tattoo before. The dragonfly perched amid delicate vines and tiny flowers that wrapped around Bree's shoulder. The wings were fully spread, as if it were just about to take flight. He traced the outline of a wing. He could feel the ridges and puckering of the scar under his fingertips, the dents where the dog's teeth had sunk deep into the child's flesh.

The tattoo was a mural painted on a blighted building. Its beauty covered an ugly event. Through it, Bree had taken ownership of the painful past that still haunted her, the past he already knew had caused tonight's torment.

He kissed her shoulder. "Are you going to tell me what happened tonight?"

She rolled onto her back and flung one hand over her head. "I had a dream. It was more of a flashback. Harley was there." In a few sentences, she outlined the nightmare.

Matt took a couple of seconds to digest it. "Do you remember what your dad and Harley were fighting about?"

"No. Not yet, anyway. Who knows what I'll remember tomorrow? All I know today is that he was there the day my mother died and that he made my father angry."

"Do you have any other memories of Harley?"

"Not yet." She rolled to her side and faced him. "How could I have forgotten Harley? He was obviously part of my family. How could I have blocked an entire person from my memories?"

Matt ran his hand down her biceps. "Frankly, it's a wonder you didn't suppress more of your childhood."

She frowned. "I thought I'd only blocked that day and other memories directly related to it. But this couldn't have been the only time Harley was at the house. When he was challenging my father, it felt familiar, like it had happened before. I had the sense that he was family. He talked to my father like no one else did, like only someone who'd known him since their childhood could have gotten away with."

"But your father didn't go after him?"

"No." Three wrinkles formed between her eyebrows. "In my dream—or flashback—or whatever it was, I wasn't afraid for Harley. He was the one arguing with my father, but I knew my mother, my siblings, and I would be the ones to pay the price."

Matt squeezed her shoulder. "It sounded like he wanted to help."

"But even through the perspective of a little kid, I knew he was making everything worse." Bree shook her head. "You know what they say about good intentions."

"You had no other feelings about Harley?" Matt asked.

Melinda Leigh

Bree was quiet for a couple of minutes. "I wasn't focused on him. He was just . . . there. I wanted him to go away."

"You didn't want to go with him?" Matt didn't understand how Bree had survived her childhood. Sheer courage, he suspected.

"I did, but I didn't want to leave my mother." She spread her fingers on his chest. "It was a confusing dream."

"Sounds like it makes sense to me." Matt couldn't fathom what it had been like to grow up in Bree's abusive, dysfunctional family, but he understood loyalty. "You were sticking with your mom, even though you didn't want to."

"The dream was messed up, but so was that part of my life."

He rubbed her shoulder. "I'm sorry."

"I'm sorry I woke you." She smiled and scooted closer, sliding one long leg over his. "Actually, I'm not. Not at all."

"Good." He kissed her.

He'd been waiting for her to come to him like this, but it hadn't been easy. He'd been running out of patience, hoping she came around.

Hoping he hadn't fallen in love with a woman who couldn't love him back.

He hadn't fooled himself. It wasn't just about her job. Her reluctance to commit to him went all the way back to her childhood. The soul-deep scars that left her reluctant to trust. He respected her honesty, and her refusal to allow their relationship to move faster than she felt ready. She'd been nothing but transparent with him.

But now, hope bloomed in his heart.

She rested her head on his chest. "I'm not used to *needing* someone. Not this way."

He stroked her back. "I want you to come to me for whatever you need." He brushed her arm with his knuckles. "I've been worried that you didn't *need* me at all."

"Why would you think that?" She lifted her head.

"Because you don't want to acknowledge our relationship publicly. You still want to drive twenty miles out of town to eat in a restaurant."

Bree winced. "I'm sorry."

"I don't want apologies. This is the first time you've actually reached out to me first." It felt like a breakthrough to Matt. "The kids will always be your number one priority. I totally understand that. I don't mind coming in second. But eventually, I was hoping we would reach a point where our relationship became more important than your job."

Bree rested her head on his shoulder. "You're right. I've let the politics of my job get between us."

Matt continued. "A huge part of your identity is wrapped up in law enforcement."

"Yes and no." Bree levered up on one elbow. "I feel like that's changing. In the past, I never had anything else to live for. Now I have more than I thought possible. Maybe this case will force me to move beyond my childhood. I need a balance between work and my personal life. I need to actually have a personal life." She met his eyes. "And I need you in that life."

"Good." Matt kissed her on the mouth. "Because there have been times when you've acted like a martyr, and that's damned scary. Do you know what happens to martyrs? They die."

He searched her gaze. She was so very hard to read, but not because she was dishonest. Although he'd seen her lie quite adeptly when necessary to suspects, in all other dealings Bree was forthright almost to a fault. Even playing the necessary political games required of her public office was distasteful to her. But her best coping mechanism was to bury her feelings. She wasn't hiding them. She couldn't find them either.

Tonight, he saw a new clarity in her hazel eyes.

She stretched out a hand and grabbed her cell phone from the nightstand.

"Are you leaving?" he asked, knowing she would want to be home for the kids, but not liking it.

"No." She set the phone down. "Just setting an alarm. I'll go home before the kids get up." She stretched out and closed her eyes. "I think I'll sleep better here."

He smiled and tucked her against him, honored to keep her nightmares at bay.

Chapter
Twenty-Seven

Monday morning, Matt carried his files and coffee into the conference room. Despite getting only a few hours' sleep, he was energized. Todd was already at the table. His laptop was open, and files were piled around him. Bags underscored his eyes, but his gaze was bright.

Matt set down his take-out cup. "You found something."

"Wasn't me." Todd scrolled on his computer and clicked. The printer in the corner hummed, and he got up to grab the printout.

Bree walked in. She carried a mug of coffee and a glass food container. She set down the container and peeled off the silicone lid. "Dana sent scones."

"What kind?" Setting aside the paper, Todd reached for the container.

"Chocolate cherry." Bree sipped her coffee.

Matt met her gaze. She flushed and the corner of her mouth curved. He felt his own mouth mirroring her intimate smile. Todd looked up from digging into the scones, raised a surprised brow, then suppressed a grin before returning his attention to his breakfast.

Bree cleared her throat. "Todd, you look like you have something to say."

Todd washed a bite of scone down with coffee. "I do." He tapped the open lid of his laptop. "Forensics transferred the VHS tapes to digital format. They managed to clear up some of the graininess on the surveillance video of Jane Parson and an unknown male leaving the bar a week before her disappearance." He wiped his hands on a napkin and slid a printed photograph across the table. "Does he look familiar?"

Bree bent over the image and swore. "That lying bastard."

Matt pulled the image toward him. "That's Richard Keeler."

"He said he barely knew Jane." Bree's eyes went cold. "I want to question him again."

"Do you want to bring him in here?" Matt thought there was a better way.

"No. He'll bring his lawyer, and we won't get anything out of him." Bree drummed her fingertips on the table. "Where will he be on a Monday morning?"

Matt checked the time. Seven thirty. "If we hurry, maybe we can catch him at home."

Bree's eyes took on a cagey look, like a tiger sizing up a deer. "His wife might be there too. We should talk to her as well."

Matt lifted a shoulder. "Only one way to find out, unless you want to call him first."

"Hell no." Bree stood and stretched. Todd's news seemed to have reanimated her more than her coffee. "I can't wait to see his face when we show him this picture."

"What do you want me to do?" Todd asked.

Bree wrapped a scone in a napkin. "I'd like you to review all the surveillance tapes from the country club the night of the charity event. See if you can spot Richard Keeler entering and leaving the club."

"Will do," Todd said with a sigh. "There's hours of video."

"Recruit a deputy if you need to," Bree said. "I'll leave the scones. Where's the picture of Keeler and Jane at the event?"

Todd handed it to her, and Bree made several copies. Matt gathered his files and followed her from the conference room. Bree stopped to check in with Marge before they left via the back door. Then they drove the SUV out to Keeler's place. Bree ate her scone on the way. Morning sunlight shimmered on the shiny coats of grazing horses. Two gangly yearlings chased each other up and down the fence line. Bree parked, and they walked to the house, where no one answered their knock.

Standing on the porch, Matt gazed out over the land. A horse's whinny drew his attention to the barn. The doors stood open, and he could see the silhouettes of a horse and three people inside. Two of the shapes looked female. He pointed. "Someone is in the barn."

The crack of a bat on a ball sounded.

"Sounds like Keeler is practicing again." Bree started toward the porch steps. "Why don't you see if that's Mrs. Keeler in the barn? You're more charming than I am. Give her that smile."

Matt jogged down the steps next to her. "What smile?"

She paused on the walk. "Picture me naked."

He did.

She blew a loose hair off her forehead. "Yeah. That's the smile. Mrs. Keeler is toast."

"I was unaware I wielded such power."

"You have no idea." Bree shook her head. Turning away, she said over her shoulder, "Now go use it on Mrs. Keeler."

Wiping the grin off his face, Matt headed for the barn. He stepped through the doorway into the cool dimness of the aisle. A white horse stood on cross ties. Two women and a man stood next to it, murmuring in worried tones. Matt walked closer.

All three people turned toward him. He recognized the groom he and Bree had spoken to on Saturday. The two women were clearly related, mother and daughter, Matt guessed.

The older woman's dark hair was shoulder length and tucked behind one ear. The daughter wore hers tied back in a long, sleek tail.

Both women were dressed in breeches, polo shirts, and worn English riding boots. Neither had bothered with makeup or nail polish. Matt knew Keeler's wife was in her midfifties, but she could have passed for ten years younger. The daughter looked to be in her late twenties.

The older woman stepped forward. "Can I help you?"

Matt extended a hand holding a business card. "I'm Matt Flynn, a criminal investigator with the sheriff's department. Are you Mrs. Keeler?"

She accepted the card with a mix of curiosity and caution. "I'm Susanna FitzGeorge. I'm Richard's wife, but I didn't change my name. This is our daughter Becca."

"Ms. FitzGeorge," Matt said to the older woman.

"Call me Susanna," she corrected.

Matt gave her a professional half smile, *not* the smile Bree had suggested he use. "Susanna, I'm investigating an old crime. I'd like to ask you a few questions."

One perfectly arched brow lifted. "A crime?"

"Yes, ma'am."

"Excuse me, Miss Becca?" the groom interrupted. "Do you want me to make the poultice?"

"Yes. I'll hose his leg while you prepare it," Becca answered, then turned to Matt. "Do you need me?"

"No, ma'am." Matt shook his head. "I suspect the crime is older than you."

Susanna's brows drew together. "Let's go up to the porch." She turned to her daughter and touched her arm. "He'll be all right. Give him a few days' rest."

Becca nodded, but looked worried.

With long strides, Susanna led the way up the back lawn.

"What's wrong with the horse?" Matt asked.

"Probably just an inflamed tendon. Mr. Sparkles was Becca's first horse. He's twenty-six now."

Matt grinned at the name. It didn't fit the snooty stable. "He looks great for his age."

"She babies him. He's more pet than mount now, but she still takes him out for a hack once or twice a week. The exercise is good for him." Susanna smiled. Pride for her daughter shone in her eyes.

"How many children do you have?" Matt asked.

"Three. Becca is the youngest. My oldest is going to be a father soon, so I have my first grandchild on the way." She climbed the steps to the back porch and sat in a wicker chair. A fat old cat waddled across the planks to rub on her ankle. She stroked the animal, and it began to purr. Then it plunked itself into a patch of sun at her feet.

"Congratulations." Matt eased onto a chair facing her. He'd come here to poke an old wound but found he didn't want to. He liked her. You could tell a lot about a person by how they treated animals. She'd passed his first litmus test.

Reluctantly, he began. "Do you remember Jane Parson?"

"I do." Susanna crossed her legs. "Our families have known each other forever." She froze, her hands flattening on the armrests. "You're investigating her death."

"Yes."

"How can I help?"

"Jane disappeared after a charity event in June 1990."

"Yes. I remember." Her tone grew wary.

"Did you attend?"

She shook her head. "I was pregnant with my oldest and not feeling well enough. He was born just a few weeks later."

"But your husband attended," Matt said.

She stilled. Irritation flickered in her eyes. "Yes. He did. I remember a police officer interviewing us a day or so later."

"Do you remember what time he left for the event and what time he got home?"

"No." She blinked and looked at the barn for a few heartbeats. "I think the officer asked me the same question back then. I'm sure I gave him an answer, but it's been thirty years."

Matt sensed the first crack in her armor. "How well did your husband know Jane?"

"Why do you ask?"

Matt tugged two photos from his pocket. He handed her the picture of her husband and Jane at the event, the one with Keeler's hand on Jane's hip. Her mouth twitched into a brief frown, and anger lowered her eyelids. But she didn't look surprised.

She gave it back. "Yes. I saw this photo back in 1990. I won't pretend it doesn't still bother me."

"Did Richard have an explanation?"

"He said it was nothing. She'd had too much to drink and was all over him. I knew Jane well enough to believe him." But doubt crept into her eyes. "If you're thinking Richard killed Jane, you're wrong. He isn't smart enough to successfully pull off a murder, and he doesn't have the balls. He has a position with my family's office, but it's not a real job. He's fairly useless."

The Keelers' marriage was clearly not a happily-ever-after. What would keep Susanna from incriminating her husband? Matt hoped nothing.

"Did you ever suspect your husband of having an affair?" He offered her the image of Keeler and Jane in the bar parking lot.

She hesitated, as if sensing the picture would change her life. But she was no coward. Her chin came up and she accepted the paper. Her eyes glittered with unshed tears for a moment. Then she blinked them away and hardened her features. "You know what? I suddenly remember that night in 1990 very clearly."

CHAPTER
TWENTY-EIGHT

Bree found Keeler in his batting cage. Like during her first visit, he glanced at her, then hit several more balls before shutting off the machine. He clearly wanted her to know he was in control and that he'd talk to her when *he* was ready.

"Mr. Keeler?" She didn't have time for his ego-driven bullshit. "I need to speak with you."

He set the bat on one shoulder and turned to face her. His expression was one of cool hostility. "I already answered your questions."

"I have more." Bree stared him down.

He walked over and checked the time on a fancy watch. "You have two minutes."

"That's all I need." She showed him the photo of him and Jane from the country club. "Remember this picture?"

He waved it away. "I explained that picture. Jane was drunk. She was all over me."

Bree squinted at the photo. "You're the one touching her."

"Timing. A few seconds before that was snapped, she was hanging on to me."

"What about this one?" Bree pulled out the enhanced still of him leaving the bar with Jane.

He snatched the image from her hand. White flashed around his eyes as he shook it in her face. "Where did you get this?"

"This was taken outside the Railway Tavern." Bree plucked it from his grip. "Do you remember that night? It was the week before Jane disappeared."

He leaned closer. Fury glittered darkly in his eyes. His voice dropped as his composure slipped. "Why are you here?"

Bree gave no ground. "Jane Parson was murdered a week after you left a bar with her."

"How dare you!" A tendon in the side of his neck bulged.

"How dare I what?" Bree maintained the pressure. "Were you having an affair with her? Did you go home with her that night?"

"I don't have to tell you anything." His nostrils flared, and his chest rose and fell as he took a deep breath, visibly trying to calm himself.

Bree kept going. She wanted him to lose his cool. "Did your wife know? Did Jane threaten to tell her?"

"You have no fucking idea what you're talking about."

"Enlighten me."

Instead, his fingers tightened on the bat over his shoulder.

Bree took one step back. "Drop the bat."

"Fuck you." A drop of spit flew from his mouth. "You can't come here and ruin my marriage over a thirty-year-old picture."

"I came here to find out the truth about a woman's death, but maybe I should ask your wife about this night." Giving the photo a shake, Bree returned it to her pocket.

He went still except for the fingers flexing on the bat. "You can't do that," he said in a flat, dead tone. His muscles tensed, his body preparing to strike.

Bree shifted her weight to the balls of her feet, softened her knees, and pressed the final button. "My criminal investigator is talking to your wife right now."

Rage bulged a vein in his forehead, and his face flushed impending-stroke red. "You fucking bitch," he roared.

The bat came down off his shoulder and swung at Bree's head. Ready, she ducked and weaved. The bat swished in the empty air over her head. She yanked her baton from her duty belt. One flick of her wrist expanded the rod to full length. Bringing the weapon to her chest, she struck him behind the knees with a short backswing.

His legs buckled. He dropped the bat. It hit the ground with a *thunk* at the same time he went down onto his knees. Bree collapsed her baton and returned it to her belt. She used an armbar to guide Keeler onto his belly. Then she planted a firm knee into the small of his back and cuffed him.

"You're under arrest for assaulting an officer of the law." She didn't have enough evidence for a murder charge.

Yet.

"Let's go." She grabbed his biceps, helped him to his feet, and marched him toward the house.

"I'll sue you," he spit. "You're going to lose your job. You can't treat me like this."

Bree ignored him. As they approached the house, she spotted Matt and a middle-aged woman on the back porch. They rose. Matt's brows lifted. The woman stared at Keeler with unexpected hostility.

"Mrs. Keeler?" Bree introduced herself.

The woman nodded. "I'm Susanna FitzGeorge."

Bree almost smiled.

"Call our attorney, Susanna," Keeler sputtered. "This is an outrage."

Susanna regarded him with a cool glare. "Find your own attorney. David's firm won't be representing you."

Keeler's face paled, the anger sliding from his face as if it were melting as his wife turned and went into the house. She didn't slam the door but closed it with a deliberate motion. It shut behind her with a final, firm *click*.

Matt jogged down the steps. "What happened?"

"He swung the bat at me." Bree tugged Keeler toward the front of the house.

Matt's brows dropped and he shook his head at Keeler. "That was monumentally stupid."

Bree felt her lips peel away from her teeth in a predatory grin. "He's under arrest for assaulting an officer."

"Then let's take him in." Matt kept pace beside them.

They returned to the driveway and loaded Keeler into the back of the sheriff's SUV. Bree fastened the seat belt across his body. She climbed behind the wheel and drove to the station. Keeler stared out the window and seethed.

At the station, Bree handed him off to a deputy. She wanted to give him a few minutes to marinate in his own mistakes. "Put him in interview room one."

The deputy led him away.

Bree and Matt went into her office, where Bree dropped into her chair behind the desk. Dissatisfaction rumbled through her.

"What's wrong? You made an arrest. Keeler is a good suspect for Jane Parson's murder."

"But so far, there's no link between him and Frank Evans."

Matt paced while he summarized his interview with Susanna FitzGeorge. "She's recanting her previous statement. Now she says Keeler came home around three o'clock in the morning, not midnight, after the charity event. She also said he claimed to have had car trouble the night he was with Jane at the bar. He gave the same excuse the following week when he was three hours late after the charity event. He doubled down on the lie by putting the car in for service the next week."

Bree paged through a pile of pink message slips, then set them on her blotter. Pressing both palms to her desk, she pushed to her feet. "Let's find out where he was for those three hours."

"How do you want to play it?"

"He has a huge ego. He might think he can talk his way out of this."

Matt agreed with a nod. "He'll play his *this is a misunderstanding* card."

"You start. I was already mean to him today." Bree opened her door. "Give him the opportunity to run his mouth all he wants."

They stopped in the break room for a bottle of water, then filed into the interview room. The room held a table and four chairs. Keeler slumped in the closest chair. His obnoxious bravado had evaporated.

"Are you going to remain calm?" Bree asked with a stern look.

Keeler nodded.

"Then stand up and turn around." She removed his cuffs.

He rubbed his wrists, then sank back into the chair.

Matt and Bree took the opposite chairs. Matt set the bottle of water in front of Keeler, who opened it and drank with an air of *that's more like it*. He shot Bree a look, then addressed Matt. "The assault charge is bullshit. I didn't strike her."

Bree ignored his statement. "Tell us about the night of the charity event. How was Jane that night?"

"We've already gone over this," Keeler protested.

"Indulge us," Matt said. "We weren't there."

"She was drunk, as usual." Keeler set the bottle on the table. "She was hanging all over every man she could get her hands on."

"What time did you leave the country club?" Matt asked.

"Around eleven forty-five." Keeler drank more water, his gaze wary. "The event ended at midnight. Everyone was leaving."

Matt followed up. "And what time did you get home?"

"I don't recall." Keeler shifted his position in his seat, trying to get comfortable with his lie.

Matt leaned his forearms on the table. "Your wife says you didn't come home until three o'clock in the morning."

Keeler leaned back in his chair to recover his personal space. "She wouldn't know because she was asleep."

Bree wondered if he was aware he'd just argued against his own alibi.

"She says she was only pretending to be asleep to avoid talking with you." Matt let the point sit a few seconds before hammering it home. "She was angry because you were missing half the night while she was home pregnant."

Keeler froze for a few seconds. Only his eyeballs moved. His gaze darted from the water to the table and back again as he tried to think of a response. In the end, he must have come up empty, because he said nothing.

Bree set down the photo of Keeler leaving the bar with Jane.

Keeler's gaze landed on the photo and stayed there. He knew he was in deep trouble.

Bree tapped the photo over Jane's head. "Were you having an affair with Jane?"

Keeler hesitated, then his mouth twitched. "No."

She sensed Keeler was skating around a lie. She rephrased her question. "Did you ever have sexual relations with her?"

Keeler met her gaze, his eyes stubborn and defiant. "I didn't kill her."

Bree shook the photo. "Did you meet with her after the charity event?"

He didn't hesitate and maintained angry eye contact. "No."

"So where were you for three hours?" she pressed.

He shifted his ass in his chair. "Jane was supposed to meet me afterward. I went to her place and parked behind the house so no one would see my car. She didn't show up, so I went home."

Bree sat back. "You were having an affair with her?"

With a hard puff of air through his nose, he gave her a curt nod. "I won't be saying anything else without an attorney, except that I didn't kill her."

"OK." Bree rose, opened the door, and called in a deputy. "Book him for assaulting an officer."

The deputy snapped cuffs on Keeler and took him away.

Bree watched them disappear down the hallway. "I hope he has to spend the night in jail, but rich people always seem to get bailed out fast."

Rising from his chair, Matt shot her a sly smile. "Booking will take a while. Then he has to find his own attorney."

"His wife turned on him in record speed." Bree went through the doorway. "Well done."

Matt followed her from the room to her office.

Bree went behind her desk. "Was she worried about the false statement she gave in 1990?"

Matt shook his head. "Not at all. I doubt the prosecutor will go after her, and I assume she has the kind of attorney who can make that issue go away. At the time, she was almost due to give birth. She didn't want to believe he would have cheated on her. Now she's angry and embarrassed that she let him fool her all these years." He hesitated. "But she still doesn't think he killed Jane. She said he's not cunning or bold enough."

Bree rolled back her chair and sat. "He was bold enough to swing a bat at my head."

"He definitely has a hot temper, but that's not the same thing as premeditated murder." Matt stood, as if his brain were too busy for his body to be still. "Maybe she made him angry and he killed her accidentally."

"I don't see how a bullet in the head can be accidental," Bree said. "And then there's Frank's murder. How did they get in that grave together?"

"All good points." He walked the length of her office and back. "But we still have Shawn Castillo as a suspect as well."

"If we can find him," Matt said.

Three raps sounded on Bree's door.

"Come in," she called.

The door opened and Todd walked in. He carefully shut the door behind him. Bree didn't like his frown or worried eyes.

"We have a problem." He stopped at the corner of her desk. "You're not going to like it."

"What is it?" Bree shifted forward. Dread coiled in her chest like a spring.

Todd said, "Forensics called. Some of the evidence from the original scene and also from Shawn Castillo's house is mislabeled."

"How much of it?" Matt stopped pacing.

Todd touched his forehead, as if the answer pained him. "Enough to be a serious problem."

"Who collected the evidence?" she asked.

Todd frowned. "Deputy Oscar."

"Is he here?" Bree asked. This was Oscar's third strike, at least. *Damn it.* She'd given him so many chances. Would he ever learn?

"Yes," Todd said.

She scrubbed a hand down her face. "I want to talk to him after I call the DA."

"Yes, ma'am. I'll get him." Todd left the office.

"What are you going to do?" Matt asked.

"I have to talk to the DA." She reached for her phone. "And then I'll deal with Oscar."

"I'll go get some coffee." Matt walked out of the office, closing the door behind him.

The DA picked up his line. "Sheriff Taggert. I was just going to call you."

"I hear we have a problem."

"We do." Bryce Walters was a politician down to his soul. But he was also an excellent prosecutor. He was good-looking in a respectable way and had a courtroom presence that held a jury's attention no matter how boring the evidence.

For the last six months, Bree had worked with him repeatedly without issue. She respected his skill and his opinion, but today, she knew she wasn't going to like what he had to say.

"A significant amount of the evidence from the crime scene and Shawn Castillo's house was mislabeled."

"How?"

"The dates are incorrect, and some of the labels are not clearly marked with the case number. Two envelopes weren't properly sealed."

Shit.

The DA continued. "I'm going to drop all the charges. A first-year attorney could get all of the evidence thrown out."

"Even the assaulting an officer and trespassing charges?"

"I've already been contacted by Mr. Castillo's attorney," the DA said. "Mr. Castillo says he didn't hear you identify yourself as the sheriff and was acting in self-defense."

Bree suppressed an eye roll at the absolute ridiculousness of the statement, but she felt her eyes narrow. "He was trespassing on my brother's property."

"The property is not marked private and borders county-owned open space." The DA's tone was unyielding.

But Bree couldn't decide if the DA actually believed his own bullshit. "He was inside a barn he doesn't own. It was clearly not open space."

"The county has bought other vacant pieces of property in the past twenty years as part of the open-space program. His argument is not completely without merit."

"What about the drug charge?" Bree knew the answer before he spoke.

"Mislabeled evidence reeks of corruption, and all the charges against Mr. Castillo will carry the stench."

Frustration welled in Bree's throat. "A narcotics addiction isn't going to go away on its own."

"I understand that, and I don't disagree with you, but this charge is not going to happen." The DA paused.

Bree chewed on the DA's statement. There was no point in arguing with him. The prosecutor had the ultimate say in whether a suspect was charged. "What if I found additional evidence?"

"Do you want some advice, off the record?" he asked.

"I don't know. Do I?" Bree asked in a wry tone.

Walters chuckled. Even though he was giving her news she didn't want, she couldn't help but like him. *Which is why he gets reelected every year.* Most people liked him. *Hell, even most of the defense attorneys like him.*

"Elias's attorney would fight every little charge as if Shawn were being charged with a dozen murders. Ultimately, he would win. He knows all the judges. He would play Shawn as a victim of your overreach. He would present the mislabeled evidence as proof of your incompetence and corruption. He would make you look like a bitch. I've gone up against him in court before. I know how he operates."

"So, I should just let him win without a fight?" Bree bristled. "That won't be good for my career long term either."

"No." Walters sighed. "But don't engage in fights you can't win. In a perfect world, Elias would care more about his brother's addiction than his own reputation. But we both know the world is far from perfect." He exhaled hard. "You could win this one battle and still lose the war. Elias is well liked in the community. He's been here forever. You are a newcomer. He has the power to ruin your career."

"I hate politics." Bree sat back and let the DA's words simmer for a few seconds. If she insisted on pressing minor charges against Shawn, she would irritate the judge, who was Elias's friend, and be painted as corrupt by the media. She was backed into a corner, but the only way out felt like a hammer to the funny bone.

"That's because you have integrity," the DA said. "You're a good sheriff. The best one we've had in decades. The county needs you, and selfishly, I much prefer working with an honest sheriff. Your predecessor made my job very difficult."

Bullshit or truth?

Bree couldn't tell. She swallowed her distaste. "Fine."

Walters said, "Good. It's the right decision."

Then why did it feel so completely wrong?

"What if Shawn Castillo is the person who killed the two victims?" she asked.

"Then we have a very big problem. You'll need evidence that hasn't been tainted." The DA ended the call.

Bree got up, opened her door, and spotted Oscar at a desk. "Oscar. My office. Todd, you come too."

When they entered, she gestured for Oscar to take a chair facing her desk. Todd leaned on the wall next to Bree, positioning himself on her side.

Bree settled back in her chair and leveled a hard gaze at Oscar. "You've been given both verbal and written reprimands about following procedure after your lack of follow-through has caused dangerous incidents. I just heard from the forensics lab and the DA. You mishandled evidence and compromised our charges against Shawn Castillo. I'm putting you on administrative leave. Hand over your badge and gun."

Oscar's mouth opened and closed. How could this possibly be a surprise?

"You can't," he finally stammered.

Bree flattened her hands on her desk. "You've left me no choice."

He stared at her for a full minute, the shock and anger in his eyes gelling into hatred. His jaw sawed back and forth as if he were barely holding back a retort. Finally, he rose suddenly. His chair scraped backward, his movements jerky as he relinquished his gun and badge. His face was rage-red as he stormed out of the office.

Todd waited until she'd locked the gun and badge in a desk drawer, then he moved closer, standing next to her desk. "You should have fired him. He's careless, lazy, and arrogant."

"Believe me, I wanted to. But that's not protocol." She swiveled her chair to face him. She was so tired, her eyes ached. "His case will be reviewed. If the charges hold, then I'll fire him. I expect my staff to follow procedure, so that's what I have to do as well."

Todd nodded. "Oscar was the old sheriff's lapdog. I never trusted him. Watch your back." Her chief deputy left the office.

Matt walked in the open door, and she filled him in.

"What does that mean for our investigation?" he asked.

"I don't know yet, but if the DA is dropping the charges, then we have no grounds to pick up Shawn Castillo."

Her cell phone buzzed, and she glanced at the screen, surprised to see the name EVANS and a phone number. "It's Curtis Evans."

"He's actually calling you?"

"Seems like." Bree answered the call. "Sheriff Taggert."

She expected to hear a male voice and was surprised when a raspy female one said, "This is Wanda Evans, Curtis's mother."

"Yes, ma'am. I remember you."

"Curtis." The older woman's voice caught on a sob. "He's missing."

CHAPTER TWENTY-NINE

Matt watched Mrs. Evans adjust her oxygen cannula with shaking hands. Her eyes were red-rimmed and swollen, and her pallor concerned him. They sat in the small living room of the house she shared with her son. Digger lay on the floor at her feet, her soulful eyes watching the old woman.

Looking equally concerned, Bree perched on an ottoman facing Mrs. Evans. "When was the last time you saw Curtis?"

"Yesterday morning." Mrs. Evans sniffed. "He went to work. Usually, he comes home in the evening."

Matt scanned the inside of the house. Everything looked roughly the same as the last time they'd come here.

"Does he always come right home?" Bree asked.

"No." Mrs. Evans's voice trembled. "Once in a while he stops for a beer, but he usually calls me to let me know. Last night, I fell asleep early. I'm on a new medication, and it wipes me out." She paused for a breath. "I didn't wake up until late. I thought maybe he'd been home, slept, and left for work again, except that Curtis usually wakes me up to give me my morning pills and a piece of toast. None of that happened this morning. When I came out to the kitchen"—she pointed to a pill organizer with all its compartment lids open on the counter in the adjoining kitchen—"I knew for sure he never came home last night. Every single morning, he sets up my pills for the day. He makes my coffee too. Decaf, because I'm not allowed to have caffeine."

"Maybe he was running late," Matt suggested, but he knew in the pit of his gut that something had happened to Curtis.

"No." Mrs. Evans shook her head hard. "He knows the medicines confuse me. There are too many of them, and they change all the time."

"OK." Bree surveyed the room.

"He would never leave me," Mrs. Evans insisted, even as panic flashed in her eyes. "Never. Curtis takes good care of me."

"I believe you," Bree agreed.

Matt nodded.

"You do? You're really going to look for him?" Mrs. Evans asked in an incredulous voice.

"Yes, ma'am." Bree took both of the old woman's thin hands in her own. "I promise we will do our best to find your son." She released her.

Mrs. Evans collapsed back in her chair. "I don't know what to do."

Matt glanced into the kitchen at the pill vials lined up on the counter. "Did you take your medicine today?"

Mrs. Evans stared at her gnarled hands. "I can't remember which ones are for morning."

Matt pushed off the wall. "Do you have anyone we could call to stay with you?"

Mrs. Evans shook her head. "It's just me and Curtis. There's no one else."

"We'll need a list of Curtis's friends," he said.

Mrs. Evans reached for the end table next to her chair. On it sat a cordless landline phone and an old-fashioned address book. She picked up the book and thumbed through it. "He cut ties with most of his friends years ago. There's only one person he hangs out with anymore, his business partner, Anders. They've been close since they were boys."

"We already have his number," Bree said. "We'd like to search the house. Is that all right?"

"Yes." Mrs. Evans nodded fiercely. "Do whatever you have to. Please find my son."

Permission was dicey in this situation. Mrs. Evans didn't own the house, but it was her residence. If they found evidence Curtis had committed a crime, they wouldn't be able to seize any of it. But they needed to look for clues.

"I'll call in a BOLO on Curtis and his truck," Bree said. "And I'll have Todd get a warrant for his phone records. In the meantime, we'll ask the provider to ping Curtis's phone." Under exigent circumstances, cell phone providers could agree to locate a user's device.

"You want me to call Anders?" Matt asked.

"Yes." Bree nodded. "Then we'll give the house a quick search." She turned to Mrs. Evans. "Hold tight, ma'am."

Matt and Bree both stepped outside to make their calls.

Anders answered his phone. "A Cut Above."

Matt could hear lawn mowers and Weedwackers running in the background. "This is Investigator Matt Flynn. Did Curtis show up for work today?"

"Hold on. Let me get in the truck," Anders said. A door slammed, and the sound of the lawn equipment quieted.

Matt repeated his question.

"No, Curtis didn't show today. He didn't call either. I texted and called him, but he didn't answer." He sounded worried. "I thought maybe his mom had some kind of emergency."

"No," Matt said. "He didn't come home last night. His mother is frantic."

"Shit." Anders hesitated. "I knew something was wrong."

"Is there anyone we can call to look after his mother?"

"She doesn't have anybody but Curtis. I'll be right over."

"That would be helpful." Matt ended the call. "Anders is coming here to stay with Mrs. Evans."

"Good." Bree shoved her phone into her pocket. "Marge is going to try and get a social worker out here as well. Mrs. Evans needs to sort out her meds."

They went back into the house. Matt searched the kitchen while Bree went through the living room. Neither found anything unusual. They headed for Curtis's bedroom together.

The full-size bed was neatly made with a plain navy blue quilt. The tops of the dresser and nightstand were dust- and clutter-free. A wicker hamper held dirty clothes. Bree began with the dresser. Matt took the closet. Curtis's jeans and work pants were folded on shelves. His shirts hung in a neat row. Matt checked his pockets. Empty.

"Look what I found," Bree said.

Matt turned.

She was standing next to the bed holding a photograph. A photo album sat open on the nightstand. "It's a copy of that same picture with Frank, Curtis, my father, and Harley. But this picture was in the album and isn't as faded as the one that was in Frank's missing persons file."

"Let's ask Mrs. Evans what she knows about it."

Matt carried the picture into the living room. Mrs. Evans hadn't left her chair. She didn't seem to have moved at all. He knelt beside her chair. "Do you recognize this picture?"

She reached for a pair of glasses on the table at her elbow. Putting them on, she squinted at the picture. "Yes. I gave a copy of this to the police when Frank went missing." She pointed to Bree's father, then to Harley. "I always thought one of these two men had something to do with Frank going missing."

"Do you know anything about them?" Matt asked.

Mrs. Evans shook her head. "All I know is that Frank did *jobs* for them now and again, when he was hard up for cash."

The way she'd said *jobs* made Matt think the work was sketchy. "What do you mean by *jobs*?"

She pursed her lips. "I don't know. Frankie would never tell me. But he always came home with too much cash for a day's work. I told him, 'Frankie, if something seems too good to be true, it probably is.' But he would shrug me off. He didn't like being out of work. He didn't want to be a burden on me. *He* wanted to help *me*, not the other way around." She went quiet, staring at the photo.

A knock at the door interrupted her musing. Anders walked in.

Mrs. Evans reached her hand out to him, and he took it.

"Did you eat breakfast?" he asked.

"I'm not hungry," she said.

"You need to eat anyway." Anders went into the kitchen, opened a cabinet, and pulled out a loaf of bread. He put a slice in the toaster, scanned her medication, and rolled up his sleeves. "Don't worry, Mrs. E. We'll sort this out together."

Leaving Mrs. Evans to Anders, Bree and Matt returned to the SUV.

Bree's phone buzzed. She read the screen. "The cell provider pinged Curtis's phone."

She fed the location into the GPS and stomped on the gas pedal. The light bar flashed as they sped down the country roads. About ten minutes later, Matt spotted the old pickup parked on the shoulder. Bree pulled up behind the vehicle, and they got out. The sun beat down on Matt's head, and heat radiated off the pavement in waves.

With one hand on her weapon, Bree jogged to the driver's door. Matt headed to the passenger side. The pickup's cab was empty. The driver's window was smashed. Glass shards littered the seats, floor, and dashboard. The front tire was flat.

Matt bent to inspect it. "There's a nail in the tire."

"His cell phone is on the passenger seat," Bree said. "Can you grab it?"

Matt put on gloves and opened the door. He picked up the cell phone. "It's passcode protected."

Bree stabbed her own phone screen, then put the device to her ear. "Todd, do you have Curtis Evans's cell records yet?" She waited, then nodded. "Any recent calls? Text me the address." She ended the call. "Curtis's last phone call was to a landline in Scarlet Falls. Guess who the number is registered to?" She paused, her mouth set in a grim line. "Darren Taggert."

Bree stared at Curtis's truck, but she was clearly focusing on some internal thought.

"Do you have a relative named Darren?" Matt asked.

"Not that I remember, but then I didn't remember Harley until recently." Bree circled the truck. "What do you think happened?"

"Someone drove a nail into his tire, then followed him until the tire went flat."

"Then they nabbed him?"

"That's my best guess." Matt went back to the truck's cab and stuck his upper body inside the vehicle. "I don't see any blood."

"Then maybe he's still alive." Bree headed back to her SUV. "We'll have the truck towed to the county garage. Forensics can go over it there. We're going to see Darren Taggert."

While Bree drove, Matt used her Mobile Data Computer System to run Darren Taggert. Among the information Matt could access were motor vehicle records, the NCIC, and the Division of Criminal Justice Services.

"Darren is sixty-five years old. Five foot ten, hazel eyes. He drives a 1999 F-150. Driver's license and registration are valid. No outstanding warrants."

"Criminal record?" Bree asked.

"Long and distinguished. He was in and out of jail multiple times back in the '80s and '90s. B and E, burglary, theft, trespassing. No violent crimes, no drug convictions, and nothing recent." Matt scrolled through the information. "In fact, he hasn't been arrested in twenty-five years."

"Maybe he learned his lesson." The SUV careened around a bend as Bree barely slowed for the turn. "Is he married?"

"Doesn't seem like it." Matt scanned the screen. "He works for ABC Auto."

Ten minutes later, Bree turned into a solidly middle-class suburban development. Trees and basketball nets lined the street. A small playground on the corner contained a slide and a few swings. A mother pushed a baby stroller on the sidewalk away from the playground. A little boy toddled beside her. He squatted, picked up a rock, and shoved it into his pocket.

The neighborhood was quiet, well groomed, and family friendly, not the sort of place he'd expected to find someone with a criminal record as lengthy as Darren's.

Bree cruised to a halt in front of a well-maintained one-story home. Matt took in the structure. White with blue shutters, the house had a mailbox in the shape of a barn. The garage doors were styled like barn doors.

"You sure this is it?" he asked. "It looks so . . ."

"Normal."

"Exactly." Matt double-checked the address. "This is the right place."

They stepped out of the vehicle, and he joined her on the sidewalk, standing on a child's chalk drawing of a giant daisy. From the sidewalk, Matt could see the shadow of a tall vehicle through the narrow windows of the garage door. "There's the truck. Looks like he's home."

Before they could start up the driveway, the air resounded with a solid *pop*. Matt startled, and a cold ball solidified in his gut. He knew exactly what that sound was.

Gunshot.

He crouched, scanning their surroundings.

Where was the shooter?

And who was the target?

CHAPTER THIRTY

Bree's heart did a double tap as she reached for her weapon. She'd been shot two months before. The wound had been superficial and had healed well, but the gunshot brought back the memory. The scar seemed to sting.

"Did it come from inside the house?" Matt asked.

"I think so." Scanning the front of the house, she whipped out her cell phone and called for backup and an ambulance. Behind her, Matt retrieved the AR-15 and Kevlar vest from the SUV. He was still fastening the Velcro of his vest as they jogged up the driveway. She was wearing her own body armor under her uniform. They both knew they should wait for backup, but if someone had been shot inside the house, those extra minutes could mean the difference between life and death.

Narrow panes of decorative frosted glass framed the front door. Bree and Matt automatically flanked the entry. Bree tried the knob, which was locked. She turned her ear to the door, but the house was dead quiet.

If someone was exiting the house, they would likely use the back door, where they'd be less visible to the neighbors.

Raising one hand in the air, Bree signaled for them to go around back. Matt went left, and Bree ran to the right. Weapon in hand, she crouched as she passed in front of a picture window. She paused beneath it, lifted her head, and tried to peer inside, but the blinds were closed. She kept moving.

Adrenaline sprinted through her veins as she passed in front of the garage door. She rose onto her toes to look inside. The F-150 occupied the right half of the garage. On the other side, a workbench and rolling tool cabinet were lined up against the wall. She scanned the concrete floor around the F-150, but the garage looked empty. She saw no one inside the cab of the pickup. Continuing, she rounded the corner and jogged along the side of the house. A side door clearly led into the garage. As she passed, she checked the knob. Locked. She hurried along the side of the house until she came to the rear yard.

She peered around the corner. Darren's lot wasn't fenced, but all three adjoining properties were enclosed with six-foot-tall fencing. She listened for sounds of a person fleeing, but all she could hear was the echo of her own pulse. In the far corner, four Adirondack chairs faced a brick firepit. She saw no one, and the grass was too thick for visible footprints.

Bree moved into the backyard just as Matt was coming around the opposite corner. She jogged to the patio and passed a gas grill to stand at the side of a set of french doors. Matt put his back to the house on the other side.

Bree peered around the doorframe. The reflection of sunlight on the glass obscured her view inside the house. She shielded her eyes with a hand to block the light. She could see into a small but nicely renovated kitchen. White Shaker cabinets and marble countertops gleamed. The floor tiles looked like planks of driftwood. A dark patch on the floor caught her eye. She moved her head. Her stomach rolled over as the dark patch glistened red. "I see blood."

"We need to get inside."

Bree tried the doorknob. Locked.

Matt used the butt end of the rifle to break a glass pane in the french door. Reaching through, he popped the doorknob lock and opened the door.

The house was small. Bree could see all of the kitchen and adjoining family room. A man's body lay behind the kitchen island, but she and Matt quickly searched the two bedrooms and single bathroom.

They wouldn't be able to help anyone if they were also shot.

After they'd cleared the house, she returned her weapon to its holster and crossed the tile to the victim. She dropped to one knee beside him. Blood pooled around his head. His eyes were closed, and his skin was the pasty color of skim milk. His features had aged, and his brown hair had gone mostly gray, but he was familiar. She knew him. She'd seen him at her childhood home many years before. An ache formed in the center of her chest. "That's Harley."

She pressed two fingers to the side of his neck. From the size of the blood puddle, she expected him to be dead. The faint thrum against her fingertips surprised her. "He's alive."

The blood was coming from his head. She leaned closer, separating his wavy gray hair until she found the source, a wound just behind his temple. "He's been shot in the head."

Just like Jane and Frank.

"How bad?" Matt leaned over her.

"There's too much blood. I can't see anything. I need something to stop the bleeding."

Matt rummaged through the kitchen drawers. He rushed back to Bree and handed her a short stack of folded dish towels.

"Call dispatch and get an ETA on that ambulance." She pressed a towel to the side of Harley's head and applied pressure. How had she not remembered him?

She looked him over. He wore jeans and a Rolling Stones T-shirt. His feet were bare. His hair was shoulder length. Gray patches colored his short beard.

Matt brought a blanket from the bedroom and spread it over him. "If he's your father's cousin, does that make him your second cousin?"

"I think so." Blood soaked through the towel. Bree added another.

Harley's eyes fluttered open. He looked up at Bree with unfocused eyes in the same shade of hazel as her own. He blinked hard a few times. Then his mouth twitched, and he breathed out, "Bree."

"Who did this?" Bree asked.

But that one word was all he could say. His eyes drifted closed again. She gave his shoulder a small shake. "Stay with me."

Emotions choked her. She didn't know what kind of relationship she'd had with this man, but she wanted to find out. There was so much she couldn't remember. Could he help? Had she liked him? He'd been an adult when she'd seen him last. Sure, he'd aged, but his features had been fully developed. It seemed odd that he'd recognized her. Her appearance had changed profoundly over twenty-seven-plus years. She didn't know why she remembered him as Harley when it seemed he now went by the name of Darren.

Please don't die.

Todd and Deputy Collins arrived right before the ambulance. Bree stepped back to let the EMTs take over.

Then she updated her deputies. "Canvass the surrounding homes. The shooter must have parked elsewhere and walked to this house. Matt and I were out front when the shot went off. We know the shooter didn't leave through the front door. He must have run out the back and gone over a fence. Try the three houses with attached yards first. I also want the neighbors' impressions of Mr. Taggert. Show photos of Curtis Evans, Shawn Castillo, Bradley Parson, and Richard Keeler. See if anyone recognizes any of them. Also ask if Mr. Taggert has any regular visitors or if he had any unusual company recently."

Todd and Deputy Collins hurried off. Bree knew the shooter was long gone, but someone must have seen something. This was a tight neighborhood.

"Keeler couldn't have shot Mr. Taggert," Matt said. "He's still in jail."

"I know, but I want to cover all the bases in case he's involved. Maybe he was here in the past. He could have hired someone for his illegal activity. Maybe Harley knows him from business dealings. I'll check the windows and doors for signs of forced entry."

Matt nodded. "I'll take the outside."

The EMTs loaded Harley onto a gurney and strapped him down. They'd started an IV.

"How is he?" Bree asked as they rolled him toward the front door.

The EMT shrugged. "Alive."

Bree nodded and hoped he stayed that way.

Technically, she didn't have a search warrant for the premises, but she could claim exigent circumstances to check entry points for signs of an intruder. She couldn't take anything as evidence until the warrant came through.

After donning gloves, she walked through the kitchen and living room, getting an overview of Darren/Harley Taggert's life. She found no evidence of a significant other or children. He lived like a bachelor. He liked frozen chicken potpies, oatmeal, and bananas. He drank coffee and stocked his fridge with Fat Tire Amber Ale and Diet Coke.

She went into the small bathroom. He was a tidy man. There were no beard hairs or dried bits of toothpaste in the sink. The shower curtain and the tiles around the tub were mold-free. One toothbrush and a tube of toothpaste stood on the vanity. The top drawer held an electric beard trimmer, a comb, and a stick of deodorant. The next drawer was full of basic first aid supplies, but the bottom drawer held a zippered toiletry kit full of female products, a toothbrush in a travel case, and bottles of girly-smelling shampoo and conditioner.

She opened the medicine cabinet. A prescription bottle with Darren Taggert's name on it held a common blood pressure medication. She found a tube of prescription poison ivy cream. The strongest painkiller was ibuprofen.

She walked through the second bedroom, which had been converted into a home office. Bree inspected a row of framed photographs that hung on the wall. She was surprised to see a picture of her mother, smiling from a field of wildflowers. Grief clogged Bree's throat. Had she ever seen her mother smile like that? Her mother was young, maybe eighteen. Bree instantly knew this was how her mother had looked before she'd married Jake Taggert, before he'd stolen her happiness and stamped out her joy.

Bree closed her eyes for one breath. Then she moved on to the next picture. She and Erin stood in front of a Christmas tree. Neither of them was smiling. In the photo, Bree was six or seven years old. Erin was a toddler. Adam hadn't been born yet. There was another picture of the whole family. Bree's mother held a newborn that must've been Adam. Bree and Erin huddled close, looking as wary as small prey. Behind them, Jake Taggert glared at the camera. Bree's father hadn't been a particularly big man, but his temper had made him seem larger. She studied his face for a few seconds, trying to reconcile this moment with the one a year later when he killed his wife and then himself. Had he been born mean?

What was Harley like? Would he know the answers to Bree's questions? Her lack of knowledge about her family felt like a gaping wound. Was this how Adam felt? She touched the photo of her mother. Harley would have memories of her he could share.

Please don't die.

She ripped her gaze off the walls and went to the desk. Current mail was stacked on the top. The drawers held paid bills and bank statements for Darren Taggert. She scanned the desktop. A piece of glass covered the surface. A few snapshots had been placed under the glass. Bree's hand traced one of Harley as a young man sitting on a motorcycle—a Harley-Davidson—and she realized Harley had been a nickname.

A recent photo of Harley and a gray-haired woman caught her eye. They were standing on the beach of a lake, his arm slung around her shoulders. Both of them were smiling. The girlfriend?

Bree moved into the main bedroom. A queen-size bed and two nightstands faced a dresser. She searched the dresser drawers and found clothes for a man of Darren's approximate size. His wardrobe leaned toward jeans and T-shirts. The last drawer contained women's clothes: a few T-shirts, underwear, socks, one pair of jeans, one pair of pajama bottoms, and one pair of yoga pants.

It appeared as if Harley had a regular female guest, but their relationship hadn't reached a solid commitment.

She opened the bifold closet doors. A shelf held a short stack of black work pants. Five red polo shirts with the logo for ABC Auto hung in a row. He owned one navy blue suit and one dark-red tie. A few pairs of boots and sneakers stood underneath the hanging clothing. Bree checked jacket pockets and slid clothing to inspect the walls behind it.

The carpet in the closet moved under her foot. Bree stepped back and tugged up the corner. A section of subfloor had been cut. She raised the loose square to reveal a secret compartment. A black backpack sat in the hole. The fabric was covered in a thick layer of dust. Bree photographed the pack, then she lifted it out and unzipped it. Dust billowed, and she turned her head to sneeze into her elbow. Under a few changes of clothes, some protein bars, and a basic toiletry kit, she found a handgun, an envelope full of cash, and a fake driver's license. She thumbed through the bills and counted at least $10,000.

Plenty of people kept a go-bag, but the fake ID and gun made this one more of a getaway bag. The protein bars had expired eleven years before. Had he not opened this secret hatch for close to a dozen years?

She stared at the gun. Could this be the weapon used to kill Jane and Frank? Maybe it had been sitting under Harley's floorboard for decades.

She checked the remaining compartments, then zipped the back-pack, left it on the floor of the closet, and went looking for Matt, who was outside searching the yard. She found him examining the fence line behind a juniper bush.

As she approached, he gestured to the neighbor's fence. "We think this is where he went over the fence. There are some broken branches on a bush on the other side. There's nobody home."

Bree described Harley's getaway bag. "It's been there a long time. I suspect he hasn't opened it in many years."

"Most people don't keep a gun and ten grand in a bug-out bag under their closet floor."

"So, what was Harley into?" she mused. "I didn't find any evidence of drugs." She explained her theory about Harley's name.

"Makes sense," Matt said.

Todd entered the yard. Spotting Bree, he hustled over. "We canvassed the whole block. No one saw anything."

"What do they think of Mr. Taggert?" Bree asked.

"He's a quiet neighbor," Todd said. "Keeps to himself, maintains his yard, and doesn't cause any problems. No one had anything bad to say about him. The guy on the corner says Darren helped his teenage daughter when her car wouldn't start."

"Did anyone recognize Curtis Evans, Richard Keeler, Bradley Parson, or Shawn Castillo?" Bree asked.

"No." Todd pointed to the white house next door. "The Averys think he has a girlfriend. Sometimes they see him sitting at his firepit with a woman. She's about sixty years old and slim with short gray hair."

The woman from the photos.

"Let's get a search warrant for the house, plus warrants for Harley's phone and financial records," Bree said. "I'd also like to find the girl-friend, but we'll need a warrant to access his cell phone records. I didn't see a cell phone lying around anywhere. On the bright side, we have a potential murder weapon for the killings of Jane and Frank." She told Todd about the backpack.

Todd's eyebrows rose. "Do you think Harley is our killer?"

"I don't know." Bree should remain objective, but she hoped Harley wasn't guilty for purely selfish reasons.

"Harley didn't shoot himself," Matt pointed out. "There was no gun anywhere near him."

"This is true. Someone else shot him today. Who and why?" Bree rubbed at an ache in her temple.

"Maybe he knows who the killer is," Matt suggested.

"He could have been there," Todd added. "He spent time at your family's farm, right?"

Right.

"Let's get the evidence bagged as soon as the warrant comes through." She wished they had bullets or bullet casings from Frank's and Jane's murders. There was no way to determine whether Harley's gun had been used to commit those crimes.

They didn't know where Shawn or Curtis were or if they had gone willingly or had been taken.

They had no idea who had shot Harley Taggert.

Or if he would survive to identify his shooter.

CHAPTER
THIRTY-ONE

It was afternoon before Matt and Bree made it back to the sheriff's station. While Bree checked in with Marge, Matt carried the café take-out bag and cardboard tray of coffee cups into the conference room.

Todd looked up from flipping through the murder book. "Is that coffee?"

"And food." Matt handed the chief deputy a wax paper–wrapped sandwich and a cardboard coffee cup. As tempting as it was to work nonstop, they would function better with adequate food and rest.

Bree carried an armload of files and a bottle of water to the conference room. She set her pile on the table and accepted coffee and a sandwich. She ate robotically while she sorted her files.

Matt slid into a chair and scarfed his lunch while he flipped through the murder book. Unable to focus, he got up to pace. "If we assume for the moment that the same person killed Frank and Jane *and* shot Harley, then where are we with the investigation?"

Todd began. "We have multiple suspects: Shawn Castillo, Richard Keeler, Harley/Darren Taggert, Bradley Parson, and Curtis Evans."

"Let's take them one at a time." Bree opened her laptop. "Can we rule anyone out?"

Matt turned on his heel. "Richard Keeler definitely didn't shoot Harley."

"But he did have an affair with Jane," Bree said.

Todd shuffled his papers. "We've established no relationship between Keeler and Frank."

Matt took three strides and pivoted again. "What about Mrs. Keeler? She would have been jealous and feeling betrayed."

Bree tapped a file with a fingertip. "Mrs. Keeler gave birth a few weeks after Jane and Frank were killed. I doubt she was in any condition to kill two people and bury their bodies in a shallow grave. We also haven't uncovered any relationship between Frank and Mrs. Keeler."

"Could she have hired Frank to kill Jane?" Todd asked. "Anders thought Frank did illegal jobs. Maybe he killed for hire."

"If Frank was the killer, then how did he end up getting his fingertips snipped off and being buried with Jane?" Matt couldn't connect those dots. "I don't think Mrs. Keeler did it. Richard, though, I can totally see killing Jane if she threatened to tell his wife. He has a nasty temper."

"Agreed," Bree said. "But then, who shot Harley today? Richard is still in jail waiting on his arraignment."

A moment of silence passed. No one had an answer.

"So, we're back to Frank's and Jane's murders." Matt continued his pacing. "What about Bradley Parson? He didn't like his sister."

"Jane was mean to Bradley's wife and kids," Bree said. "But did Bradley know Frank? They didn't move in the same social circles." She flipped through several pages in her files. "We have nothing on Bradley. His record is clean. He's never had as much as a parking ticket."

"But he benefited from his sister's death." Matt stroked his beard. "His inheritance doubled."

"He has an alibi," Todd said.

"His wife." Bree all but rolled her eyes. "Still, I put Bradley on the bottom of the list. The fact is, we have motive for several people to have killed either Frank or Jane, but no link between the two victims and no actual evidence. The crime was committed thirty years ago. It's damned hard to solve cases that cold, which is why it's interesting that Curtis and Shawn have disappeared. Yet Kayla was targeted to threaten me, and someone shot Harley."

Matt nodded. "Shawn is the best suspect so far."

Todd turned several pages in the murder book and skimmed his interview report. "Some of what he says is nonsensical. He seems too scattered to have successfully committed a double murder."

Matt considered his point. "Now look at the photo of him at the charity event in 1990. He looks perfectly normal there."

"True," Todd admitted.

"He had just graduated high school in that picture." Bree tapped the end of a pen on the table. "According to Elias, Shawn started using drugs in college, and then he flunked out."

"He started college in August 1990," Matt said. "Could committing those murders be what drove him to drugs?"

"As a coping mechanism?" Bree sighed, dropped her pen, and rubbed her temples. "The timing is right, but all we have is speculation."

Bree's phone buzzed and she picked it up. "It's Mrs. Evans." She answered the call. "This is Sheriff Taggert." Bree closed her eyes as she listened. "No, ma'am. Not yet. I'm sorry. I'll call you with an update as soon as I have one. Is Anders still there?"

Matt couldn't hear the words, but the old woman's voice was high-pitched with worry.

Bree nodded. "Good. If I have any news, I'll call you immediately. Otherwise, you'll hear from me in the morning." She ended the call, looking devastated. "I don't want to give Mrs. Evans another death notification. We have to find Curtis."

"Is Curtis still a suspect?" Matt asked.

"Yes, but he's not on the top of my list," Bree said. "Maybe it's personal, but I can't imagine him killing his brother. Not all siblings have family bonds, but they seem to."

Matt did understand family bonds, and he agreed. Then he stopped and said, "So, where *is* Curtis?"

"I can't imagine him leaving his mother willingly," Bree said. "He takes too much care with her day-to-day life to just abandon her. He's trying to keep her from dying in a nursing home. He manages her meds. I can't reconcile that person with a murderer who runs when police ask questions about his brother's cold case."

Matt nodded. "Frank's fingertips were snipped off before he was executed. Jane was lying on the ground when she was shot in the head. They were buried in a shallow grave. Their killer was definitely cold-blooded."

"Yes," Bree agreed. "Shawn Castillo knew Jane. He was at the charity event. We found him at the burial site. He ran off after being arrested. He had bones in his possession. He was camping with the skull of one of the victims. His house was full of those weird drawings of people being tortured."

"Shawn wins the creep award, for sure," Matt said. "We haven't tied him to Frank."

"Yes. We need the link between the victims." Bree propped her elbows on the table and rested her chin in her hands.

Matt dropped into a chair. "We need to review everything."

Bree shifted forward. The front feet of her chair hit the floor with a thud. Frustration and exhaustion lined her face. "You're right. We must be missing something."

She divvied up the files and reports among the three of them. Matt took the thumb drive with the surveillance videos from the charity event. "I'll start with these."

"I noted appearances of our suspects." Todd slid his laptop and a notepad across the table.

Matt spun the notepad right side up.

Todd pointed to the columns. "Name. Arrival time. Departure time."

Matt inserted the thumb drive into his laptop. He ignored the list. He'd rather view the videos fresh without any notations. The cameras had captured the doors of the building, so everyone had been filmed going in and out of the event.

Matt fast-forwarded to the end of the night. For the next forty-five minutes, he watched a party of rich people break up. Jane and Shawn left about ten minutes apart, along with a bunch of other people. Jane was clearly hammered drunk. Shawn wasn't walking too steadily either. Neither one of them should have been behind the wheel of a car. Keeler departed near the tail end of the event. At least he looked stone-cold sober as he climbed into his BMW.

More people streamed from the building. Matt switched to slow motion and looked at every face. Many were senior citizens. The guest list had favored older rich people, but then, he supposed they were the ones with money and free time. He spotted numerous guests who'd clearly consumed too much alcohol.

Matt was ready to stop the video when he saw Elias Donovan rushing from the exit. He hurried to the curb in front of the valet stand and pressed an old, bulky cell phone to his ear. His head swiveled as he searched for something. Then he raised a hand and signaled. A few seconds later, a sedan pulled up to the valet stand. At first, Matt thought the driver was the club valet, but instead of getting out of the car and handing the keys to Elias, the driver remained behind the wheel. Elias opened the passenger door and jumped in. As he pulled the door closed, he motioned toward the windshield for the driver to go. As the car drove away, Matt saw the back of a third passenger's head in the back seat. He squinted but couldn't make out the license plate.

So, Elias had a driver that night. No big deal. He'd been a local big shot for decades. Maybe he didn't want to drive drunk. But something about the clip bugged Matt. He replayed the minute of tape in slo-mo. Elias's mouth was tight, his expression strained. He didn't look like a guy who'd just spent the evening drinking and schmoozing. Elias had looked like he'd been in panic mode.

After a third view, Matt touched Bree's arm. "I want you to watch this and tell me what you see."

She set down an interview summary and gave him her full attention. "Did you find something?"

"I don't know." Matt turned the laptop to give her a better view of the screen. He pressed "Play."

Her brows drew together, and her head cocked.

"Maybe it's nothing." Matt's eyes burned from staring at the computer screen. He squeezed them shut several times to clear his vision. "But he seems agitated."

"Wait." Bree hit "Play" again, then suddenly flinched. Her mouth dropped open and she paused the video. "I can't believe it."

Matt scanned the screen. She'd frozen the video on the frame where Elias had just slid into the passenger seat and closed his car door. "Believe what?"

Todd got up from his chair and walked around to stand behind Bree. He leaned over her shoulder. "I watched this video three times. What did I miss?" His forefinger landed on his list. "The time stamp on the video matched the time I noted Elias leaving the event. He does look upset."

"Don't look at Elias." Bree pointed to the driver. "Look at who picked him up."

Matt squinted at the screen. The camera angle caught the driver through the windshield. Matt's breath locked up in his lungs for a few seconds as he ID'd the driver.

He nearly slapped his own forehead. The answer was so simple. "Frank Evans."

"Anders said Frank did rough work for someone local," Todd said. "That must have been Elias."

"He denied knowing Frank." Matt met Bree's gaze.

"He lied." Her eyes sharpened like those of a wolf that had spotted its prey. "We need to find Elias."

CHAPTER
THIRTY-TWO

It was early evening before the search warrant came through. Bree had had to work hard to convince the judge. Thankfully, the one on call did not seem to have a particularly tight relationship with Elias, but to issue a warrant on the residence of one of the county supervisors was a big deal. He had grilled Bree and made sure every *i* and *t* in her affidavit were addressed. If Elias turned out to be innocent, that judge would never sign another warrant for her.

But he'd signed it.

Elias had ties to both of the victims, and he'd lied about knowing Frank both when Bree had recently questioned him and back in 1990.

Now, standing in the circular driveway, Bree scanned the front of Elias's huge brick house. Despite the approach of twilight, the heat refused to abate. Sweat dripped under her body armor, pooling under her breasts and at the base of her spine.

Matt stood beside her, his Kevlar vest strapped over his torso, an AR-15 in his grip. Behind them, Todd and Deputy Collins waited for their signal. Bree circled her hand in the air. Todd and Collins headed alongside the house. They'd make sure no one escaped out the back while Bree was knocking on the front door. Two additional deputies waited for instructions.

Bree had donned a radio and shoulder mic for the search. Todd's voice came over the radio a minute later. "In position."

She touched her shoulder mic. "Ten-four. Proceeding."

Matt put his shoulder to the doorframe and settled the butt of the rifle firmly into his shoulder. He nodded to Bree.

She drew her weapon and rang the doorbell. Deep chimes sounded on the other side of the thick wooden door. She waited, but no one answered. She rang the bell again, then used the handle of her baton to knock loudly. The sound reverberated inside the house. "Sheriff! We have a warrant. Open the door or we will force entry."

In order to serve a warrant, she was required to announce herself and wait a reasonable length of time before entering. Bree repeated the knock-and-shout routine one additional time. She breathed deeply. It was important she appear calm and collected to her team, no matter what was happening inside her.

Matt shot her a look, his eyes fierce. "Can we breach the door now?"

She nodded, signaled to one of the remaining deputies, and updated Todd via her radio. The deputy fetched a breaching ram. Bree heard a noise inside the house and gestured her team back to their original positions. The door opened.

A young woman stood on the threshold, slightly breathless, as if she'd run for the door. In her early twenties, she was curvy with long dark hair tied back in a ponytail. She smelled like bleach, and her black yoga pants and ratty gray T-shirt were white-streaked. Her eyes opened wide in alarm as she took in Bree and her deputies on the doorstep. "I'm sorry. I was upstairs cleaning the shower. What's going on?"

"I'm Sheriff Taggert. We have a search warrant for the premises." Bree moved into the house, forcing the young woman back. "I'll need your name."

"I'm Maria Young." She moved out of the way with no resistance. "I clean for Mr. Donovan once a week."

"Is Mr. Donovan here?" Bree asked, her voice echoing in the two-story foyer.

"No, but when I turned onto the road"—Maria pointed to the west—"I saw his car going the other way."

"How long ago was this?"

Maria checked the time on her Fitbit. "Twenty or thirty minutes ago."

Bree eyed the setting sun. "Do you always clean in the evening?"

"I had a class today, so I'm behind. Mr. Donovan usually has a meeting on Monday evenings. As long as I'm out of here by ten, he doesn't care."

"Can you really clean this big house in just a few hours?" Bree asked.

"Mr. Donovan only uses a few rooms on a daily basis. I trade off with the other spaces."

Bree pulled out her notepad. "I'll need your contact information."

"Of course." Maria provided her address and phone number. "Do you want me to leave or stay?"

"It would be best if you stayed. We might have questions." Bree didn't want to waste any time finding her if she needed more information. "How long have you been working for Mr. Donovan?" Bree herded Maria to one side of the foyer so the team could pass. They knew what to do: start with a quick sweep of the entire house.

"A little over a year," Maria answered, but her attention was on the deputies and Matt filing through the foyer.

"How well do you know him?" Bree asked.

Maria shrugged. "He doesn't interact with me very much. He's rarely here when I am."

"You have a key?" Bree asked.

Maria's ponytail swayed as she shook her head. "The mudroom door has an electronic lock. I do have the passcode for the alarm system, though."

"Have you noticed anything unusual lately? Either with Mr. Donovan or his brother?"

Maria shook her head. "No."

"Have you seen any unusual visitors?" Bree watched her eyes but saw no sign that Maria was lying.

"No. Like I said, the house is usually empty when I clean."

"Do you know Mr. Donovan's brother?"

Maria pushed a piece of hair away from her sweaty face. "Not really. I've seen him here a few times, but I didn't interact with him. I sometimes do Mr. Donovan's grocery shopping. Twice, he asked me to leave supplies on his brother's doorstep, but I wasn't supposed to knock."

Bree frowned at her. "Didn't you think that was unusual?"

"I work for rich people. They're all weird." Maria's gaze shifted to the team assembling in the kitchen. "I mind my own business, and they pay me."

Bree had one final question. "Do you have any idea where Mr. Donovan is right now?"

Maria returned her focus to Bree. "No. I assumed he went to his meeting."

"OK." Bree looked around. "I'll find somewhere for you to wait."

"I can sit on the patio. May I get my purse?" Maria asked.

"Where is it?" Bree followed her to the kitchen. The room's sheer size—along with its commercial-grade everything—struck her again. Large windows overlooked the expansive rear yard, artfully illuminated by landscape lighting.

Maria pointed to a small purse on the kitchen island. Her yoga pants and T-shirt didn't have pockets. Her phone would be in her purse. Bree couldn't take the chance that Maria would call or text a warning to Elias. She met the woman's gaze with a hard, flat stare. "As long as it doesn't contain any evidence in it, you'll get it back when we're finished here."

"OK." Maria's head dipped, and she stared at her tattered canvas sneakers.

Technically, Bree's right to hold on to the purse was a gray area. Maria's purse wasn't listed on the search warrant, and she didn't live on the premises. But Maria didn't challenge the decision. With Curtis missing, Bree would do whatever it took to find him.

Maria walked out onto the patio and sat in a cushioned chair. Bree didn't have the extra manpower to babysit Maria, and the woman seemed cooperative and more than a little intimidated. The night was warm and clear. She'd be fine. Bree turned back to the search.

While Bree had questioned Maria, her team had already split up and done a quick run-through of the interior looking for Elias. Now they reassembled in the kitchen.

"He's not here." Matt lowered the AR-15. "The basement door was locked."

"Weird," Bree said. "What was down there?"

"Home gym, storage." Matt lifted a shoulder.

He and Bree went upstairs while the two deputies searched the first floor. Typically, people kept their most personal possessions in their bedroom. That's where Bree would go first. On the second-floor landing, Bree spotted a set of double doors standing open and headed that way.

She and Matt searched the main bedroom. Bree went through the drawers at a fast clip, shoving aside clothing and feeling around the edges. She didn't find anything unusual, not in the nightstand or his dresser.

Matt emerged from the closet. "It's a sea of polo shirts. They're arranged by color. Who does that?"

"Not me." Bree closed the nightstand drawer. "Did you find anything relevant?"

"No." Matt dropped to his hands and knees to look under the bed. "I doubt he would keep anything incriminating anywhere the cleaning lady could see it."

"He probably has a safe somewhere." Bree moved into the attached bath. Maria had been in this room when they'd knocked. A bottle of bleach-based cleaner stood in the shower. Next to it, a pair of rubber gloves had been abandoned. Bree checked the vanity drawers. Elias took one medication, a common cholesterol drug. Bree opened the linen closet. Folded towels were stacked in precise columns. She left the bathroom.

Matt lifted the mattress. "I like a clean house, but this is a little obsessive."

"Agreed. We're not going to find anything in obvious places."

They walked through the remaining bedrooms, but it was clear they weren't used very often. Closets and dressers were empty. Bathrooms were stocked with towels that matched the bed linens. Every item was neatly stowed in its place.

Bree closed a vanity drawer stocked with travel-size hotel toiletries, wondering if Elias had guests often. "I feel better about all the hotel shampoo I've shamelessly hoarded."

With the upstairs finished, Matt and Bree moved downstairs. She checked in with her team. Todd was rummaging through the desk in the home office. Collins knelt on the floor, shifting books on the shelves in the library. The additional two deputies were searching the gigantic kitchen.

"It doesn't even look like anyone lives here," one said.

Matt and Bree headed for the basement door, now dented from the battering ram. The wooden frame was splintered and cracked near the lock.

Bree flipped the light switch and started down the steps. Matt was right behind her.

She stepped down onto a rubber-matted floor. The room was only a small portion of the basement and had been outfitted as a large home gym. A treadmill and fancy stationary bike faced a TV. A metal rack held free weights and dumbbells.

"Why would he keep the basement locked?" Matt asked. "It's a gym, not an office."

Bree spied a door on the other side of the treadmill. "There's more."

The door was not locked. The second room was used as storage. Plastic containers held Christmas and other holiday decorations, plus random discarded household items. After months of working investigations together, she and Matt functioned as a team. They began at opposite ends of the room and started digging through boxes.

"I see nothing down here worth locking up." Bree lifted lids and moved cardboard. Each one contained exactly what was listed on the label. After she shoved the last box aside, she stood, doubt nagging at her. "This room feels wrong."

Matt closed the lid on the last container on his side of the room. "What do you mean?"

"It's not the room that feels wrong. It's the *space*." Bree turned in a circle. "It's not big enough. The house is huge. The ground floor has to be three thousand square feet."

Matt nodded. "The gym probably takes up half the space, but this storage room doesn't make up the rest of the footprint."

"Right." Bree went to the metal shelving and began tugging on it. "It's possible that it's only a partial basement."

"Or that there's a separate entrance to the other side."

But Bree's instincts sent a little burst of adrenaline into her bloodstream. They moved from shelf to shelf, tugging at the metal frames. When they pulled on the center shelf, it moved.

"Bingo." Matt pulled harder, and the entire shelf moved. "It's not attached to the wall."

He dragged the shelving unit away from the wall to reveal another door. "No reason to conceal a door unless you have something to hide."

Bree tried the knob. "Locked from the inside." She pulled her weapon from its holster. She used her radio to call for a deputy to bring down the battering ram.

Matt regripped his rifle.

The hairs on the back of her neck quivered. The deputy hurried into the storage room, and she signaled toward the door. She and Matt flanked the doorway. Then she raised her gun as the deputy moved forward and swung the heavy metal tool. The end of the battering ram hit the door near the lock with a solid sound, and the door flew open. He stepped to the side.

From the darkness, a gunshot blasted.

CHAPTER THIRTY-THREE

Wood splintered behind Matt as the shot went wide and hit the doorframe. He hadn't seen a muzzle flash. The shot must have come from the side of the room he couldn't see. On the other side of the doorway, Bree took aim into Matt's blind corner.

"Police! Put down your weapon!" she commanded.

"Fuck you!" a man's voice shouted.

Another gunshot barked. This time, Matt saw a quick brightening of orange from the direction Bree's weapon was pointed. She returned fire, then retreated around the doorframe.

"Put down your weapon," Bree repeated.

"No! Get out!" a man screamed. The gun went off again.

The bullet went through the opening and hit the opposite wall.

Bree swung her handgun around the doorframe again and pulled the trigger.

A high-pitched cry sounded.

"You shot me! You shot me!" the man wailed.

"Put down your weapon!"

"It's down," he moaned. "I'm bleeding."

Matt shone his flashlight in the direction of the groan. The beam fell on the kneeling body of a man. He was cradling one arm. His body curled protectively over it. His face tipped down.

Bree shouted, "Let me see your hands!"

The man raised them in the air. Matt could see a handgun on the floor next to the man's right knee. Blood dripped from his forearm, and his body swayed.

"Do not move!" Bree swept into the room. She kept her weapon on the man until she stood over him.

Matt moved with her, flanking the man between them. With the rifle trained on the man's head, Matt kicked the gun on the floor away.

"Do you have any more weapons?" Bree pushed him to the floor facedown. Then she pressed a knee into his lower back, handcuffed him, and patted down his pockets.

"No," he said in an oddly flat voice.

Light flooded the room as recessed lights in the ceiling turned on. The deputy with the ram had flipped the wall switch. Everyone blinked at the brightness.

The man on the floor looked up.

Shawn.

Blood welled from a wound in his forearm. Matt scanned him but saw no other injuries other than the facial bruises from his tussle in the sheriff's station when he was arrested the previous Thursday.

"Is anything in your pockets going to cut me?" Bree asked.

Shawn shook his head, his movements abnormally slow.

Bree turned out his trouser pockets. "Are you shot anywhere else but your arm?"

His answer was a low moan.

"Get a first aid kit and call for an ambulance," Bree said to her deputy.

"Yes, ma'am." He hurried away.

Todd and Collins rushed into the room, guns drawn.

While Bree gave them a rundown of the shooting, Matt surveyed the windowless room, which seemed to be another storage area. Shelves lined one wall. A cot stood in the middle next to a folding snack table outfitted like a nightstand. A sleeping bag had been draped over the cot. A case of bottled water stood in the corner, next to a brown-paper grocery bag. Matt crossed the room and checked the bag. "Pretzels and cookies."

"How long have you been down here?" Bree asked Shawn.

When Shawn didn't answer, she touched his shoulder. "Shit, he's unconscious." She rolled him onto his side. "Shawn! Wake up!"

Matt went to the snack table and rummaged through the items on it. He found a bottle of pills behind a stack of books and a plastic bottle of water. "Oxy." He lifted the bottle and squinted at the label. "The prescription was written to Elias Donovan last year."

Shawn's next breath was shallow. Bree took his wrist. "How many pills did you take, Shawn?"

"I don't know," he mumbled.

Matt looked at the bottle. The prescription had been written for thirty tablets, but they had no idea how many had been in the bottle today.

Bree radioed the deputy fetching the first aid kit to also bring Narcan, a drug that would reverse the effects of the opioid. She grabbed Shawn's arm and shook. "Shawn!"

He groaned but didn't open his eyes. She shook him harder. "Wake up. Where's Elias?"

Shawn's eyelids cracked, then drooped again.

Bree gave his cheek a light slap. "Where's your brother?"

"Bad things," Shawn moaned. "He does bad things." He licked his dry lips. "But it's all my fault."

"How is it your fault?" Bree pressed.

But Shawn's eyes went vague. They didn't have time for a full confession anyway.

Bree turned his chin so he faced her. "Does Elias have Curtis Evans?"

Shawn's nod was nearly imperceptible. "Gonna die. Tonight." His eyeballs rolled up into his head.

Bree grabbed the bottle of water and shook some onto his face. Shawn sputtered. His eyes opened again.

Bree caught and held eye contact. "I need to know where Elias is. Where did he take Curtis?"

Her voice edged between frustration and desperation. Matt knew the very last thing she wanted to do was go to Mrs. Evans and tell her her only remaining son was dead. If the news didn't kill the woman, it would certainly break her.

Bree focused on Shawn. "Stay with me. Where is Elias?"

"I don't know." Shawn's voice was thick, and his words slurred together. "He's gonna kill him, but he hasta make him pay first. No one crosses Elias. He makes everyone pay."

Matt thought of Frank's snipped fingertips and Jane's broken bones. What would Elias do to Curtis? "Come on, Shawn. Do the right thing. Tell us where he went."

A tear leaked from Shawn's eye. "He went back to the killing place." His eyes rolled back in his head and he went limp.

The deputy raced into the room with the Narcan nasal spray. He administered half of the contents in each nostril.

They couldn't wait. Bree ordered the deputy to stay at Elias's house and take charge of what was now a crime scene. "If Shawn doesn't come to in five minutes, give him a second dose."

Narcan worked only if a person had opioids in their system. It wouldn't hurt him.

"Todd, Collins, you're with me. We have to go before Elias kills Curtis." She turned and headed for the door. Matt was close behind her.

"Where are we going? Where is the killing place?" Todd asked as they rushed from the basement.

Bree didn't break stride. "My family farm."

◆ ◆ ◆

Matt checked his vest. They stood on the rural road a quarter of a mile away from the Taggert place. They'd come in with no lights or sirens and parked their vehicles on the shoulder of the road. The night air remained hot and humid, and he'd already sweat through his polo shirt. His blood hummed with anticipation. He settled his rifle into the crook of his arm.

Bree slid her Glock from its holster. Next to her, Todd and Collins checked their weapons.

Bree touched the mic clipped to her chest, and her voice spoke in Matt's carpiece. "Check, one, two, three."

Matt touched his own mic. "Check."

Todd's and Collins's voices replied next.

"Move out." Bree's hand moved in a chop-down motion, signaling them toward the house.

On foot, they turned into the driveway. The moon shone, but as they approached the house, the tree branches curved over their heads, blocking out the light. They moved at a careful but steady pace, opting for quiet over speed, trying to minimize the crunch of dirt and gravel under their feet. By the time they reached the house, Matt's eyes had adjusted to the darkness, and he could make out the major elements in the eerie landscape.

He scanned the clearing. Elias must have used a car to transport a kidnapping victim, but Matt didn't see a vehicle. He wanted to check the ground for tire tracks, but he didn't want to risk turning on a flashlight while they were out in the open.

They didn't want Elias to know they were there.

His right hand ached, and he loosened his grip on the rifle. They crept forward, and his blood hummed with tension. Backup from the state police was on the way, but they couldn't wait. Shawn had said that Curtis would be killed tonight, and it was already dark. Bree would not accept Curtis being murdered while she sat on the sidelines waiting for the big guns.

Matt agreed. He'd been raised in this rural area. When you lived in the country, you learned to do for yourself.

They crossed the clearing. The house squatted in darkness, and the barn loomed in the background. The buzz and chirp of insects filled the night. The air smelled of forest, earth, and decay. A mosquito landed on Matt's neck. He ignored it and focused on the structures ahead, his eyes, ears, and Spidey senses all tuned to his environment.

As planned, they headed for the house. Todd and Collins went around back to cover the rear exit. Bree crept up to the front door. She tried the knob. It was locked, but she'd picked up the key from her brother. Matt peered through a window. Inside, the house was dark and empty.

She drew the key from her pocket, inserted it into the lock, and pushed open the door. She stepped inside. Matt was right on her heels. The scent of mold and dust hit his nose, and he suppressed a sneeze. They both turned on their flashlights and swept the beams around the room but found it empty. Walking through to the back door, Matt saw the shadows of Todd and Collins. He opened the back door for them. The house was small. They split up and searched the bedrooms in a few minutes, then reassembled in the kitchen.

Bree waved one hand toward the barn. They filed outside and crept across the yard. As they approached, Matt's instincts kicked in, as if he could feel someone's presence. His senses sharpened, until it seemed as if he could hear the rush of blood through his veins.

They crouched behind a tree and scanned the facade.

Was that a faint glow in the loft window?

Matt nudged Bree's arm with his elbow. He leaned close to her ear and whispered, "Do you see the light?"

She nodded and turned to put her lips to his ear. "Faint. Like a camp lantern."

She circled her hand in the air. Todd and Collins went around to the back of the barn. Bree and Matt moved toward the main door. They stopped behind a huge oak tree. She motioned for him to stay back and cover her. Matt swore. She should be sending deputies into the danger zone, not heading into it herself. She might be learning to delegate, but she would always lead from the front.

She crossed the ground, pressed her shoulder to the barn door, and put her eye to a crack in the rotting wood. Her body stiffened, and Matt heard her slight, involuntary intake of breath. What did she see?

CHAPTER THIRTY-FOUR

Bree's stomach twisted as she stared into the barn. Only a narrow slice of the interior was visible. But in that limited view, she saw Curtis.

The barn had been built primarily for equipment storage. Six stalls and an open loft lined one wall. The rest was one big space. Curtis stood at the very edge of the loft. A portable spotlight was trained on him, as if he were a piece of art on display. A noose was tied around his neck. The rope rose from his neck and disappeared into the darkness over his head, probably tied to an overhead beam.

He stood on his toes, the noose and rope clearly tight enough to make him strain to breathe and struggle to balance. His head tipped back slightly, and his lips were open and pursed. He was sucking air like a goldfish that had jumped out of its bowl. If he slipped forward a few inches, he'd fall out of the loft and be hanged.

He turned his head slightly and looked in Bree's direction, as if he knew she was there. She pulled away a few inches. He couldn't possibly see her.

A low groan came from his lips. It was the guttural sound of an animal in pain, reduced to its base instincts. His wrists were bound behind his back. A crude, blood-soaked bandage was tied around one hand. Blood dripped to the raw wooden floor of the loft. Sickness rose in Bree's chest and burned her throat as her mind conjured images of his torture.

Elias was a monster.

She had to catch him, stop him from hurting anyone else.

She wanted to rush inside and free Curtis, but she quelled the urge. This could be a trap.

Elias had set a stage. Why? He had something planned. Where was he?

She backed away from the board and spotted a knothole a few feet to her left. She eased over and peered through it. But it was no use. She couldn't see into the corners of the barn. The spotlight blinded her to the rest of the interior. Elias could be anywhere.

She glanced around her. After staring at the spotlight for several minutes, she'd lost her night vision. She eased back a step, slowly sliding her feet and avoiding twigs that could snap and announce her presence. Two more steps and she could update Matt on what she'd seen.

"Sheriff." Elias's disembodied voice came from inside the barn. "I know you're there. Please come inside."

Bree froze, then took another step back. Was he watching her? She had a sense of eyes on her, but it could be her imagination. She hesitated, unable to contact her team. Matt was only a handful of yards away, but she was unable to communicate with him either, not if Elias was close enough to overhear.

The less Elias knew, the better.

He might have seen all four of them arrive. In that case, there would be no surprising him. But there was a chance he didn't know about the rest of her team.

"I'm waiting." Elias's voice sounded oddly hollow. "I could hurt him some more. You don't want that to happen, do you?"

Conflict tugged at Bree. How long could Curtis maintain his balance? He looked close to passing out. She couldn't let him hang, but walking into a trap would be pointless and stupid. She couldn't save anyone if she was dead.

A sharp scent cut through the warm night. Gasoline. Bree's pulse kicked up. She scanned the barn, and her gaze locked on a pile of wooden debris below Curtis's feet. Alarm and fear sent adrenaline streaking through her.

Elias wasn't going to rely on Curtis losing consciousness or his balance failing. He was going to burn his victim alive.

Elias's voice rang out again. "You have ten seconds to open the door or he's dead. Ticktock."

CHAPTER THIRTY-FIVE

Matt's muscles coiled. He couldn't see what was happening in the barn, but it had to be bad. He readied himself to lunge for Bree to keep her from walking into the barn—into a likely death trap. But she was out of reach. He'd never get to her in time.

She didn't move toward the barn, but he could tell by her posture that she wanted to. Bree wasn't stupid, but she was self-sacrificing. She *would* risk her life for another's.

Her voice rang out clear and confident. "What do you want, Elias?"

"I just told you what I want," Elias called out. "You. In here. Don't you want to save Curtis?"

Matt tried to pinpoint Elias's location, but he seemed to be moving.

Todd's voice sounded in Matt's ear. "We found Elias Donovan's Jeep behind the barn."

Matt couldn't respond. He was too close to the barn. Elias would hear him.

Bree raised her voice. "Send Curtis out. Then I'll come in."

"I'm not stupid," Elias snapped. "Fine. Have it your way. I'll just kill him."

Matt heard something *whoosh*. Bree lunged forward, throwing open the barn doors and exposing a living nightmare.

High above, Curtis Evans was in a state of semihanging, his toes barely touching the floor, inches from the edge of the loft. There was no play in the rope, no drop for a merciful neck break. If his toes slipped over, he'd die by strangulation.

A fire raged at his feet. The screams he emitted were choking, high-pitched, and primal. They were the sounds of someone who had been stripped of their humanity.

They were the sounds of sheer, unadulterated terror.

Bree started toward him, but Matt shoved the rifle into her hands. "Cover me." He raced past her.

"No," she protested.

Matt hesitated and looked over his shoulder. "Can you carry him out?"

"Shit! No. Wait." She ran through the barn doors, dropped behind a barrel, and aimed the rifle over the top. From there she would have a decent view of most of the barn. "Go!"

The pungent smell of gasoline hit his nostrils as he sprinted for the ladder to the loft. In front of him, flames ate at what once had been stalls. Soon, they'd reach the ladder. Then there would be no way to get to Curtis before he was either hanged or burned to death.

In his peripheral vision, Matt saw the rear door opening. Gunshots sounded. He flinched but kept running. If he didn't reach Curtis in the next few minutes, the man would die.

Matt reached the ladder just as the fire licked at the base. Another gunshot went off. Matt leaped for the rungs. Smoke billowed as he climbed. By the time he hit the top, he was coughing. He stumbled forward, the smoke burning his eyes.

Ahead, Curtis was slumped, unmoving, the noose around his neck pulled tight.

Matt lunged toward him. Was Curtis still alive?

CHAPTER THIRTY-SIX

Bree searched for the origin of the gunshots but saw no one. Smoke billowed through the barn and out the open rear door, the barn aisle acting like a chimney. In her peripheral vision, she saw Matt make it safely up the ladder.

Please, let him get Curtis and get them out alive.

Static snapped in her earpiece, and Todd's voice sounded in her ear. "What's going on?"

She slapped her mic. "What do you see?"

Todd said, "All we can see is fire. Fire department and ambulance are en route."

Bree pressed her mic again. "Matt is in the loft. Where is the shooter?"

"Too much smoke. We can't see anything."

Damn it.

Where is that bastard?

Something moved to her right, and she caught a glimpse of a man running. She swung the rifle. Her finger twitched on the trigger guard. Then the wind shifted, and the smoke blew across the space between them. She was blinded.

Smoke burned her eyes, blurring her vision.

Had he gotten away?

Probably.

She turned back to see Matt running toward Curtis. The man hung on the end of the rope. The fire had nearly reached the base of the ladder. Grabbing Curtis's shoulders, Matt pulled a folding knife from his pocket and sliced the rope. The wounded man fell into his arms. Matt didn't waste time assessing him. He turned and dragged the unconscious man toward the ladder, but it was gone. The old wood burned like kindling. In another minute or two, the entire loft would be on fire. Bree pointed toward the other side of the barn. When she was a child, there had been a ladder on each end of the barn.

Now she could only hope it was still there.

"Get out!" Matt shouted to her.

But she would not leave him.

He heaved Curtis over one shoulder into a fireman's carry. Matt strode across the loft, wood cracking and embers hissing as the fire grew. Bree rushed to meet him, turning to provide cover in case she'd been wrong and Elias was still in the barn. Half of the second ladder's rungs were missing or broken. Matt turned and started down. If he weren't as strong as an ox, he wouldn't have made it. He had to jump the last five feet. Curtis's body bobbled and jolted as Matt's feet hit the ground.

"Is he alive?" she shouted over the roar of the fire.

"I don't know." Without checking, Matt headed for the door.

Wood groaned, and a deafening crack blasted overhead. Bree looked up in time to see a burning beam hurtling toward them. She grabbed Matt's arm and pulled him out of the way. The timber crashed to the ground, sending a shower of sparks into the air.

Bree turned and tented her arms over Curtis to protect him from the embers as they rained down on them. When the embers stopped falling, she looked up. A huge pile of burning wood blocked the front exit. In unison, she and Matt turned to run for the rear door.

More timbers crashed to the ground. They covered their faces with their arms. Smoke clogged Bree's throat and choked her. Tears streamed from her eyes. She blinked to clear them. Ahead, the rear exit was covered with an impenetrable wall of thick, black smoke.

They were trapped.

CHAPTER THIRTY-SEVEN

Matt shifted Curtis's heavy weight on his shoulder and came to a sliding stop. He didn't even know if the man was alive or dead, only that if they didn't get out of this burning barn, all three of them would die. He scanned the interior of the barn, looking for additional exits. There must be a window . . .

The only windows were in the stalls, and they were set six feet up in the wall.

But fire and smoke surrounded them.

The wind shifted and carried away some of the smoke. Bree tugged on his arm. Coughing, she pulled him toward a break in the fire. They ran, dodging falling embers and burning piles of debris. The huge piece of ceiling timber that had fallen lay on an angle, propped up by the remains of the exterior wall. Flames crackled and popped over their heads as they ran beneath it. The heat seared the exposed skin on Matt's cheeks. They reached the door and stumbled through it. Fresh air hit Matt's lungs like a bucket of ice water.

He gulped it in, setting off a coughing fit.

Next to him, Bree coughed and gagged. Todd was at his side in a second, helping carry Curtis away from the fire. They set him down on the ground. Someone thrust a bottle of water into Matt's hands.

"Rinse your face and eyes," Deputy Collins said.

Matt poured the water over his eyes, then rinsed his mouth and drank deeply. With his vision cleared, he could see Bree next to him doing the same.

Todd was on his knees next to Curtis, checking his pulse. "He's alive."

Relief and surprise hit Matt with equal punch. He'd expected the poor man to be dead after near strangulation and smoke inhalation.

"Where's Collins?" Bree asked.

Curtis gagged, and Todd rolled him onto his side. "Getting a first aid kit."

"Did anyone see Elias get away?" She met Matt's gaze.

"No," Todd said. "The smoke is too thick to see anything."

Matt glanced back at the barn. The entire roof was in flames. The fire howled, the wood moaned, and the side wall caved in. Sparks shot into the air. They'd just made it out in time.

"I might have seen him run that way." Bree pointed toward the woods.

"He didn't take his Jeep." Todd rinsed Curtis's eyes. "I disconnected the battery."

"So, he's on foot." Matt caught Bree's gaze.

In the middle of her smoke-blackened face, her lips peeled back into a snarl. "Let's get him." She turned to Todd and swept a hand toward the barn and Curtis. "Handle this."

"Yes, ma'am," Todd said.

Bree picked up the rifle and handed it back to Matt.

Matt held it at his hip. "Let's go."

"He went that way." Bree pointed toward the woods.

Matt pulled out his flashlight and shone it on the ground. Flattened weeds and broken underbrush indicated a recent trail into the forest.

Bree set off without waiting for Matt. He quickened his strides to catch up.

Touching his mic, he spoke in a whisper. "Do you know where he's going?"

"I do." Bree plunged into the woods.

CHAPTER THIRTY-EIGHT

Bree knew the way. She hadn't lived on this land since she was a child, but years of running wild in the woods had left an imprint on her mind. Her feet knew the trail that led from the barn to the dogs' yard.

Despite their smoke-tinged lungs, she and Matt should be able to catch Elias. He was much older than they were. Plus, both Bree and Matt were in excellent condition. They ran regularly. No doubt Elias had expected to be fleeing in his Jeep, not on foot.

At the edge of the clearing, she stopped and listened. Behind them, the fire crackled and roared. Something rustled to her right, and the hairs on her arms stood.

Matt had his flashlight out. He crouched and examined the ground. "He went this way." Matt indicated a slight veering off to the right. Bree followed him. The excavation was just ahead, a gaping scar in the earth where two people had been buried.

"Hold on," Matt said, his voice barely audible in her earpiece.

She turned and walked back to him.

He pointed to a rusty metal stake in the ground. A heavily rusted chain lay coiled next to it. Matt indicated the end of the stake. Bree looked closer.

Blood.

And it was fresh.

Elias must have cut himself. Had he tripped in the darkness? She hoped he was hurt badly enough for it to slow him down.

Keeping his light close to the ground, Matt moved to the right. Underbrush crunched as they walked. Bree scanned the woods around them, readjusting her grip. This couldn't be right.

A trail of blood drops led them in a U-turn that took them right back to the house.

Bree stood in the woods looking at her family home. The back door stood ajar. This was the place where her father had murdered her mother. Inside, another killer waited. She hesitated for barely a few seconds before working her way around the yard. She stayed in the trees until they'd reached the side of the house.

Only a dozen yards of weeds separated them from the back porch. Her gaze dropped to the missing board and the gap she'd crawled through all those years ago. A gunshot blasted in her mind.

It had been in her mind, right?

She glanced at Matt. He hadn't flinched, so she was reasonably certain the gunshot had been her imagination. Being back at this house, under fire, was seriously messing with her head. But this was one fear she had to face.

With a sweep of her hand, she led the way across the ground. At the corner of the house, she motioned for Matt to go around to the front door. She didn't want Elias getting away. He'd hurt too many people, and tonight, he was both armed and out of control.

They needed to stop him.

At the back steps, she took care to be quiet. Matt jogged away and disappeared around the front of the house. Bree approached the back door as she would any other dangerous situation. She avoided the center of the doorway. Holding her gun close to her chest, she stepped inside.

She could still hear the fire from the barn, but it had faded to background noise. Her ears echoed with her own pulse—and with the past.

Smoke from the barn fire had seeped inside and filled the air with a gray haze. She swept her gun around the kitchen. No Elias. Bree struggled to not see the house as it had appeared twenty-seven years before. The kitchen table had been there, and Bree had coaxed her little sister out from under it. She could hear her parents fighting in the bedroom. Daddy's curses. The fleshy slap of an open hand on a face. Mommy's sobs.

Bree shook her head to clear it. No one was in the kitchen. She turned down the hall that led to the bedrooms. She stepped one foot into the room she'd shared with Erin and swept the barrel of her gun from corner to corner. Her hands were shaking. Empty. Hall bath, also empty. At the end of the very short hall, the nursery faced her parents' bedroom. Adam had been in there, crying, screaming. Bree had lifted him out. She'd carried him from the house, with her little sister in tow.

Adam's not here.

But in her mind, he wouldn't stop wailing.

Get your head in the game.

Where is Elias?

But she couldn't refocus. The past continued to call to her. Bree turned around. Across the hall from the nursery was her parents' bedroom. She pictured her father pinning her mother against the wall, one hand around her throat, the other holding a gun.

You're going to end up dead in the very house from which you once escaped death.

The crackle of fire caught her attention and brought her back to the present. Her heart kicked as she scanned the room. A small cloud of smoke drifted from what had been Adam's nursery, and it was not smoke carrying in the air from the barn.

The smoke was dark and concentrated and spreading right toward her.

CHAPTER
THIRTY-NINE

"The fire jumped to the house," Matt said in his mic. "Get out."

Outside, the fire had spread across the grass and into the trees around the barn. Wind carried embers to the house. The roof and one wall were already blazing. There was plenty of dried, rotting wood to burn.

Smoke filled the living room. Matt couldn't see into the adjoining kitchen. Staying low, he moved through the room, his rifle firmly pressed into his shoulder. In the kitchen, he swung the barrel 180 degrees. Empty.

Where was Bree?

Matt turned into the hallway that led to the bedrooms. He moved into a wall of thicker smoke. His eyes and throat burned. Flames glowed in the first bedroom. He paused in the doorway. Fire engulfed the exterior wall and licked at the floorboards.

Soon, it would consume the entire house.

He turned back to the hall. The smoke thickened, choking him and obscuring his visibility. He could barely see two feet in front of him. He couldn't suppress a cough. He gagged as he continued down the hall.

Bree had to be here somewhere. He wouldn't leave this house without her.

CHAPTER FORTY

An orange glow brightened the smoke-filled air. Bree's eyes were tearing, and she could barely see. The fire was spreading fast. Coughing, she began backtracking. She had to get out of here. Her team would cover the exits. The fire would drive Elias from the house.

Or it wouldn't and he would die.

Before she took two steps, something swung at her from the right. A board. Bree ducked and blocked the blow, but it hit her wrist. Pain sliced through her arm and numbed her fingers. Her gun flew out of her hand, skittered across the floor, and stopped at the base of the wall. She lunged toward her weapon.

"Stop!" Elias was right next to her. The muzzle of his gun pressed into her temple.

Bree's breath locked in her lungs. Her heart thundered like a team of Clydesdales.

"Move." Elias forced her a few feet backward into her parents' bedroom, where the smoke was thinner. Soot blackened his face, and blood soaked his pant leg. He yelled into her ear, "This is where your father shot her. She was standing right where you are. He shot her in the head. She was dead before she hit the floor."

Fear gripped Bree, but her mind whirled. How did he know all this? Maybe he'd seen her parents' file. Maybe he'd talked to the sheriff or a deputy who'd responded. He'd been around long enough.

A slight scuff sounded in the other room. *Matt? The fire?*

"His brains and blood splattered all over this wall." Elias pointed behind her.

"You knew my father?" Bree coughed.

"He was a useful bastard. The only person I knew—besides me—with no conscience." Elias sounded impressed.

"Which one of you killed Jane and Frank?" Bree asked.

"You think I'm going to blab all my secrets?" Elias wheezed. He wiped his face on his shoulder, as if trying to clear his eyes. "Fuck you. I'm not confessing."

He was too calm. Bree needed to throw him off. "Shawn overdosed."

Elias flinched, then flattened his lips. "It was inevitable. Is he alive?"

"I don't know, but you're going to prison."

Elias bared his teeth. "It's been thirty years. You'll never prove anything."

"Harley is still alive." She actually had no idea if he was alive or dead. She hadn't had time to call the hospital, but Elias didn't know that. "So is Curtis."

She hoped.

Elias froze; his mouth opened, then closed again. His teeth were white in his soot-streaked face. She held his gaze.

"I won't go to prison," he said in a calm voice.

"You won't get away with this," Bree said. "There are additional deputies here. Put down the gun, Elias. This house is on fire. We need to get out."

"No. That's not what's going to happen. I have an overwhelming sense of déjà vu." He stared at her, and she understood. He was going to kill her, then himself. He wouldn't surrender. He wasn't the kind of man who could go to prison. He'd spent his adult life as a pillar of the community, a respected leader. His ego would never let him accept his downfall.

Bree suppressed a flashback, but panic encroached on her nerves. Her memories were ingrained. They didn't require conscious thought. Her body recognized the danger on a primal level.

She couldn't die. She couldn't do that to Kayla and Luke. Could she disarm Elias without getting shot in the head?

Over Elias's shoulder, a shadow appeared. *Matt?*

Bree needed to distract Elias. "So, you're going to go out in a blaze of glory?" She uttered the clichéd words with contempt.

Elias sneered. "I'll go out the way I've lived my entire life—on my own terms."

An old board squeaked under Matt's weight. Elias turned. He and Matt fired simultaneously. Matt clutched his chest and went down. Fear barreled through Bree. *Matt!* But she couldn't go to him. She needed to stop the threat.

She sprang at Elias, shoving at his gun hand. He fumbled but didn't drop his gun. Bree's momentum carried her another step. Her boot caught on a loose floorboard, and she lurched forward. In her peripheral vision, she saw Elias swinging his gun toward her.

Bree landed on one knee, drew her backup piece from her ankle holster, and shot Elias in the dead center of his chest. A large spot of blood bloomed on his shoulder. A smaller one appeared high on his chest. He staggered backward two steps, until his back hit the corridor wall, then he slid down to a sitting position. He might survive her 9mm slug to the chest. But Matt had shot him with a high-velocity rifle. That bullet entered the body with a hole the size of an olive. The exit hole would be as large as an orange. If they didn't help him, he would bleed to death.

He might bleed to death anyway.

Bree grabbed Elias's gun from the floor. Then she dropped to her knees beside Matt.

"Vest," he wheezed and slapped his own ribs. "I'm OK."

She didn't have time for an exhale of relief. "We have to get out of here. Can you walk?"

Matt nodded, and she helped him to his feet. They each grabbed one of Elias's arms and dragged him down the hall and out of the house through the back door.

Outside, they crossed fifty feet of grass and let Elias fall onto his back. On the other side of the yard, she could see Todd and Collins with Curtis. The fresh air cut through the gunk in her throat and lungs, and she began to hack up disgusting things. She gagged and spit out a mouthful of soot. Next to her, Matt removed his vest and rubbed his chest.

Elias groaned. "You should have left me inside."

Bree pressed both hands to the shoulder wound. "I want you alive to go to prison."

She wanted to be relieved she cared enough to save his life, but she actually thought death would be the easy way out. Elias deserved to pay for what he'd done for the next twenty years.

A parade of emergency vehicles arrived. The next minutes were controlled chaos of firemen dragging hoses, EMTs taking charge of the wounded, and state police arriving.

She and Matt relinquished the weapons they'd used to shoot Elias. The guns would be returned after the state police ballistics lab was finished with them.

Since Bree and Matt had both been involved with the shooting, the state police would take over the scene and investigation. For once, Bree was perfectly fine with letting go. One of her deputies brought her a canister of sanitizing wipes, and she used them to clean Elias's blood from her hands.

"Here." Matt handed her a bottle of water.

"Thanks." She dumped half on her face, then drank the rest. Then she turned and splayed her hands on his chest. "Are you all right?"

He grimaced, rubbing his solar plexus. "I feel like I've been hit with a sledgehammer, but I'll take it over a bullet hole."

Thankful for body armor, she kissed him hard on the mouth, then pressed her forehead to his. Somehow, their fingers became intertwined. They stayed that way for several minutes. A truckload of gratitude rolled over Bree. She and Matt were both all right. They'd saved each other.

A state trooper approached. Matt tried to pull his hand away, but she held on. She didn't care who saw them. She wasn't ready to let go of him yet.

Chapter Forty-One

The next morning, Bree stood in the hospital elevator answering Nick West's email on her cell phone. As much as she hated media exposure, she arranged the interview she'd promised him. He'd kept his word. She would keep hers. Hitting "Send," she approached Curtis's hospital room. Anders stood in the hallway, leaning on the wall just outside the door.

Bree stopped next to him. "Everything OK?"

"Yeah." He pushed off the wall. "Mrs. E just had to see him for herself."

"I understand." Bree cleared her throat. She'd sucked down some oxygen the night before, but her throat and lungs still ached from inhaling smoke.

"You want me to get her?" Anders offered.

"No. I can wait." Bree would not interrupt Mrs. Evans's reunion with her son. Now that she had the kids, she understood what these minutes would bring to the older woman.

"Good. She can't be out of the house long anyway. She gets tired."

"You're a good friend," Bree said.

Anders flushed and averted his eyes.

"Anders?" Mrs. Evans's voice sounded thin and weak.

Anders turned into the doorway. "Yes, ma'am?"

"I'm ready." She sounded short of breath.

Anders went into the room. Bree heard Mrs. Evans say goodbye to her son.

"I'll see you tomorrow." She emerged from the room, leaning on a walker with a portable oxygen converter strapped to it. She saw Bree and shuffled closer.

The old woman's eyes glistened with unshed tears. "Thank you. You said you'd find him, and you did." Mrs. Evans reached out and touched Bree's forearm. "I'm sorry I slapped you."

"Apology accepted." Bree nodded. "I received an email from the medical examiner. The DNA match came through, confirming Frank's identification."

Mrs. Evans squeezed her eyes closed for a few seconds before opening them again. "Does that mean we can bury him?"

"The medical examiner will contact you about releasing Frank's remains."

Mrs. Evans sighed. "At least I'll be able to put him to rest before I die."

Bree's heart ached for her. "Is Anders taking care of you?"

"He's a good boy." Mrs. Evans's eyes brightened. She lowered her voice. "They're more than friends, you know."

"Really?" Bree wasn't surprised.

"They think I don't know, but I'm not blind." She rolled her eyes. "Years ago, it might have bothered me, but even an old gal like me can learn. I'm happy Curtis won't be alone when I die. In the end, all a parent can hope for is that their kid is happy, right?"

"Right." Bree's eyes went misty. She thought of Luke and Kayla. Would they be happy? "Are you going to let them know you know?"

"We'll see." Mrs. Evans looked thoughtful. "It's their secret to tell, not mine. I'll find a way to make it clear that I support them."

Anders appeared in the doorway. He leaned back in to speak to Curtis. "I'll take your mom home and come back." Then he strode into the hallway and stopped next to Mrs. Evans. "Are you OK?"

"I am." She shuffled toward the door. "Let's go."

Smiling, Bree went into the room. Curtis sat propped on pillows. A rolling tray in front of him held a plastic cup of water. His face was pale. One hand was wrapped in bandages. His voice was barely a rasp. "Thank you for saving me."

"I wish I could have found you sooner." Bree stopped next to the bed. "Are you supposed to talk?"

He shook his head and croaked, "Not much."

Bree took her notepad and pen from her pocket and set them on the tray. "If it hurts too much to talk, you can write your answers."

He nodded.

"How did he kidnap you?" she asked.

Curtis wrote: *Put a nail in my tire. When I stopped for the flat, he pulled up next to me with a gun, forced me into his Jeep.*

"Do you know why?"

A tear leaked from Curtis's eye. He looked away and took a minute to compose himself. He set the pen down and spoke in his painful whisper. "Elias killed Frank."

"You saw it?"

Curtis nodded once. "Frank took me out for pizza that night. He got a call from Elias while we were out. When Elias called, Frank went running."

Bree leaned in to hear him better. "Because he paid so well?"

He nodded again. "We picked up Elias at his club." He paused for a sip of water.

Bree remembered the third passenger in the surveillance video.

Curtis exhaled a shaky breath. "We drove out to a country road. Elias's brother had hit a woman with his car. She'd pulled over on the side of the road to throw up and he hit her. The kid was plastered. The woman was in bad shape. She wasn't moving." He drank more water. "I thought she was dead, but she wasn't. Another guy, Jake, came with a truck to tow the woman's car. He had his cousin with him. They all argued about what to do. Elias told the men to put the woman in the car. Frank said they had to call an ambulance, but Elias said no. Frank got in his face. Elias didn't like that. He pointed a gun at Frank and had the other guys tie him up and put him in the trunk. Then he pointed the gun at me and told me to drive the drunk kid's car and follow them. I poured the kid into the passenger seat and did what I'd been told."

His voice sounded horrible, scratchy and raw, as if every word were scraping its way out. Bree wanted to stop him, but she also wanted to hear the rest of the story.

"At the Taggert place, they marched Frank into the barn. Someone carried the woman. I brought the drunk kid. Elias wanted him to watch so he'd learn that actions had consequences. Elias told me to wait outside, but I could see everything through a crack in the wood. What they did to Frank . . ."

Bree's gut chilled as he described the men holding Frank while Elias cut off his fingertips.

"The drunk kid was screaming and vomiting. Frank was on his knees. He was bawling and bleeding, and Elias shot him in the head." Curtis closed his eyes and breathed. "Then he shot the woman." He opened his eyes and lifted his own hand. "I deserved this. I deserved to die tonight. I stood there and did nothing while a bunch of goons tortured and murdered my brother."

Bree's father had been one of them.

"Were they all armed?" she asked.

Curtis nodded. "Afterward, Elias told me I could go, but I had to remember what happened to people who betrayed him. He knew I had a mother to look after. He told me if I ever said a word, he'd make me watch him cut her up into small pieces, then he'd do the same to me."

"Did he say why he kidnapped you now? You kept quiet all these years."

Curtis shrugged. "He was convinced that you were going to figure it out, and that he had to get rid of the only evidence that could still put him away: witnesses."

Bree touched his uninjured arm, careful of the IV line. "You didn't deserve what happened to you back then or now. You did what you had to do to survive. We all do."

Curtis threw his uninjured arm over his eyes and cried silently. A nurse came into the room and chastised Bree for upsetting him and allowing him to talk. She injected a shot into his IV line and made a shooing gesture at Bree. "He needs to rest."

The shot must have been pain meds or a sedative, because Curtis's eyes closed, and his breathing evened out within minutes.

When Bree left the room, she was glad to see Anders on his way back in. She wondered if Anders knew the burden Curtis had been carrying all these years.

She took the elevator to the next floor. A deputy stood guard outside Elias's ICU room. Bree went in. Monitors beeped as she crossed to the bed. One of Elias's hands was cuffed to the bed rail.

His eyes opened and immediately filled with hate as he focused on Bree. His voice was stronger than she'd expected it would be just a few hours after surgery. "Shawn died. I did it all for him, and he died."

Decades of drug abuse had taken their toll on his body.

Bree tried to summon compassion but came up empty. His brother had been the most important thing in his life. "You murdered two people. You shot Harley. You frightened my eight-year-old niece." She had to stop for a breath. The thought of Elias putting his hands on Kayla made her want to shoot him again.

"I didn't hurt her."

"You tortured and tried to kill Curtis."

There was no remorse in Elias's eyes. "If you think I'm confessing to anything, you're wrong. I'll take the Fifth Amendment, bitch."

"What about Shawn? When did your brother become obsessed with medieval torture?" Bree remembered Elias saying that his brother had turned to drugs in college, which would have been shortly after the murders. She suspected that in the very act of protecting Shawn, Elias had destroyed him. "Let me guess. He couldn't deal with what he saw. Is that when he turned to drugs?"

Elias glared. If looks could kill, lightning would have struck Bree on the spot. Through gritted teeth, he said, "Fuck. You."

Bree turned and started to walk away. She'd reached the doorway when he asked, "Why couldn't you just let me die?"

She smiled at him over her shoulder. "Because I want to see you in prison. That's where you're going to spend the rest of your life."

Her step felt lighter as she left the ICU. At Elias's age, he would never taste freedom again. She hoped he suffered every day for the pain he'd inflicted on others in the greatest display of selfishness and entitlement she could remember. If that made her a bad person, so be it. No one was perfect, right?

She'd saved Harley Taggert's interview for last. He'd been very lucky. Rather than penetrating his brain, the bullet had grazed his skull. He'd lost a good deal of blood and suffered a concussion, but he'd be all right. He was propped up on a pillow, his head bandaged. Just like Elias, one of Harley's wrists was cuffed to the bed frame. When she walked into the room, he studied her as intently as she studied him.

"You look like your mother, but you have your old man's eyes."

"I don't know how I should feel about that." Bree paused at the bedside.

"Are you like him?" Harley asked.

"I hope not." With every fiber of her being.

"Then they're just eyes." He shrugged.

They stared at each other for a few minutes, assessing, comparing, remembering.

Finally, he said, "I guess you want to hear about that night."

"Yeah." She settled into the chair by the bed and watched him. His features, his shape, his body structure . . . all reminded her of her father. But there was one quality missing.

Meanness.

Bree's father had been cruel and short-tempered. He hadn't just hurt people. He'd enjoyed it. She sensed none of this from Harley. In comparison, Harley seemed . . . emotionally flat.

He began with a deep inhale. "Your dad and I did some work for Elias Donovan back in the day. If he wanted to buy a property, and the owner didn't want to sell, we paid them a visit. If someone owed him money, we encouraged them to pay him back."

"You beat people up for him."

"Yeah." His lips pursed, but he didn't look remorseful; nor did he make excuses. "Elias's dumbass younger brother got shitfaced and ran over a woman." His story about the happenings in the barn matched Curtis's. "I've never met anybody as cold as Elias." Harley shook his head. "He never raised his voice or broke a sweat."

"What about his brother? How did he react?"

Harley's eyes dimmed. "That kid was fucked up. Elias made him watch everything. Wouldn't even let him look away or close his eyes. By the time it was done, the kid had puked all over. He was raging and incoherent." He shook his head. "It was like something inside him broke."

After a few heartbeats of silence, Bree asked, "What happened next?"

"I disposed of her car. Jake was supposed to take care of the bodies."

"What did you do with her car?"

"Took it to a chop shop in Albany," he said. "But your father was as lazy as he was nasty. He buried them right in his own backyard. He said no one dared go back there because of the dogs. Of course he was dead three years later. But I guess he was right. No one found them for thirty years."

"But they were found," Bree said. Buried secrets had a way of working their way to the surface.

"Yep." Harley stared at the handcuff on his wrist. He might not have pulled the trigger, but he'd helped commit and conceal two murders. The law saw little difference. "Your daddy and me did a few more jobs in the next couple of years, but after he died, I went straight. I haven't broken the law since."

Bree nodded. "Do you think he planned to kill my mother?"

"I don't think he planned much. He was a hothead, and he liked hurting people."

"Were you surprised that he killed himself?"

"I knew him better than anyone. No one will ever convince me that he did." He shook his head. "Jake was a mean one. He was homicidal, not suicidal." He sighed. "I'm sorry about what he did to your mom. She didn't deserve that."

"No."

"I tried to get her to leave him."

"I remember."

He frowned at her. "You do?"

"I remember more than you'd think."

"Not sure if that's a good thing."

"Me neither," Bree agreed. "Do you want me to call you Darren or Harley?"

"Darren would be good. I tried hard to forget Harley. He wasn't a good person. *I'm* not a good person. If you're looking for some father substitute, don't bother. That's not me. I don't do relationships."

Bree had a feeling he kept his lady friend at arm's length, just as she'd been tempted to do with Matt. Watching Harley—Darren—try to weasel out of being her relative made her overjoyed that she'd chosen to raise Erin's kids, to embrace their love, to risk her heart. She could easily have made the wrong choice. She could have retreated from their needs and turned her back on them. She could be the one nursing a hollow emptiness.

But she wasn't. Instead, her heart and her life were full in a way she'd never expected.

"Let me explain something to you, *Darren*. If I was looking for a father figure, I sure as hell wouldn't pick a man who helped murder two people. You haven't been in my life for twenty-seven years. I'll survive without you." Bree left the room without looking back.

Anyone who could do what Harley had done could never be trusted. He was right about one thing: he wasn't a good person. She'd embraced life and love with Adam and the kids, but sometimes it was just as important to know when to walk away. She knew better than anyone that just because someone was family, that didn't mean they weren't toxic.

CHAPTER FORTY-TWO

Later that afternoon, Bree knocked on Adam's door. For the last hour, she'd debated whether to tell him about Harley. Adam was desperate for news of their family. Would he pursue a relationship with Harley? Would Harley reject Adam and cause him more pain? Deep down, she didn't want Harley anywhere near Adam, but that wasn't her decision to make.

Adam answered, bleary-eyed. He shoved his curly hair off his forehead. "Hey, come on in."

"I'm sorry if I woke you." She stepped into his house. "You cleaned."

"Yeah. Cleaned and crashed."

She walked back to the studio. Sunlight streamed through the windows onto the canvas, creating a heavenly effect. "You didn't change it."

He cocked his head and stared at it, a bemused smile curving his mouth. "I promised I wouldn't."

"This is your best work yet."

"I guess we'll see, won't we?" He turned away from it. "The gallery is picking it up next week."

She noted a new canvas propped against the wall. "When will you start another?"

"I don't know. I was thinking about taking some time off, maybe getting a horse of my own. Then we can all ride together. What do you think?"

She grinned. "I think it's a great idea."

"Will you go to the livestock auction with me? I want to pull a horse from the kill pen, like Erin always did."

Bree's eyes burned. She blinked away a tear. "I would be honored."

He grinned wide, something the serious Adam rarely did, and Bree hated to ruin his day. But she had to treat him like the adult he'd become.

"I have something to tell you." She told him about the investigation, the murder minus the gory details, and about their newly discovered cousin. "He doesn't want anything to do with us. He likes to be alone. Considering his crimes, I don't want him anywhere near Luke or Kayla, but it's not my place to speak for you."

"I can understand wanting to be alone." Adam inhaled and sighed deeply. Then a touch of anger flashed in his hazel eyes. "*He* always knew about *us* all this time, though, right?"

Bree had expected him to be hurt, not mad. "He did."

Adam considered her answer for a few seconds, then huffed. "Our family has a terrible history. Who knows how messed up he is?"

"Good point." Bree wasn't as nice as her brother. She had little empathy for their cousin.

"That said, he helped kill people." Adam gave her a curt nod. "I don't want him anywhere near Luke or Kayla either."

"OK. Good." Relief swept over Bree. "I know how much you want to connect with Mom and all."

"The house burning down is a sign that I need to let go of what I lost and appreciate what I have." Adam slung an arm over her shoulder. "We don't need anyone else. We're OK."

Bree leaned her head on his shoulder. "That we are."

CHAPTER FORTY-THREE

Tuesday evening, the summer sun shone hot on Matt's head. "Relax your arm. She'll sense your tension."

Bree loosened her grip on Greta's leash. In the field next to her barn, the black German shepherd trotted at her side. Bree stopped and commanded the dog to sit in German. Greta obeyed. Bree continued walking, and Greta fell into step beside her.

"She did it." Bree smiled as she led the dog toward Matt.

"Of course she did. She's brilliant."

Excitement lit Bree's eyes. "I want to work with her more before she goes for training. Nothing too complicated. I just want to know how she thinks and how she responds."

"You have time. The earliest she'll go for training is September. Have you decided who will be her handler?"

"I'm leaning toward Collins." Bree used a hand signal to command the dog to lie down. When the dog obeyed, she rewarded her with a tug toy. A quick flash of alarm crossed her face as Greta lunged for the toy. But Bree held on as Greta's mouth clamped shut and she pulled hard. "Oscar also applied, but even if I wasn't going to fire him, I wouldn't trust or reward him with a dog."

Matt smiled at the change in her perspective. Six months before, she wouldn't have considered acquiring a dog to be a reward. He loved watching her challenge her fear. She was the strongest person he'd ever met. "You're definitely going to fire him?"

Bree walked Greta over and let the leash go long. "Todd called this morning. Elias's cell phone records showed multiple calls back and forth with Oscar."

Everything clicked. "He fucked up the evidence labels on purpose so Shawn wouldn't be charged."

Bree nodded. "I also suspect he did his best to smudge fingerprints."

"Aunt Bree!" Kayla and Ladybug came running from the house.

Bree tried to shorten Greta's leash.

"Don't." Matt stopped her. "She's fine with kids and other dogs. Watch her body language. She's happy, confident, and curious."

The two dogs greeted each other with wags and sniffs. Greta dropped into a play bow. Bree visibly relaxed. Ladybug wanted Bree's attention, so Matt took Greta's leash.

Kayla pointed at Greta and asked Matt, "Can I pet her?"

"Sure." Matt casually stepped on the leash to keep the dog from jumping on the child. Greta liked kids, but she could get excited, and the dog was bigger than the little girl. When everyone had quieted down, he pulled a tennis ball from his pocket. "Do you want to play fetch with her?"

"Yay!" Kayla threw the ball as hard as she could. It went about fifteen feet. Matt unsnapped Greta's leash. The dog fetched the ball in two big strides, brought it back, and dropped it at the little girl's feet. Then she backed up two steps and barked.

Matt stifled a laugh. "Try again."

Uninterested in fetch, Ladybug stretched out on the grass to watch.

"Luke is coming." Kayla picked up the tennis ball and wiped it on her dirt-and-grass-streaked jeans. "He can throw it really far."

When Luke arrived, the kids and the German shepherd moved into the field. Luke took the ball and pitched it far out over the meadow. Greta sprinted after it.

Bree turned to face Matt. The setting sun burnished her hair. She squinted, the lines around her eyes fanning out.

Matt's heart swelled. He took both of her hands in his. "I'm going to tell you something. Do you promise not to freak out?"

Her eyes widened. "Why would I freak out?"

"You'll have to trust me." Matt had never felt this close to anyone, but he had to face the fact that he had no control over her feelings, and he couldn't hold the words inside any longer. They just burst out. "I love you."

Tears brimmed in her eyes.

The pressure inside his rib cage grew, seemingly to a breaking point. Had he made a huge mistake? Had he rushed things?

Joy filled Bree's heart. She wiped her eyes. It felt like a stupid time to cry, but she couldn't stop. Matt's face fell, and she wanted to tell him that she was happy, not sad, but emotions tightened her throat. She had to swallow before she could speak.

"I'm sorry." Matt rubbed his chest. "I didn't mean to make you uncomfortable."

"Shh. Stop." She pressed a finger to his lips. "I love you too."

With a wry smile, he pulled his head back. "Do I hear a *but* in that statement?"

"No. No qualifiers. I love you." She took a few seconds to find the right words. This moment was too important for her to screw up. "Please be patient with me. I want you. I want our relationship to work. I've never felt this way about anyone before."

His smile widened. "I'm a very patient person."

"You are." Bree laughed, then sobered. "My family has a horrible legacy. They suck at being happy. They suck at relationships. I'm trying, Matt, but I guarantee I will mess up. Some days, I wonder if I'm just too damaged to ever have a healthy adult relationship, but I don't want that. I want to move forward and put my entire past behind me. When I talked to Harley, I realized how much I didn't want to be trapped in his lonely world. I want to break the Taggert curse. I want those kids to learn how to love. I want it all." She lowered her voice. "Did I tell you Luke likes a girl?"

"No." He grinned.

"They're *hanging out* next week." The thought of Luke having a normal life made her almost too happy, as if joy could be ripped away at any second. *No.* She wouldn't be afraid of the future. She would learn to be an optimist, not an easy feat when one handled crime for a living.

Her department's budget would be approved in some way, and she'd live with the funds she received. Greta would become their next K-9. The kids would be all right. They had plenty of people to love and support them. Bree would look forward, not back.

Matt looped his hands behind her back. "So, you really love me?"

She leaned into him, content. He was solid and strong, and she knew that she would be able to depend on him no matter what happened. She had complete faith in him, a sentiment she'd never thought she'd feel about another person.

She looked up into his eyes. "I do."

He brushed a knuckle across her cheek. "Then everything else will be OK."

Acknowledgments

Right Behind Her was written in the time of Covid lockdowns. There were days I didn't think I would finish this book, but I managed it, with the support and assistance of a whole community of people. Thanks to my family for helping me make the best of everything 2020 threw at us. Special thanks to writer friends Rayna Vause, Kendra Elliot, and Leanne Sparks for various technical details, moral support, and plot advice. I'd also like to thank Kendra, Leanne, Toni Anderson, and Amy Gamet for the virtual happy hours that helped get me through the months of isolation. Cheers, ladies! As always, credit goes to my agent, Jill Marsal, for her continued unwavering support and solid career advice. I'm also grateful for the entire team at Montlake, especially my managing editor, Anh Schluep, and my developmental editor, Charlotte Herscher. As far as teams go, I am lucky to have the best.

About the Author

Photo © 2016 Jared Gruenwald Photography

Number one Amazon Charts and number one *Wall Street Journal* bestselling author Melinda Leigh is a fully recovered banker. Melinda's debut novel, *She Can Run*, was nominated for Best First Novel by the International Thriller Writers. She's garnered numerous writing awards, including two RITA nominations. Her other books include *She Can Tell*, *She Can Scream*, *She Can Hide*, and *She Can Kill* in the She Can Series; *Midnight Exposure*, *Midnight Sacrifice*, *Midnight Betrayal*, and *Midnight Obsession* in the Midnight Novels; *Hour of Need*, *Minutes to Kill*, and *Seconds to Live* in the Scarlet Falls series; *Say You're Sorry*, *Her Last Goodbye*, *Bones Don't Lie*, *What I've Done*, *Secrets Never Die*, and *Save Your Breath* in the Morgan Dane series; and *Cross Her Heart*, *See Her Die*, and *Drown Her Sorrows* in the Bree Taggert series. She holds a second-degree black belt in Kenpo karate, has taught women's self-defense, and lives in a messy house with her family and a small herd of rescue pets. For more information, visit www.melindaleigh.com.